It Takes Teamwork

to Tango

By

Russ King

"The greatest thing you'll ever learn is just to love and be loved in return."

Giver's gain – If I give you business you'll give me business and we'll both benefit as a result.

'It Takes Teamwork to Tango'

Copyright © 2007 by Russ King,

First published in 2007 by;

Ecademy Press

6, Woodland Rise, Penryn, Cornwall, UK. TR10 8QD

info@ecademy-press.com • www.ecademy-press.com

Cover Design and photography by Martin Coote
martincoote@googlemail.com

Typesetting by Charlotte Mouncey in Warnock Pro 10 on 12pt

Printed and Bound by;

Lightning Source in the UK and USA

*Printed on acid-free paper from managed forests. This book is
printed on demand, so no copies will be remaindered or pulped.*

ISBN 10 - 1-905823-14-2

ISBN 13 - 978-1-905823-14-7

*Any dialogue or behaviour ascribed to the characters in this book
is entirely fictitious. This is a novel and all the characters in this
book are fictitious, and any resemblance to actual persons, living
or dead, is purely coincidental. The businesses that the characters
work for, or run, are also entirely fictitious.*

It Takes Teamwork to Tango' is a highly amusing and extremely valuable journey through the world of networking and the cyber world of the internet. In today's business environment there is not a single person who does not need to network, children are learning it in their droves on MySpace and BeBo, this will not go away just by ignoring it! To hide from it would be a catastrophic mistake for anyone's career and business. Russ will entertain and teach you all you need to know, he walks the walk and talks the talk, why not learn from a master!
Penny Power, Founder and Director Ecademy Ltd.

Just like our BNI meetings this book is both entertaining and informative – well worth getting up for!
Dr. Ivan Misner, Founder of BNI and NY Times Best selling author.

I often wonder about the strange characters that come to Beermat Monday. Jonny was stranger than most! 'It Takes Teamwork to Tango' is a wry look at the wacky world of networking - highly recommended!
Mike Southon, co-author of 'The Beermat Entrepreneur' and other business books.

A delightful mix of business and pleasure! An enjoyable glimpse of what can be achieved through social and business networking and how we can all have fun on the way.
Helen Grant Founder of the Hezine Network

As a reader of just non-fiction for over twenty years, I approached 'Tango' with a sense of trepidation. I don't do novels! However, I thoroughly enjoyed it and, to be honest, didn't want it to end. After years of running and attending networking events, it was amusing to see them through the eyes of people new to the process. And I recognised so many of the traits of fellow networkers. Anyone who has been through the process of leaving corporate life to set up on their own and trying to find their way around the sea of networks, will enjoy this book.

I haven't yet found my true love through networking, but at least I now know I may be only three degrees of separation away!

Andy Lopata. Business Networking Strategist and co-author of Amazon.co.uk bestseller '...and Death Came Third! The Definitive Guide to Networking and Speaking in Public.'

Russ King is one of my favourite authors. His sense of humour knows few boundaries, if any. Having read and reviewed his earlier book 'We All Fall Down', I was delighted when he asked me to review 'Tango' and if I stop laughing long enough I might actually reach the end with my stomach muscles intact!

Dianne Stafford DevelopGrowth and Reiki-insight.com

A warm and funny look at the problems faced by entrepreneurs, sole traders and anyone who would like a bit more romance in their life. I meet people who are passionate about their business every day – now it's your turn!

Wendy Funnell (Adviser Manager – Peer Group Learning) Business Link Hampshire & IOW.

About the author

Russ King is grumpy in the mornings, never buys meat from supermarkets and often sings to himself. He provides a wide range of writing services from an office above his garage in a tiny village in the Scottish Borders.

Russ co-wrote the business novel We All Fall Down that shows how businesses, large or small, can discover their core problem – the one that causes all the day-to-day firefighting – and solve it.

Meet and network with Russ via Ecademy, MySpace, LinkedIn etc at www.russwrites.net

For my wonderful wife Liz who is my biggest fan,
my harshest critic, my muse and my mentor.

To access the free e-book that accompanies It Takes Teamwork to Tango please visit www.russwrites.net/tango. It contains the story behind using networking to write this book, find a publisher, and my networking experiments for promoting both this book and my business.

I'd like to thank my network for all the support, encouragement and advice I have received and especially:

- Lesley Morrissey of www.thebookcooks.com for editing some of my over-creative impulses and for pointing out the fact that would be impossible for Sarah to walk confidently if she had her knickers round her knees!

- Charlotte Mouncey for the typesetting and for sorting out all my different fonts.

- Martin Coote for the cover design.

- Mindy Gibbins-Klein and Andy Coote of Ecademy Press for publishing the book so promptly.

Contents

The House of Fun Blog

Diary of a mad house
Date 19th June 2006

Curry Challenge

VIKING – Abandon hope all ye who enter here! This blog is mainly self-centred, self-opinionated and self-obsessed. It's written for us, by us; with contributions from quite a few strange people out there.

We are about to conduct a live experiment that the Spaniard claims will destroy the common cold once and for all.

There are few phrases that really raise fear on a Sunday night. Occasionally the Celt might say "Let's watch *Antiques Roadshow*" – apparently it reminds her of her 'wee' Gran. Or the Spaniard might exclaim "My bastardo iron isn't working, how am I going to go to work?" (He has a phobia about not having an immaculately pressed shirt for each day of the week). However, this pales into insignificance after the Spaniard's recent announcement **'I have a cold!'**

We are going to attempt to give an ongoing commentary so we can remember the experience properly – we have a nasty feeling it's going to be messy. I have set up the technology necessary for 3-way blogging – one lap top and the Celt's fancy phone. The Spaniard will have to fight for access.

The Celt and I are currently hiding in the lounge while the Spaniard cooks up his special recipe 'curry cold cure.' The theory is that the super hot curry burns the

cold virus away and the copious quantities
of wine that he insists we drink with it,
oxidises any viral genetics, making them
unable to reproduce. No doubt it's a passion
killer for humans too.

CELT - He's just brought in an opened bottle
of red wine for us, each!!!!

CELT - The Viking has made a rubbish attempt
to escape by claiming that he was supposed
to meet up with a pal from work. We know the
poor wee man has no friends!!

VIKING - The smell of chillies and onions
from the kitchen are making us cry and we've
only had a few sips of booze.

VIKING - The first glass of wine has been
finished and the plate of medicine has been
brought out. It's bright red and lumpy and
may, or may not, contain something that
resembles meat, broccoli and sweetcorn.

VIKING - First taste and it's HOT!

VIKING - Celt has run out of the room in
search of water. I have pleaded with her to
bring in a bucket of water for me. Spaniard
is sweating, but grinning.

CELT - Ohmigod it's hot! Viking's cheeks
have turned scarlet, we're downing water and
wine to quench the fire - it's not working.

VIKING - Spaniard has finished his medicine!
His bottle of wine is half gone too, but
it's hard to see through the steam coming
out of my mouth.

IT TAKES TEAMWORK TO TANGO

VIKING – Celt is losing the battle to keep taking the evil concoction, sweat is trickling down her face and she's taken her cardigan off. The Spaniard is having a fit of sneezes, if we didn't have his cold before we certainly do now.

CELT – Stop typing and eat Viking you beetroot! And ladies don't sweat, we perspire!!!

VIKING – The Spaniard is still sneezing and is now jettisoning unfeasibly large quantities of snot into extra soft, pink bog roll. The Celt is lying on her back on the floor, it's definitely sweat rather than perspiration, she seems to be struggling for breath. My mouth is on fire and I've just realised that I've downed half a glass of wine to try and calm it down. I need water!

VIKING – The Celt has ripped off her top and is flapping it fiercely at her face. In case anyone is interested, her bra is white and lacy. The Spaniard is in the kitchen, he went to get me some water 10 minutes ago, but has not reappeared; I hope he's still alive.

VIKING – We have confirmation that the Spaniard lives – he is swearing copiously in the kitchen. Apparently his stomach is on fire. If he doesn't bring me my water soon I'm going to combust.

CELT – Don't you DARE describe my underwear on-line Viking!!!

VIKING – Ouch! That wee Celt has a mighty meaty right hook!

VIKING – Just finished the medicine. The Spaniard has returned with a jug of cold water. We have all practically finished our bottles of wine, and at least two pints of water each. My mouth is stinging and my stomach isn't a happy chicken either. This is insane!

VIKING – The Spaniard has just poured the jug of water over the Celt's head. I'm not sure that was a particularly wise move. She's gone from shocked to furious in less than a second. All I can say is don't try this at home.

GUEST- HornyBoy: Come on, dont stop there! Did the water make her bra go see-thru? Can you see her tits!

VIKING – What!? Think you have the wrong type of blog here mate.

CELT – Bog off pervert!

SPANIARD – Get lost and find yourself a girlfriend!

GUEST - HornyBoy: Youre kidding me? Your blogs called house of fun and its about two blokes and a bird who takes her top off.

VIKING – No porn here mate.

GUEST – Ute: Have 2 say that U were asking 4 that comment Funsters!

IT TAKES TEAMWORK TO TANGO

GUEST - HornyBoy: Yeah! Post some photos!

VIKING – Repeat. No porn here mate. I suggest you check out the 'About us' section **here.** We're logging off now to die in peace. We'll leave you to your imagination.

About the House of Fun

The House of Fun is actually a flat, but let's face it, The Flat of Fun sounds crap. The flat is owned by the **Spaniard,** a fast-talking, schmoozing Estate Agent (his capitals, not mine) who is happily forging his new career after trying out a few dead ends since leaving university.

However, one fateful weekend, his old university flatmate, the **Viking,** came to sink a few beers for old time's sake. The Viking had just suffered a painful break up with his long term girlfriend and enjoyed being in a completely new town, with an old mate. He spotted a job advert for a media-related job in a large multi-national company and moved in a few months later.

The plan was to drink beer, chase women and by pooling resources to pay the mortgage, save up enough money for the Spaniard to move up the property ladder, and for the Viking to actually get on the property ladder.

The problem was that the Spaniard actually caught a woman, the **Celt,** who has since become an honorary member of the *House of Fun.*

We hide behind nicknames because we're just ordinary people living ordinary lives. The Viking is using this opportunity to develop his blogging skills as one day he wants to escape from the corporate world and break out on his own.

People have asked for descriptions of us so here is a bit of info to let you understand about some of the in-jokes etc.

The Viking is so-called because his mother is Swedish. He is quite bemused by his nickname, but it's better than being named after a root vegetable. According to the other flatmates he is:

- 'A long-haired, speccy, sex-starved bookworm who is obsessed with women wearing short skirts and boots' - Spaniard

- 'A Viking God!' - Celt

The Spaniard has for some reason lived in the UK for eight years despite telling anyone who will listen how much better it is in Spain.

- 'An over-preened, capitalist salesman' - Viking

- 'The best I managed to pull in a dingy nightclub - Celt

The Celt is a wee Scottish lassie who has an unhealthy obsession with Irn-Bru

- 'Much too good for the likes of the Spaniard' - Viking

- 'The best lay ever' - Spaniard

Chapter 1

Jonny knew that he was going to have a bad day from the moment he woke up. He isn't a psychic, he doesn't believe in them. He recently went out with a girl who claimed to be able to predict the future, but things got predictably frosty after he pointed out that she always looked both ways when she crossed the road.

Jonny's personal network reduced from 78 to 77. However, he also lost access to his psychic girlfriend's substantial network of 327. In terms of Jonny's ability to influence the world he had made a bad decision, especially as her network included a number of other well connected people. One of which was a Welsh girl with a dirty laugh and sparkling eyes. Jonny wished he had met her first but you can't control these things. Can you?

Two things that Jonny was currently failing to control were his eyes. They were refusing to open properly despite the fact that he was now vertical and grasping a sharp implement. He was undergoing the painful sensation of waking up with the sort of hangover that feels as if someone has peeled your head apart by the ears. Unfortunately, there was no cure for this, just the ability to say no to curry-laced binge drinking sessions the night before.

Jonny sighed as his murky reflection in the bathroom mirror slowly misted away. "Why did I agree to that dodgy curry cure," he groaned at his reflection. He scowled and rubbed at the mirror with his hand, clearing the condensation so he could see his reflection. It wasn't a pretty sight, his bright blue eyes were puffy and bloodshot and sported an intense, dark shadow.

He splashed his face with water and smeared shaving cream liberally from ear to ear. By the time he was ready to brandish his razor, the mirror had misted over again. He wiped the mirror with his spare hand and attempted to shave one side of his face without injury before the mist descended again.

Jonny may not have a high opinion of his toxic body at this early hour, but his genetic pool had dealt him an even hand that was worth having the occasional flutter on. He had inherited white-blond hair from his Swedish mother that stopped just shy of his shoulders. His maternal genes had also passed on pale, unblemished skin and startlingly blue eyes that just happened to be short-sighted. His penultimate ex, who had an unhealthy addiction to fashion, not to mention a personal network of 277, persuaded him to spend a fortune on a pair of trendy, oblong, thin-rimmed glasses that accentuated his eyes.

His father's genes had conspired to give him a chunky physique that, now he was nearing the end of his twenties, was threatening to inflate at the slightest provocation. However, he usually reacted to these threats and kept his food and drink intake under reasonable control. Last night had been an error of judgment; downing a whole bottle of wine and forcing down an extra hot curry on a Sunday night was definitely not a wise move.

He was discovering that even routine tasks like shaving are an effort when it feels like someone has injected pressurised vodka jelly behind your eyes. He managed to focus his eyes on the razor and noticed how it was trembling in his hands. If he hadn't already ploughed a furrow through the stubble he would have given up and gone to work unshaven.

The mist obliterated his reflection before the razor met his chin and he splashed water at it from the sink in irritation. A scum of shaving foam slithered down the mirror and coated the untidy medley of assorted beauty products around the sink with a film of foam. Although the sink looked as if a polluted high tide had been and gone, the tactic was more effective at keeping the mist at bay than the inept ventilation fan that rumbled and coughed like a chain-smoking *Tyrannosaurus rex* with bronchitis.

A few minutes later he stumbled out of the bathroom, a damp towel hitched around his waist, only to bump in to an equally sleep-ridden, petite, brown-haired goddess who had a personal network of 178.

Heather is one of those women who perpetually looks like a fashion catalogue model. Despite her Scottish roots, her smooth skin was a healthy gold and her face was framed with long, lustrous brown hair. Her pale brown eyes had an appealing rim of chestnut around the iris. She was size eight slim with small, pert breasts; it was the type of body that could slip on nothing more than a long T-shirt and still look charmingly relaxed.

She covered her decency by sporting a bright red, over-sized Spanish football top that just about reached her mid-thighs. It was a collision fit for a single man's fantasy, but in Jonny's case it was less about unleashing hidden passions and more about the impact reminding gravity that it had a job to do. Jonny froze as his towel slumped over his feet. Heather responded to the jolt of wakefulness, by joining his gaze at his damp heap of towel on the floor before her eyes travelled slowly upwards.

"Shite, put it away, Jonny," Heather mumbled. "It's seven in the bloody morning!" She stumbled past him and bumped her way into the bathroom.

Jonny quickly bent over to grab his towel off the floor, but stopped halfway as his head's abrupt change in altitude caused his fermenting vodka jelly brain to launch sharp bursts of pain round the insides of his skull.

"And that bastard has given mae his poxy cold!" Heather grumbled as she stuck her head back around the door. She was met with that very special rear view of a naked man that not even the most lovelorn lady could possibly grow to admire. She ducked back into the bathroom, bashing her head on the door frame in her hurry to escape.

"Bastardo!" An indignant male voice with an over-emphasised Spanish accent declared in mock horror. Antonio emerged from his bedroom in a blaze of good health.

He was dressed in a sharply pressed white shirt that contrasted with his olive skin and dark brown eyes. A blindingly bright tie with a fashionably wide knot and a jacket artfully slung over his shoulder completed the ensemble. His shoes outshone any other footwear outside an army barracks.

His network was just as impressive. He had the contact details of 1,232 people at his disposal – if he was prepared to walk a fine line on the Data Protection Act. The only facet that let down his razor sharp first impression was his optimistic attempt at growing a goatee beard with a severely restricted stubble line. The resulting mess looked as if his razor had by-passed most of his chin, rather than representing a serious attempt at chin-wig cultivation.

He looked at Jonny who was cautiously completing the rest of his towel retrieving manoeuvre in slow motion and grinned. "You flashing at my senora hombre? This has got to stop!"

"How come you look so bloody well?" Jonny mumbled.

"Antonio's super curry cure!" Antonio laughed as he marched down the hall. "Yesterday bad cold, last night ridiculously hot curry bathed in sunny Rioja and now; no cold! Perfecto! Works every time. Adios hombre, it's time for me to make some serious cash!"

Jonny watched him jaunt down the stairs to the accompaniment of three successive sneezes from Heather in the bathroom. He paused to allow the pounding of his jelly head to calm down to manageable levels and went to see if he could get away with wearing Friday's shirt again.

*

Twenty minutes later and Jonny was accelerating down his street in the one part of his life that was always clean and tidy, his Mazda MX-5. He turned up the radio as he enjoyed the kick back of the gear changes, his thoughts briefly moved ahead to the likely tasks of his working day. However, within seconds he was listening vacantly to the radio DJ give the country a blow-by-blow account of exactly what he did last night. This appeared to be mostly sitting in front of the television complaining about all the reality programmes that, despite his criticisms, still seemed to feature heavily in his radio airtime.

"You should try a curry challenge. That would give you

something to complain about," Jonny muttered.

In no time he was pulling into the company car park. He opened his window on automatic pilot and inserted the security card that persuaded the barrier to slowly rise and let him in for another day's work.

He drove through the tarmac desert of empty spaces that within thirty minutes would be temporary homes for a wide array of cars. The tardy owners who took advantage of the flexi-time scheme, would have to pay for their delayed arrival in the form of a significantly longer walk to their respective buildings.

He swept round to his usual area, as close to the pedestrian security gates as possible, and headed towards the nearest available space. As he parked his car he noticed an attractive, immaculately presented woman in her late thirties getting out of her flashy BMW and his heart managed a few extra toxin-laden thumps.

His eyes were irresistibly drawn to her knee length boots, and perhaps just as important, the gap between the top of the boots and the bottom of her skirt that finished a few inches above her shapely knees. Of course, looks are not everything and this career woman had something else more important to boast about – a personal network of 712 that included some high-flying individuals who had industry leaders and celebrities in their networks. She had an influential network and a work ethic to go with it.

Jonny was unaware of her network value. He fancied her because he was drawn to stylish older women. He also had an innocent fetish for that particular boots and skirt combination. This suited-and-booted vision represented almost total perfection in the snotty-totty genre, it was the ideal distraction from his half-hearted fantasies about Heather.

In fact, the woman walking briskly towards the security gates was the real cause of his recent decision to come into work ten minutes earlier. Her confident walk made her carefully coiffured, wavy, blonde hair bounce gently with each stride.

With her aristocratic nose lifted ever so slightly in the air and her Cleopatra-style eyeliner she resembled a Queen entering her castle.

Jonny suddenly went into overdrive. He parked his car sharply, leapt out and dashed towards the security gate. The jelly in his head wobbled and protested, but he shot through the pain barrier. His efforts were rewarded as, despite the booted woman's impressive speed, he managed to beat her to the gate. He turned and smiled as he reached for his pass.

"Morning! After you." He said brightly as he swiped his security card across the sensor, his eyes searching for some type of meaningful contact with hers. They take security very seriously at in the pharmaceutical industry and the turnstiles were over two metres high with thick, metal bars running across the width. It was often joked that they were built to be formidable enough to keep the employees in, as much as keeping the undesirables out.

The snotty-totty half smiled as if this was an everyday occurrence, but didn't slow down, her carefully manicured hand reached out to push the large turnstile open. Unfortunately Jonny had tried to open the gate with his 'Super Film Nites' video club card and while it allowed him to rent 3 films for the price of two on a Sunday afternoon, it didn't impress corporate security systems.

The gate remained locked and the woman's momentum resulted in her elegant nose colliding with one of the metal bars with the sort of force that has a bloody nose written all over it.

She dropped her smart, yet feminine, executive briefcase and blinked as her hand went instinctively to her nose.

"I'm so sorry," Jonny stammered. "I thought that was my pass. I must have left in the car."

She was too shocked to speak, distracted by a thick rivulet of crimson that trickled from her damaged nose, passing a contrasting line over her subtle lipstick to leave a lasting signature on her crisp, white blouse.

"Oh!" She mumbled as she looked in horror at her ruined blouse.

Jonny hurriedly pulled out a hanky that had not seen the inside of a washing machine for some time. He looked desperately between his grubby offering and the injured object of his affections, and wished he had listened to the complaints of his hangover and had attacked the day at a more leisurely pace.

*

By the time Jonny stepped into his large, open plan office area he wished he had pulled a sickie. He had flashed at his best mate's girlfriend and bloodied the nose of the snotty-totty he had been trying to chat up for ages. He took a deep breath and started the daily 'morning' ritual.

"Morning."

"Morning Jonny."

"Morning everyone."

"Hi Jonny."

"Oh dear Jonny, big weekend?"

"Was a bit."

"Morning Jonny."

"Morning."

"Ah, Jonny. Can you come in for a minute?" It was his manager or editor, whatever you like to call it. The most accurate description could be 'the woman who took the credit for your work while deflecting any blame back at you'. She had a network value of 402, almost all of which were in the company.

Jonny's job title was 'In-house journalist'. This meant he was responsible for updating Sunshine's internal news web site. It was a strange name for a pharmaceutical company, but it had undergone so many 'mergers', otherwise known as takeovers, that the original name had more double barrels than a weekend shooting party. They had hired a PR consultancy firm and, after travelling to all the sites concerned and invoicing a huge sum, suggested that as all life is dependent on the sun, Sunshine would be the perfect name to associate with good health. They apparently failed to realise that one of the company's biggest products was used to help prevent skin cancer.

The internal news that Jonny reported was mainly about the 'jewel in the crown' of the European sites, the recently re-named Sunnyview site in the 'green and pleasant' Hampshire Downs of England.

Jonny followed his boss through the maze of open plan desks exchanging 'mornings' with the people he had yet to acknowledge today and a few he probably already had. The network value of the room was in excess of 12,000, although a number of people shared the same contacts.

His boss was uptight and withdrawn with pinched features that gave the impression that she was always holding something in. In fact, she usually was, and it tended to be information, as she believed it to be the currency of a large organisation. If she was skilled at hoarding information, she was equally adept at extracting the smallest bit of news that could be of use to her empire building programme.

Jonny sat down in the low chair opposite his boss and looked around the featureless office.

"So, how's the article coming on about the company creed?" His boss asked, a hardcover exercise book grasped firmly onto her lap.

"It's not," Jonny replied with a touch of petulance. "People see them for what they are, token efforts to appease staff and control the masses."

His boss jumped out of her seat and hurriedly closed the door of the small office.

"I do hope you have not been saying that…" she paused, "out there!"

"Of course not," Jonny rolled his eyes. "That's the response I'm getting. No-one wants to give me a quote, let alone have their photo taken to go alongside it."

"You must be able to get a quote from someone," his boss insisted.

"No-one below senior manager level," Jonny sighed. "The closest I got was a quote about 'Sharing' from someone who admitted to farting in the canteen queue. I suppose I could also list the quote under 'Innovation' as he claimed to jump to the head of the queue when everyone evacuated the area."

"This is not funny, Jonny," his boss reprimanded.

"You're telling me?" Jonny sighed. "I'm the one who is struggling to match this brief. The people out there want to find out about stuff that's useful to them and their careers, not what the VP's want to hear parroted back at them.

Jonny looked at his watch. "And talking about the bigwigs, I've got two interviews booked in a few minutes with 'them upstairs' discussing their favourite examples of the Sunshine Creed in action."

"Well, you had better get along then," his boss muttered. "But try and get some quotes on the way back. I promised we would have this series of articles done by next week."

Jonny 'morninged' his way back to his desk, picked up his Dictaphone and camera, 'morninged' his way up to the Senior Vice President's suite and discovered that no-one would give him the time of day.

The usually helpful PA to the Head of Research and Development (network value 326) was in no mood for flattery. He managed to coax a smile out of her before he left, but she still didn't give him any time with his target, or even offer a reason for his cancellation. She just told him that the senior management were in an *important* meeting.

The bristly hedgehog of a PA to the Head of Discovery (297) was even more prickly than usual, pointing out that there were far more important people that were infinitely more deserving of an appointment than Jonny. He found himself back at his desk before the last of the morning stragglers had arrived.

"Morning."

"Hi Jonny."

"Morning. Morning. Morning. Morning!"

He slumped back at his desk and glowered at his PC screen as he opened up his email account. There was nothing there but requests for interviews from those people so intent on their empire building strategies that they thought an article about them would be good exposure to the upper management. Then his email pinged at him with a new message. It was from a mate of his in the IT section (87). He clicked it open.

From: Allan Jenkins

To: Jonny Philips

Subject: Breaking news for your e-rag!

Oi Geezer,

Proper news for you for a change. Some bird's managed to injure herself coming through the security gates this morning. Broke her nose apparently and according to my sources she was a bit of a looker.

Perfect story eh? 'Blonde stunner Dolly Bird, 38: 24: 36 to sue Pharma giant after rogue security gate breaks her hooter'

Go on mate, publish it. I dare ya!

Tabloid Tat

Jonny shuddered, grabbed his camera and Dictaphone and scuttled away from his desk only to bump into his boss.

"Didn't you get to interview the High and Mighty?" she asked.

"No," Jonny stammered. "They stonewalled me, all of them. They're in some sort of meeting."

"I see," his boss replied. "I had better find out what the word on the street is. Where are you off to?"

"Trying to get the creed quotes you wanted." Jonny replied walking quickly away.

His boss just nodded, her thoughts already fully involved in getting one step ahead of the breaking news.

*

Jonny's sigh of relief as he eased his Mazda down his road at the end of the day was diverted into a particularly blunt swear word when he noticed Heather's shiny Peugeot 107 parked haphazardly outside the flat.

There are some people who would be tempted to describe their co-existence in Antonio's life as a love-hate relationship, but he neither loved nor hated her. It was true that he found her sexually appealing and also true that he used to imagine what she was like in the throes of passion. That was before he had experienced it first-hand. The way her lips curled back over teeth and her eyes blazed as she rode Antonio cowboy style, frantically testing the limits of their knackered old sofa. Unfortunately, Jonny was walking into the room with his Mum at the time.

If Heather wasn't a constant fixture in the flat he could imagine them having the perfect girlfriend-of-best-mate relationship. But she had all but moved in and Jonny was in a constant conflict between being irritated and entertained by her. He sometimes wished she wore more clothes in the flat, and was sometimes delighted that she didn't, but his main bugbear was the way she shagged Antonio senseless, yet turned to Jonny for the more mundane boyfriend duties. For some reason it was his job to listen to the trials of her day, agree that the colour of her new top did match her eyes, or sympathise with her period pains. Today he just wanted to eat, stare at the telly for a few hours and collapse into bed.

As he walked wearily in he heard Heather sneezing twice in succession quickly chased by a muttered, yet colourful expletive. He found her curled up on the sofa, wearing a boldly striped shirt of Antonio's and wrapped up in a duvet. If a fashion photographer had asked her to do 'ill and needy yet sensuous' she would have nailed the look to a tee.

She looked up as he walked in. "Ohmigod Jonny, I'm never gonnae sleep wi' him again after this. I'm burning up! Feel me."

She pushed back the duvet, reached for his hand and put it on her forehead. She was indeed burning hot and the shirt gaped as she leaned forward revealing the soft curve of her breasts and the dark edge of one of her nipples. Jonny looked away quickly, but it was more than the flash of her cleavage that had stirred his pulse, it was the warm heat that emanating from the duvet. It reminded him of the cosy glow of two snuggled bodies under the covers and he hadn't felt that for a long time. Too long.

"You're hot stuff Heather," he observed, quickly banishing his sudden desire to escape the reality of his less than perfect world by cuddling up in the duvet with her. "You taken any paracetamol?"

"Nae," Heather sighed as she slumped back under the duvet. "Will they help?"

Jonny shook his head in disbelief. "Sometimes I wonder how you've managed to live this long. They'll reduce your fever."

Jonny slipped effortlessly into the duties of a nursemaid, but after the stresses of his day he went for the easiest possible food option. The remains from yesterday's roast chicken lunch was lurking in the fridge, but the concept of using a sharp knife to prepare cold meat and salad seemed a dangerous undertaking.

He stuffed the carcass in a big pot, poured on boiling water and left it to turn into soup, while he had another go at washing off the smell of stale curry and wine in his second shower of the day.

An hour or so later they were sitting on the sofa together sipping their soup and complaining about their hangovers.

"I never thought I'd get through today," Heather sighed theatrically. "I double booked Mr Hendry and even Grumpy Collins noticed that I was looking shite."

"That was brave of him," Jonny smirked. "I haven't got the guts to accuse any seccie I know of looking shite. They'd probably lock me in the stationary cupboard or something."

"Watch it you!" Heather giggled. "He actually said I looked 'washed out'. And I'm a PA not a seccie." She winced as she burnt her lip on the soup. "This is just divine Jonny, so much better than that bastard's evil concoction. Tell me; in the years that you've known EO, did his cold cure ever work on anyone else?"

"Never."

"And did you always feel shite after it?"

"Always."

She sighed. "Never again."

"You two look mucho comfortable," Antonio observed with a grin as he breezed into the room. "And what is that bonita smell?"

"Jonny ma pal made me chicken soup after you tried tae kill me wi' curry last night," Heather pouted playfully. "I've got a fever and everything."

"You *made* chicken soup?" Antonio exclaimed. "You do know it comes in tins don't you?"

"It beats your curry cure mate!" Jonny said as he scurried away to the big misshapen armchair that was the only other seating option in the room.

Antonio laughed and went to get his soup.

Jonny wriggled amongst the wonky springs to get comfortable. While Antonio's housekeeping urges always meant the flat was clean and tidy, apart from the bathroom that never recovered from Heather's influence, the lounge was too small and cluttered with the essentials of male modern electronic living to feel homely when there were more than two people in the room.

Heather hurriedly groomed her long, brown hair with her fingers and effortlessly tied it into two side plaits so she would look more adorable for when Antonio returned. As she patted the last strand into place, Antonio appeared with a look of bemused surprise on his face.

"This isn't bad Jonny Boy," he admitted begrudgingly as he returned, clutching a bowl of steaming hot soup. He sat down carefully on the sofa, balancing the bowl of soup on a TV guide. "So you had a bueno day, Chef?"

"No. I won't tell you the worst of it, but I spent the afternoon trying to find someone of *pleb* level to give me a quote on the company creed of *sharing*," Jonny grumbled. "I found lots of people complaining that their bosses and colleagues always claimed credit for things they hadn't done, but no evidence of someone sharing what was theirs in the first place. In the end I had to make do with a quote from someone who claimed that he signed up to the car share initiative to pull women and is now shagging his car share partner. I couldn't find this mystery lover on the car share system, but I published it anyway."

"Nooo!" Heather screeched.

"Obviously I didn't say they were shagging," Jonny scowled. "That place is driving me mad."

"It's driving me mad too," Antonio sighed between slurps of soup. "You know you're my hombre and all that, but you're driving me loco with all this Sunshine crap. Have you ever considered the definition of office politics? It's just bickering that only applies in the office, your office! Why do we care if someone steals your thunder? It's not news, it happens to people all the time. It's part of working for a corporate company."

Antonio looked directly at Jonny, his spoon poised in mid-air. "It's all a façade, a sham. I'll tell you what it's like. It's like those rich students at uni. During term time they strut about being all grown up, fending for themselves, crowing on about how they could change the world. Then what? Mummy and Daddy come and pick them up in their big shiny cars at the end of term and take them home. It's a sham.

"What happens if you don't meet your goals? If you cock something up? Not much. Your boss might give you a bollocking, and you might not get your bonus at the end of year, but that's still peanuts. You want to try working on a commission basis, experience the fear that comes from knowing that if you don't close a sale, you won't be able to pay the rent. Now that's something to complain about."

"If you hate sales why are you an estate agent?" Jonny asked defensively.

"Ha!" Antonio laughed with delight. "If you hate working for a corporate so much why are you stuck on their treadmill? You're sleep walking through life. You need to dust off those testicles of yours and wave them about!"

"EO!" Heather exclaimed reproachfully as she put her empty bowl on the floor. "You cannae say that. Jonny's your wee pal!"

"It's because he's my honcho that I dare to say it," Antonio rebutted. "Let's face it; you haven't put your balls on the line since that tart of yours ran off with her boss."

"Very funny EO," Jonny scowled.

"It's Antonio to you Hombre," Antonio chirped. "Look at me. I had a fantastico day. Three of my properties had offers accepted on them. I'm going to be rich and I had a bastardo cold yesterday that I got rid of overnight. The hunt for the kill, Jonny Boy. That's what you need."

"You're an estate agent, not a secret agent," Jonny replied.

"Si, but I live on the edge," Antonio grinned and then started to laugh. "Then again, you were verrry close to the edge this morning. Perhaps I shouldn't tell you to get your balls out, I hear you were waving them at my senora!"

Heather giggled and Jonny blushed bright scarlet, a vivid contrast against his blond hair.

"Sorry about that Heather," he muttered.

"Nae bother," Heather giggled. "I didnae have ma glasses on anyway."

"Ha!" Antonio wheezed. "You'll need your glasses to see his dick."

"Don't be horrible EO," Heather scolded with a grin. "But, and I dinnae mean to be a whinge Jonny, you splashed shaving foam all over the place again this morning. It makes a terrible mess."

"I can't help it," Jonny protested. "It's Mr Sauna here. I can't see my own nose after he's been in there. I can't shave blind. You need to fix that bloody fan Ant."

"Don't worry," Antonio declared grandly. "When this batch of commissions comes in I'll buy a flat that has a bathroom with a window. I might even invest in a house! That's what happens when you give your balls a dusting."

He finished his soup and settled back into the sofa. Heather wriggled into him and put her head against his shoulder. He turned on the TV just as a hospital drama was starting.

"Right, I'm taking the first patient, then Heather, then you, Jonny. First one to die has to do the washing up."

"No way," Jonny retorted. "I did all the cooking!"

"Them's the rules hombre," Antonio grinned and Jonny shot him a venomous look before extracting himself from the springs of the armchair and heading to his room.

To: Sam

From Cat

Subject: RE. Is this you?

Date: Sun 19/6/2006

Dear Sam,

Wow! What an amazing surprise! Sorry I am so rubbish at staying in touch. Thanks heavens for Friends Re-united! I can't say how good it is to hear from you, even if you have escaped to the land of Sheila's and kangaroos.

So you're a Mum now! You disappear out of my life for a year and you're already popping out mini Winston Churchills! My little sister Kelly is talking about shagging without a parachute, but her and her hubby have just bought the Dog and Bacon pub – the very same one that I first got drunk in and... oh hang on, I'd better start this from the beginning. I'm afraid my life's been a bit complicated of late…

The gossip you heard was half right. I *was* engaged to 'Mr Sex on Legs' as you insist on calling him. However, the bastard broke my heart. He was having it away with my (much younger) assistant at work. I've never cried so much before in my life, but you know me, good old dependable Cat… I managed to persuade my boss to move the bitch to another department and gave the bastard's diamond to a charity shop in a bundle of last season's clothes – he was gutted, expected me to give him back his ring, so he could use it on the next fool!

Whoops, think I need to move back another step. Let's start at the beginning. Once upon a time, soon after you callously deserted me to follow the love of your life to Oz I found myself in a bit of a mess. It hit me suddenly when I actually had some time off from work. I realised that I had no-one I really wanted to call up to hang out with. I ended up staying with my parents and had such a shock! My previous visits had been so brief I hadn't really taken much notice of how the area was changing.

Remember how I used to say that our town was the armpit of Hampshire? How I couldn't wait to get out? Well, it's not anymore. It's the centre of the universe. A giant pharmaceutical company with the ridiculous name of 'Sunshine' has taken over a huge deserted warehouse site.

My boring old home town now has new houses, shops, coffee shops and a multiplex cinema, not to mention my little Sis who has finally retuned home after travelling. Sunshine advertised for an event manager and I got the job, met the man of my dreams, discovered he was a nightmare and ended up in a tiny house with a boisterous dog called Ferrero (he's a chocolate brown Labrador and he's very nutty – get it? Ferrero Rocher? My pig of a fiancée didn't find it funny either…).

Now (to return to my ramblings at the beginning) Kelly has bought the pub that used to be my local when I was a cider and black swilling teenage tearaway. It's all very strange!

So, tell me more about your life as a Sheila and whether you have learned which way to hold your baby up – you always swore that your 'front bottom' was for pleasurable activities only, what happened?!

I'd better go, just about to board my flight. I'm writing this from Rome airport.

Fantastic to hear from you Sheila!

Cat xxx

Chapter 2

While Cat was not greeting the morning with a neurone melting hangover she was in the process of enjoying a more leisurely start to her Monday than normal. She was making the most of her freedom to work from home by munching on a piece of toast liberally smeared with Marmite.   She was also watching breakfast television, checking through her email inbox, scribbling down a quick to-do list for the day and gently tickling Ferrero's chest with her foot.

Cat was supremely organised in her work life and it was because of this that she had a healthy network of 418. As an event organiser she met and emailed a large number of people and she diligently filed their contact details. There are those who would criticise her for not making the most of these contacts, but they were there should she need them.

Jonny is not in her network. Cat has never met him even though they work in the same company. She has read his work in the company's online magazine, but they have not so much as passed in the site's many corridors.

Just as they are geographically close, there are also only two degrees of separation between their networks. Put in plain English, if Jonny was psychic enough to know of Cat's existence and want her contact details he would only have to ask one of his friends, who could then ask one of his past clients, who just happens to know Cat's mobile number off by heart. They are only two introductions away from their eyes meeting and melting into mutual attraction.

Unfortunately, it is very difficult to find a soul mate and simply asking your contacts to do all the work for you would take half the fun out it. You have to leave things to chance. Or do you?

While Cat was supremely organised in her work life, the state of her home was a different matter. She felt that a regimented home life was the first step on the neatly signposted way to alphabetically arranged bookcases. She had a deep distrust of those boldly labelled kitchen jars that proclaimed to the world that they contained coffee or sugar. Why bother when coffee and sugar already come in well designed storage devices? In the same way she didn't see the point of buying style and fashion magazines to idly flick through if you set a time and a place to do it. Unfortunately, as Cat was nearly always on the go, she rarely had time for idle flicking, but the magazines always looked enticing in the shops, so her collection gradually expanded throughout the house.

To call Cat's end of terrace house a mess seems a little harsh. It was true that most of the surfaces were covered with assorted clutter that made dusting almost impossible, but there was certain style to the chaos. Many of the objects, an unusual art deco table lamp; a groovy vase bereft of flowers or the terribly delicate orchid that could really do with some water; looked as if they were meant for a better place than their current humble status. In fact, with a bit of imagination and the removal of 80 per cent of the clutter, the room could be quietly and classically elegant.

However, Cat's own appearance was blessed with a quiet and classical elegance that her home décor would always struggle to achieve, even if the clutter was spanked by the strict principles of Feng Shui. She put her breakfast tray on top of the pile of magazines and newspapers that hid her glass sculpture of a coffee table, picked up her laptop and curled her long frame up on the sofa. She could not be described as slender, her body offering the feminine curves missing from the women in the photos of her fashion magazines. However, it was an hourglass figure that earned male approval and she kept it in good running order by means of taking Ferrero for active walks and frequent trips to the gym.

Her long brown hair, artfully blended with blonde streaks, was currently tied in a casual pony tail. Her face was bereft of make up, exposing the healthy looking freckles that had broken out after yesterday's exposure to the strong sun of Rome. Her hands were adorned with understated rings and the best efforts of her nail technician.

"Why do these people feel they need to email me such trivia," she complained to Ferrero as she ploughed through her inbox. "Oh please! Listen to this one. 'Dear Cat. It was good to meet you today and I look forward to getting to know you much better over the next few weeks.' Yuck! He hardly raised his eyes from my boobs all meeting."

Perhaps Ferrero should have agreed with Cat's scathing indictment on the male shortcomings in the mixed sex workplace, but he chose to respond with his tried and tested response of tail wagging. He followed it up by moving as close to Cat as he dared, wary of being reprimanded for getting his nose too close to her food. He may have earned his name by being a nutty puppy, but now he had developed into a loving companion who did a passable impression of an expert listener. If he had been human he would be besieged by female admirers.

"Yes, yes. No need to fret pooch," Cat smiled at him. "You're still my number one fella."

Ferrero's antics dislodged a haphazard pile of style magazines that were leaning against the sofa. They slid onto the floor with a flap and thump, sending Ferrero scurrying to the other side of the room. His quivering backside dealt a glancing blow to a freestanding, extravagantly curled wine rack that was currently home to a solitary bottle of gin. It swayed first one way and then the other, before toppling over into the middle of the room. Ferrero panicked and tried to hide under the glass coffee table and conveniently left his rear end out to break the fall of the gin bottle. He jumped up in shock and yelped as his head hit the thick glass table top.

Cat giggled. "You *could* clear up a bit darling," she said reaching out for him to come to her. He dashed towards her, relieved not to be in trouble. "That was a good effort with the gin, it's good to see you have your priorities right, but I think it's time we finally did something about this, don't you?"

She looked down at her to-do list and pushed it to one side.

"They've had their pound of flesh out of me all weekend. It's time we had a major sort out." She looked around the room with distaste. "We have two problems here. Too much stuff and too many magazines. Solution: put all the stuff in the spare room and throw magazines away."

Ferrero gazed at her with a confused expression.

"I know fella, it has its drawbacks. I would lose my spare room and I don't get to read the mags. Where's the win-win solution?" She looked thoughtfully around the room. "How about we pack the stuff into boxes and put it in the garage and I use the crappy part of the mags as packing material?"

Ferrero wagged his tail at the lightness of her voice.

"Glad you agree," Cat smiled. She picked up the nearest magazine and quickly flicked through it. It landed on a skin cosmetics advert featuring a beautiful woman's face that had been airbrushed to remove any sign of character. "Now she definitely needs a few wrinkles," Cat declared and ripped the page out, crumpled it up and used it to wrap up a delicate glass candleholder. She was interrupted by the ping of an incoming email. She tutted and turned towards her laptop, saw that the email was from her sister, Kelly, (153, mostly overseas) and read it while looking for something to pack with her free hand. She tutted again, searched for the phone and quickly dialled a number.

"Ferrero sends you a lick," she said in response to her sister's 'Hello.'

"He's da man!" Kelly laughed.

"Thanks for looking after him."

"No worries mate, anytime. How was sunny Rome?"

"Didn't see much of it as usual. Straight from the airport to venue, to hotel, to venue, to airport and back home. Usual type of thing."

"Yeah right, and you didn't go shopping at all then?"

Cat laughed. "I squeezed in a quick half hour."

"You back at work already? You must be well-knackered."

"Actually I'm working from home today and I've decided just to deal with incoming emails. You won't believe this, but I'm having a sort out – the house needs less stuff."

"Now that is scary! What brought that on?"

"Poor Ferrero just caused an avalanche, so I'm packing all the clutter up and storing it in the garage."

"But you love your stuff!"

"It was bought for a bigger house. There's no room for it here and if I put it in the spare room it'll always feel as if I am just about to move. It's time for a new start."

"Good on you Top Cat, I'm proud of you."

"Now, what's all this about you reverting to your original plan of going for B&B at the pub rather than the flat?"

"Don't start this again!" Kelly wailed. "You know why. It was our honeymoon dream! Malc and I spent many a sweltering train journey through India planning it out. We made a pact that we would never work for someone else again and that we wanted to meet lots of interesting new people."

"But..."

"Stop your butting Top Cat. You don't know what travelling is like."

"I do have some idea Kel, I rack up a few air miles myself."

"Duh! You don't see anything! You go from airport to hotel to venue and take in a few fancy shops. You don't interact with real people, listen to their music, dance with them."

"Oh listen to yourself, Kelly. Are you telling me that you're intending to belly dance with your guests?"

"Don't take the piss," Kelly replied sulkily. "We want our lives to be enriched by a variety of people passing through our doors. There's also a better profit margin in B&B and let's face it, we need the cash."

"What's happened to my hippy sister?" Cat laughed. "I thought profits were just for capitalist pigs who give nothing back to the community?"

"Yeah, whatever. We're trying for a baby, remember? They cost a bit more to maintain than your darling mutt."

"Don't you want to at least get the pub thriving before you start playing Mummies and Daddies?"

"Don't patronise me Cat," Kelly snapped.

"But you've got to face reality Kel! You're running a pub which takes up, what? At least 12 hours a day? Every day. How much time are you going to have to wash sheets and clean rooms?"

"But it's good money!" Kelly wailed. "And we need the cash flow."

"It's quicker to turn it into a flat and you get a monthly cash flow without worrying about the rooms being taken every single day. You're going to meet all sorts of weirdo's through the pub anyway. You'll be dying to have some time alone."

There was an extended pause on the other end of the line as Kelly collected her thoughts. "We'll do it if you move in," she declared.

"Kelly, darling. You are my little sister and I love you to bits, but I would rather eat my new boots than live in the same building with you. Besides Malc might get his didgeridoo out."

Cat finished the phone call with a wry smile, wondering how she had managed to get roped into helping her sister run a pub, let alone the pub where she had committed a number of teenage sins. She was struck by a sudden feeling of nostalgia for those far away teenage years. Things were different then. Like most teenagers she had ranged from exuding confidence, to feeling awkward, shy and misunderstood, but she still felt as if she belonged. She was one of the gang, one of the group of rebels who were too big and ambitious for the boring town of Overchurch. Now here she was back again with a negligible circle of friends and the town had grown up without her. She hadn't left it behind; it had left her behind.

*

Cat was never down for long and by that evening she was chuckling over some of her less pleasant teenage memories. The home perm kit that made her look like a mutant poodle for a start. Not forgetting her first ever proper snog. It was with Chris Patterson (then 41, now 834) by the pool table in the Dog and Bacon, moments after he had thrown up four pints of bitter, two pickled eggs and a bag of scampi fries. She winced at the thought and bent down to pat Ferrero, who was trotting along happily beside her.

"Ouch!" Her back ached after her packing exertions, but she was pleased with the results of her clear out, both mentally and in terms of re-claiming the house. She even had a distinct jauntiness to her step.

She breezed into the pub to find Kelly idly wiping down the beer pumps and just one old man (59) sitting on his special stool at the end of the bar. He was staring at Kelly intently, his mouth slack and partly open, perhaps remembering his earlier years when he might have tried to court the maverick new landlady in front of him.

Kelly definitely attracted attention, especially as she never stayed still for more than a few seconds. Her long hair was braided tightly against her head, an effect made more powerful, by a mix of black and white braids that contrasted with her natural mousey hair.

The next effect to hit you were the piercings; one through her left eyebrow, a long spike through the top of her left ear and a tongue piercing that she tended to tap against her top teeth when she was concentrating.

Nature had not given Kelly the perfect figure, but she didn't need one. She described herself as short for her weight; she was a size sixteen and, just like Cat, she had curves in all the right places – only hers were more exaggerated. She may not be able to smoulder like Marilyn Monroe, but she certainly had an air of permanent mischief and rebellion and this was the baseline of the relationship between the sisters ever since Kelly was old enough to get into trouble.

"Hey Top Cat!" Kelly quipped. "So how's the house? Room to swing a cat yet?" She put some ice in a glass and poured a double measure of gin.

"Ha ha," Cat groaned as she eased herself on to a bar stool and looped Ferrero's lead over a coat hook under the bar. "You wouldn't recognise the place. I may even be able to invite people round now."

"Oh yeah?" Kelly cooed, pausing in her efforts to dose the glass with tonic water. "Is there something you want to tell me?"

"That you're very nosy, a pain in the arse, and barking completely up the wrong tree?" Cat said with a smirk.

Kelly grinned as she grabbed a lime from an artfully arranged pile behind the bar and deftly cut a thick slice. "See? We got limes in especially for our business advisor."

Cat smiled and Ferrero put his front paws on a ledge under the bar in order to see Kelly. He licked his chops hopefully.

"You've been feeding him crisps again haven't you?" Cat stated reproachfully. "He's getting fat, I don't want him to start waddling."

"Moi?" Kelly said innocently, patting Ferrero's broad head as she passed the completed gin and tonic to her sister. "It's on the house." She added as Cat started to open her shiny new Italian handbag. "By the looks of that monstrosity, you could do with saving the money."

"By the lack of customers in here it looks as if you should be charging me," Cat observed as she looked around the room. "It's not exactly overflowing with social interaction is it?"

"Tell me about it. Apparently there are some rumours about something going on at Sunshine."

"With any luck they'll give me the chop," Cat sighed. "I'm sick of working weekends for them."

"No way!" Kelly exclaimed. "You're not allowed to move away again. We'll miss you too much. There's so much organising to do."

"Uh-uh," Cat said as she sipped her G'n'T. "Malc's your Chief Organiser. I'm just someone to bounce ideas off."

Their conversation was interrupted by the arrival of a self imposing looking woman (427) hidden under layers of a capacious fleece jacket and wild orange coloured hair that failed to disguise the fact that her natural hair colour had been grey for some time. She peered imperiously at Kelly over her half moon glasses.

"Hello my dear," she said sweetly. "Is the landlady in? I have an important question for her."

"You're looking at her love," Kelly replied with just a hint of animosity.

"Oh, I *am* sorry," the lady replied, looking anything but. "I am afraid I don't really keep up with these young, modern fashions."

"No." Kelly agreed and leaned back while still maintaining eye contact.

"I have a favour to ask actually my dear. Your predecessors used to host the Overchurch Local Business Meetings," the lady said emphasising the capital at the beginning of each word. "It went on for over twenty years, but, when the town developed, it died off rather. Now the out of town supermarkets are taking our business we need to do something so we're going to get things going again. You must have noticed that the village centre is in danger of becoming deserted. The local shops simply can't take the competition. Can you see your way to helping us out?"

"Sure, no problem," Kelly replied. "When's the meeting?"

"Tomorrow, I'm afraid. You see. Well, we were planning to meet in the village hall but, apparently they have a problem with the ladies toilets. Flooded the place actually. Wall to wall water in fact."

"Oh. We may not be able to..." Kelly started.

"That will be fine," Cat butted in. "And we'll provide some finger food as well."

"Oh that would be wonderful my dear," the woman beamed just as the sound of a didgeridoo wafted out of the jukebox. "Oh my," she wheezed, "that *is* unusual music." She bent down to pat Ferrero on his broad head. "What a handsome young fellow. Perhaps you'll come too?" She chirped before perfecting a regal exit on her way to spread the good news.

Kelly stared at her sister, a picture of instant hostility.

Cat calmly returned the look.

"Have you considered that this music could be keeping your customers away?" Cat asked.

"Perhaps you would like to bounce your ideas off me next time before you start running *my* business?" Kelly said venomously. "We're trying to attract more alternative types here. In fact, we decided this morning to have a summer solstice celebration tomorrow night, but you've certainly squashed that. We were going to get in some scrumpy, a folk band is interested in playing a set. Malc even thinks he knows where to get some mead."

"Kelly! You're off your rocker. Overchurch is full of young professionals who want to drink lager, wine or alcopops and have a flirt on a Friday night. You would be better off getting some slutty tops for you and the barmaids; it would pull in more punters."

The reminiscing local at the end of the bar almost spat out his false teeth into his pint, while Kelly just scowled at her sister.

"Don't beetle your eyebrows at me Kel, you've got to think these things through. If you want to have a specialised night you need to set it up weeks in advance and advertise it. Have you done any of that? It's tomorrow! If you host this business meeting you're going to get all the small business owners in here. Where do they do a lot of their business? In the pub!"

"You'd better be right." Kelly said sulkily.

"I know I am, and have you booked the decorator to do your flat yet? The sooner you get someone in, the sooner you get a monthly rent cheque."

"Top Cat?" Kelly said quietly.

"Yes?"

"You really need to get laid."

The House of Fun Blog

Diary of a mad house
Date 20ᵗʰ June 2006

The Aftermath

VIKING – Thanks for the all the expressions of concern. Just for the record we got through 4 bottles of wine, several gallons of water and the plate of fire burned just as much coming out of the body as it did going in.
The result? The Spaniard's cold was miraculously cured by morning, the Celt has caught the cold and the Viking endured the worst hangover in the long and battle-hardened history of Viking hangovers. The hangover also led to involuntary public nudity and an event that it is too shocking to recount, even in an anonymous blog.
It is a sad day as it has become obvious that the 'Curry Cure' only ever benefits the Spaniard and will be avoided by the Viking in the future.

CELT – An event worse than flashing at me? The mind boggles. Tell us Viking!

GUEST – Ute: Viking flashing! Must have been bad. So – R there any pics?

GUEST – HornyBoy: Yeah we want the threesome pics!

VIKING – Give it a rest Hornyboy!

GUEST – CapnJack: Talking about you lot not wearing much, someone called Foxy Celt has just joined my MySpace friends list. See **here.** Is this you Celt?

VIKING – Phew, she takes her vitamins! But she's not our Celt. How on earth do you have so many wenches as your 'friends'?

GUEST – CapnJack: That's the beauty of MySpace, you can ask all sorts of beauties to be your friend and they say yes.

CELT – And these women who are allergic to their clothes aren't just out for publicity then?

GUEST – CapnJack: If wanton wenches want to use me then why say no? ;)

GUEST – Ute: This is all just a smokescreen, what's your secret Viking?

VIKING – No way, my housemates would never let me live it down.

CELT – Now you're going to have to tell us!

VIKING – Look up the definition of secret!

Chapter 3

Jonny (77) was lying in bed listening to Heather humming to herself as she performed the necessary ablutions to face another working day. He was already fifteen minutes later than usual and didn't feel motivated to get vertical any time soon.

It wasn't that he was drugged with sleep. Far from it. He had suffered a restless night and had been awake and reviewing his life for the last three hours. He had made a few decisions, but had the rather sickening feeling that making decisions were much easier than facing their consequences.

By the time he started his commute the traffic was considerably busier and although he was only about twenty minutes later than usual, he found himself arriving forty minutes later in the car park. He was hurrying between the ranks of parked cars that were usually just empty spaces when he got to work when his eyes fixed on a pair of knee high boots and a short skirt in front of him. His eyes rose in appreciation only to bulge with shock. The enticing rear view belonged to the snotty-totty (712) he had managed to maim the previous morning.

He stopped in his tracks, his mind taking in her slow progress. He was either going to have to be a man and apologise to her and see how she was, or be a mouse and take a detour to the next security gate and make himself even later.

After his early morning self pep talk he decided to grab life by the pointy bits. He reasoned that there might be a very outside chance that she would appreciate him playing doctor for her. He was just picking up his pace when a bustling woman with big hair, shoulder pads and impressively sturdy calves (145) appeared from behind a towering four wheel drive vehicle that threatened to block out the sun.

"Sarah!" The woman gasped, grabbing the snotty-totty's arm. "What on earth are you doing here?"

"Something big's going down," Sarah said brusquely, retrieving her arm. "I was on endless conference calls last night."

Jonny gasped as he saw Sarah's side profile. Her once elegant nose was badly swollen and even the large sunglasses she was wearing failed to hide the green rings of a developing black eye.

He turned round briskly so his back was towards them and flapped at his pockets, making a show of pretending to look for his pass. The women didn't notice him and continued to walk slowly towards the security turnstile. Jonny walked back to his car where he continued the charade of finding his pass to buy him a few extra minutes to mentally process the damage he had done to the poor woman's face.

He arrived more than fifty minutes later than usual at his desk and was greeted with the chaotic scene of people dealing efficiently with a crisis by all talking at once and dashing about carrying bits of paper. There was not a 'morning' to be heard.

"Where've you bloody been?" His boss (404) demanded. "Get up to the management suite, they're announcing another merger!"

"You're joking?" Jonny groaned as he reached for his equipment. "I can't cope with the stress of another Day One."

As soon as he reached the management suite he was whisked straight into the board room, a room he had only previously seen through the partially open door. The CEO (789) looked up as he walked in. His normally pinched features contorted by a stressed fury that turned his face red around the edges and made his bushy eyebrows dance jerkily as he barked, "Who's he?"

"Jonny Philips," Jonny replied meekly. "Internal Comms, to announce the merger news via the Intranet."

The CEO glared at him with distaste. "You're late!"

Jonny looked back at him determined to put up some kind of effort into standing up for himself. "Erm, not really, sir. Not with flexi-time."

The CEO glared at him. "No wonder this place is going to the dogs, any excuse to stay in bed. You can rehash this." He flicked a piece of paper disdainfully across the over polished table towards him. Before Jonny could start to read it, the CEO stormed towards the door. "And get Head Office on the phone!" He bellowed.

"But they'll be in bed," his PA (215) stammered.

"Good!" The CEO retorted before turning to Jonny. "And don't you dare publish anything until *I've* approved it!"

Jonny started to read the memo.

> *Sunshine Inc are delighted to announce that they are merging with MedBioBerg to form MedBioSunBerg Inc. This is a strong business decision borne out of mutually compatible development pipelines and products.*

Jonny became aware of a heavy silence in the room and stopped reading. The remaining Senior Vice Presidents in the room were sitting still and staring morosely into space.

"What's going on?" he asked. "I know that mergers are difficult, but look at this, it's good news. The share price will go up."

The Head of Finance (212) snorted. "A journalist should know more than anyone not to believe everything they read. We've been bought out, we're screwed."

"But, this place is huge!" Jonny stammered.

"It's not as big as MedBio's main site just outside London, nice and easy to fly into. And they also have a satellite sales site in the Midlands. They'll close this one in a matter of months."

"But what about all the people?"

"Oh, I'm sure they'll be jobs for a few hundred if they agree to relocate," the Head of Finance sighed with the look of someone who hadn't quite connected fully with the news he was passing on. "So Mr. Journo, the people are waiting. What are you going to write?"

Jonny looked thoughtfully at the memo in front of him and felt his courage slowly building. "My resignation," he said quietly.

The Head of Finance stood up with a sigh. "Now that's the best idea I've heard all day. Just keep quiet about this, nothing's been announced yet and you'll get your butt more than kicked if any of this leaks out."

Jonny sped back to his desk as if his feet were on fire, filled with a desperate need for speed now his plans, created only a few hours earlier had been suddenly dragged forward into reality. He was immediately accosted by his boss. Jonny took the initiative and prevented another blustering by handing her the piece of paper bearing the press release.

"There you go," he said enjoying the look of surprise on her face. "CEO wants you to re-hash that and to get his approval before you publish it."

"But... what?" His boss was too bemused to form a sentence.

"I'm afraid that I'm leaving," Jonny announced, "and since the company didn't see fit to make me a permanent employee at the last review I only have to give a week's notice."

"But..."

"My contract says that either side can give a week's notice, but that annual leave can be incorporated. I'm owed over a week's holiday so we're quits. I'll write my resignation letter now."

His boss looked at him suspiciously. "What's going on? What did they tell you in there?"

"I'm afraid I can't tell you," Jonny replied as reasonably as he could manage, he was pushing his luck with the instant departure as it was. He didn't want to antagonise her too much. "The word from the top is that I will get my *arse-kicked* if I tell anyone."

*

"I can't believe you're being so laid back about it," Antonio (1,236) said as they walked to the Dog and Bacon together. "I've known you for years hombre, and you've never once made an impulsive decision."

"You told me to dust off my danglers," Jonny reasoned.

"But you're giving up your cushy corporate lifestyle. Pension, paid holidays, regular salary."

"Not quite, I was still on a contract, remember?"

"Oh, and you don't think they wouldn't have made you permanent the next time round? So you've jumped ship, giving no notice and risked your reference. For what? Some freelance work you've kept in your back pocket that's worth, what? Three hundred quid a month?" Antonio's teasing grin faded as he saw Jonny's expression. "What's going on?"

"I can't face covering another merger."

"No. I don't buy it. There's something you're not telling me. I know these things."

"I know that you still haven't fixed the fan in the bathroom."

Antonio stopped walking and stared at Jonny. "Something mucho importanto's happened. You changed the subject. You know something you can't tell." Antonio monitored Jonny's reaction closely. "They're making people redundant?

Jonny stared back at him impassively.

"No!" Antonio declared with a sharp intake of breath. "They're shipping out! They're closing the site!"

"Will you keep it down!" Jonny urged.

"But I'm right, aren't I?"

"Nothing's decided yet," Jonny admitted.

"But unofficially, it's the most likely option," Antonio reasoned, "and you were toying with going freelance anyway, so you decided to go now as lots of other people will also try working for themselves in order to stay here with their families. People who will need a person who can write and design their web site, their marketing materials, their..."

"Are you a secret agent or something?" Jonny asked in disbelief as they crossed the road towards the pub.

"I'm a salesman," Antonio replied, "I'm paid to work out what people are thinking and this affects me just as much as it affects you. If Sunshine goes down it will take the house prices with it. People may move out, and that means sales so we need to get hold of that business."

He opened the door for Jonny and ushered him in. "Get us a drink in while I make some phone calls, I'll join you in twenty minutes or so. I'm going to have a very busy Saturday."

"Don't you dare start telling people about this!" Jonny insisted.

"Don't fret you big senora! My boss isn't going to mind me starting a big sales drive is he?"

Jonny walked into the bar in a trance. It hadn't seemed real earlier, but Antonio's perceptive take on the situation had driven it home that, in a few weeks, he would be depending on his new venture for basics like beer, food and rent.

He soon snapped out of the trance when he saw that the pub was completely packed. At first he thought that the pub had suddenly become the new 'in' place without him realising it. However, he quickly picked up that the topic of conversation was all about one thing, Sunshine. It looked as if the news had got out after all.

He took a closer look around him and realised that he was looking at a collection of very worried local business owners. He recognised very few of them, just a few familiar faces from behind shop counters, the butcher, and the owner of Jonny's local corner shop.

If Jonny was feeling self-conscious he was certainly not alone. He was witnessing the hidden underbelly of this prosperous, corporate-dependant town; the sole traders and entrepreneurs. Whilst many of them looked ill at ease, there were also a number of natural socialisers moving freely through the chattering throng, greeting friends and acquaintances with a broad smile and a firm handshake. Those not blessed with this seemingly innate confidence were thankful to be holding a glass to disguise their nervous fidgeting as they smiled uncomfortably at people they almost knew.

Jonny suddenly realised the truth in what Antonio had said about living in the security of the corporate world. At Sunshine he was Someone. He had a defined role, he was known in his department. He could crack a few jokes by the water cooler and, through his role as reporter, he knew a wide selection of people, some of them high up in the company. Here, he was a no-one, just someone having a drink in a pub, but it was obvious that business was being discussed and if he wanted to make a go of his business he should get involved. But where to start?

A small group next to Jonny broke up to disperse further round the room, or perhaps more accurately to regroup around a different outgoing character. He slipped into the space, glad to be able to put his back against the wall and escape from the constant flow of bodies trying to move around the pub. Just as he was manoeuvring himself backwards he bumped into an eclectic silver-haired lady (88) who had also set her sights on the small sanctuary. Her arty attire made her stand out from the mainly business style of casual of the other drinkers. Although her long hair was pinned back, so much of it escaped, and in such random places that it took a long, careful look to find any sign of restraint. However, it was still obvious that the shapeless, yet colourful garments she was wearing erred towards the business end of her wardrobe.

She smirked as their shoulders gently made contact. "Caught in the act of hiding eh?" She said while still backing into the wall. "Don't you just hate these business who-hars?"

"I'm not sure really," Jonny replied. "I haven't been to one before."

"Oh dear, a virgin destined for deflowering," she announced cheerfully. "I'll try and be gentle. My advice is to just lie back, think of England and leave the fools in the suits and the alice-bands to do all the talking. I'd also suggest you avoid anyone with a beard if you don't want to be backed into a corner with earnest conversation." She smiled broadly at Jonny, revealing a red jewel in one of her front teeth. "So what do you do that is going to float my boat?"

"Pardon?"

"What's your business? What are you selling? We're all selling something."

"Oh, sorry. Web sites. I'm going to design web sites."

"So you're a geek?"

"No," Jonny replied with more force than he intended. "I can provide the copy as well."

"So you're in sales?"

"No, not really. In fact I'm probably not really suited to sales at all."

"I see. So why launch yourself into copywriting? Isn't that all about sales?" The lady asked with a mischievous smile.

"Well, yes, you're right," Jonny agreed, fumbling for the right words to use. "I'm not good at the 'buy this now because the deal will be over tomorrow' pitch, but I can describe your product or service in a way that intrigues your customer."

"But isn't that sales anyway?" she asked feigning innocence.

"Er yes, you could be right," Jonny agreed desperately. "I'm off to the bar. Can I get you anything?"

"Oh no, thank you," the lady smiled. "I start singing after too many glasses of wine and that most certainly wouldn't do here."

Jonny forced his way through the ever increasing throng cursing Antonio for leaving him alone in the pub while at the same time wincing at the thought of his face as he gloated about Jonny being lost in the 'real world'. He took his place at the bar next to a wiry man in his sixties wearing a grey suit (1,273) that looked as if it was well accustomed to spending the evening in a pub. The man's greying hair was smartly combed back in a pseudo Elvis Presley quiff, but without the drama, and his fingers that were currently holding a tiny mobile phone to his ear, bore the tell-tale yellow tide mark of a long time nicotine addict.

Jonny wasn't really taking all this in. He was still fretting about his previous conversation. However, he did notice the young pretty barmaid (68) and he managed to catch her eye as he gave her his order.

"Now, I wouldn't have expected a young chap like yourself to be ordering real ale."

Jonny turned round to find the question had come from the wiry man next to him. "I prefer the taste," Jonny replied, trying to keep his roving eye on the barmaid. "And it's a local brewery."

"Aha! A gentleman with morals," the man beamed exposing yellow teeth that matched his fingertips. "Tom Stevens, Mr Wills to you." He thrust his hand towards Jonny who shook it and then tried, but failed to catch the barmaid's eye again as he paid her.

"Mr Wills?" Jonny asked.

"Absolutely, I help people to take out wills that protect their family, ensure they pay as little tax as possible and give peace of mind, all for significantly less than your distinctly average solicitor. That's me Tom Stevens, Mr Wills. And what, may I ask? Do you do?"

"Erm, I used to work for Sunshine," Jonny replied, somewhat bemused by this barrage of information. "I'm just about to set up my own writing business, web sites, press releases, copy writing, that sort of thing."

"Aha! Perfect. We have a space for a copywriter in our chapter. You must join the BNI. What's your elevator pitch?"

"I'm sorry, I'm not understanding you," Jonny started to babble and flinched as he heard his own poor use of English. "What's BNI? And what's it got to do with elevators?"

"Aha! Good point. Me, myself, I sell wills and you just heard my elevator pitch. Imagine that you, yourself share a lift with Richard Branson. You have a few seconds to get his attention and tell him exactly what you do. You use an elevator pitch, a short phrase that you commit to memory in order to get your business message across."

"Why not call it a lift pitch? It sounds better, less American or corporate." Jonny pointed out, desperate to leave his mark on the conversation in some way.

"Absolutely!" Mr Wills beamed. "You are well suited to copywriting. Yes indeed. It is just one of those phrases that has come across the pond and stuck."

"I'm afraid I don't have a lift pitch. Although going from my recent conversations it looks like I need one. I don't even have a business card yet."

"Now that I can help you with," Mr Wills beamed and grabbed a thick wallet from a very frayed inside jacket pocket. He opened it to reveal rows of business cards in plastic strips. He flicked through it and plucked out a card and handed it to Jonny. "Go and see Brian. He'll do you a good deal on some quality cards, help you stand out from the competition."

Jonny looked intently at the card.

"You see, this is what we do at BNI, the world's largest networking organisation," Mr Wills continued. "We have a network of trusted contacts and when we see someone like yourself, who needs the services of one of ourselves, we make the connection.

"You need to network sonny. Obviously this is a local business meeting, but whenever you walk into a pub you should be networking. I saw you had your eye on the filly behind the bar, but sitting over there in the corner is Tommy. He's a window cleaner. Need a mechanic? Talk to Phil. He's not here yet, but you can bet that he'll walk through the door within twenty minutes. You can do a lot of business while you socialise. You should also come and try us out at BNI, we meet every Monday in Newbury. There's time to network and then each member does a brief presentation on the type of business they are looking for. We only allow one of each type of trade in each chapter so don't wait too long." Mr Wills handed Jonny one of his own business cards. "It starts at 6.45am sharp."

"Newbury at 6.45!" Jonny yelped. "I'd have to leave the house by six."

"No pain, no gain," Mr Wills laughed. "You do get breakfast and you can still start work at a reasonable time. Think about it."

"Thanks." Jonny said and snuck back to his hiding place by the wall just as the entire room suddenly turned their attention to one end of the bar where the self-important orange-haired woman (457) who had booked the pub with Kelly earlier, was tapping the tip of a microphone, looking incongruous on a small stage that in a previous existence had been home to a DJ and some flashing lights.

"Uh-oh," Jonny's eclectic companion sighed "The mad Carrot Lady doth speaketh."

"Ladies and gentleman!" She boomed. "Your attention, if I may, as we start our first Overchurch Local Business Meeting for some time. I'm afraid, as we all now know, this is not the best of circumstances, but by working together I have no doubt that we will be much stronger."

There were some muffled agreements and Jonny's companion rolled her eyes theatrically.

"For those who are not linked into the gossip grapevine it appears that Sunshine will be closing their site here so until another company comes to town we have a number of challenges, or rather opportunities, to face. Sunshine has brought a large number of people to the area who either live here with us, or commute in from the surrounding areas. These people fuel our local economy, they hire our services, buy our products. This means that we can enjoy modern facilities like our new cinema complex and bring investment into our schools and hospitals.

"We need to ensure that Overchurch remains an area that is attractive to residents and businesses while we are in transition between the departure of Sunshine and the arrival of the replacement company."

"How do you know that another company will come in?" A voice shouted from the back.

"Let's just say that I am one of life's great optimists." The lady replied with a grand gesture of her hand.

There were some audible sarcastic mutterings from the room, which the speaker took with good grace and from that moment on Jonny's attention started to waver. The Carrot Lady demonstrated a real admiration of her own voice as she tackled the task of setting up a committee, taking nominations and telling people to sign up on specific lists that *must* include their email address to save costs.

To be fair to the speaker, his attention didn't so much ebb away as get distracted the moment the Carrot Lady made a belated thank you to the new landlady (158) who had kindly provided nibbles at short notice for later in the evening. The landlady stopped whizzing around behind the bar and gave a flushed smile in response to the muted clapping. Jonny was captivated by her assorted piercings, colourful braided hair and her cheeky smile. He quickly finished his pint and decided that it was time for another drink.

If the mild anxiety of the assembled group had given way to the resigned impatience of installing democracy, there was no sign of it behind the bar. The overworked staff were fighting to keep up with the demand for drinks caused by a subtle stream of people quietly heading for liquid refreshment.

Jonny waited quietly by Kelly's end of the bar as she hurriedly poured drinks in front of him.

"Now this must be weird for you," he observed. "You take over a pub just as the main employer in town ships out and you have the busiest day ever."

"Tell me about it," Kelly panted, clicking her tongue piercing against her front teeth as she struggled to force the lever down on the large, brass wine bottle opener attached to the side of the bar. She tugged down on the lever but nothing happened except a metallic grinding sound.

"No!" She shouted. "You can't break on me now!" She yanked the bottle out and a piece of the mechanism tumbled to the floor. She stood and looked at it, temporarily unable to move, or even think around the problem.

"You got a normal opener?" Jonny asked gently.

"Of course!" She spat, "but I'm pants at using it. Always cork it."

"Pass it over here then," Jonny replied, "and I'll open it while you serve other drinks."

Kelly's face split into a huge smile. "You," she declared, "are lovely!" She grabbed a corkscrew and pressed it into his hands along with the bottle of wine.

Ten minutes later and Jonny had opened two bottles of wine and was supping a free pint of beer. The meeting had suddenly become much more enjoyable.

Kelly was in the process of pulling a pint of ale when it spat out foam into the glass and back up into her face. At the same moment there was a show of hands in the bar as people voted on who should stand on the committee.

"Yeuch!" Kelly exclaimed, wiping her face with her hands. She turned round and bumped into a tall, skinny man with matted dreadlocks tied back from his face with a colourful bandana (208). His bare arms were decorated with tattoos and his face was a breeding ground for more piercings than Kelly's.

He looked at Kelly and laughed. "It's not aftershave babes."

"The barrel's just gone, can you change it?" Kelly pleaded.

"Not again!" The man grumbled, "I've only just done the Stella."

"Don't complain Malc!" A familiar voice boomed in Jonny's ear. "That's your wages down there."

Jonny turned round to see Antonio with Heather (178) standing beside him.

"Hey Antonio," Kelly said as she reached for another empty glass. "Checking to see if we can run the place you found for us?"

"You've certainly got the crowds in," Antonio grinned. "And I see you've met my hombre Jonny, copywriter and web designer extraordinaire?"

"You know each other?" Kelly exclaimed as she continued in her work. "Small world eh?"

"I take it you noticed her wedding ring?" Antonio whispered in Jonny's ear.

Jonny scowled, glanced quickly at the offending piece of jewellery and cursed himself. Of course, he would have been less disappointed if he realised that in making contact with Kelly he was now only one contact away from Cat. But at this point in his life she was still one of the millions of single women he hadn't met yet. He tried to move away from the scene, but Heather took his arm softly.

"How you doing hen?" She cooed. "Made any good contacts yet?"

"Erm, not really," Jonny replied. "I've met a couple of interesting people."

"You've got to get out there and talk to people," Antonio butted in. "I've been watching you. You're hiding away on the edges. You've got to sell yourself now hombre. These people here are your bread and butter. They're not going to come up to you and say 'Hi Jonny. Please design my web site and write my company newsletter."

"I know that, but my own web site will be up soon and people will be able to see my work on there. See what I'm really like, what I'm good at."

"But, they've got to find your site, have the time to read it, compare it to a few others, and then make the effort to contact you," Antonio argued. "Why not go up to the person nearest you and say 'Hi, my name's Jonny. What is it that you do?'"

"Because, it…it, just doesn't seem right."

Heather laughed. "You're a strange one Jonny. We've just watched you chat up the sexy barmaid when she's dead busy.

Some people would rather die than do that, but you're still shy of selling yourself. It's insane." She touched his elbow lightly to take the sting out of her words. "What do you normally do all day? You interview people, find out information, write things about them, yet you dinnae want to talk about your own abilities?"

"It's not that, it's just because..."

"It's a British romantic comedy cliché," Antonio butted in. "Hugh Grant always finds it impossible to ask attractive women out even though the majority of the senoritas in the audience have chosen that film purely because they fancy Senor Grant. Your problem is that you can talk to the bonita senoras, but not your clients. You have talent, hombre, you need to shout about it."

"But that's just it!" Jonny objected. "I don't know that I can do it!" He said this more loudly than he anticipated and the people around them who still had half an eye on the committee proceedings turned round to look. Antonio pulled him away to a quieter area.

"Do you think that everyone in this room is a market leader?" He hissed. "Half of these people are taking the same step as you. It's all talk. You persuade someone that you can do a job. You do the job to the best of your ability and when you do it well the news spreads and you get a good reputation. I convince someone that I can sell their house. I get as many people as possible to visit the house, especially other clients who are also selling through me. Someone will walk through the door of the house and love it. Bang! Job done. Someone in this room will love what you're planning to do, but you have to knock on the door. You know what they say: If opportunity doesn't knock, build a door!"

Jonny was in the process of trying to come up with a suitable answer when they were caught in the middle of the stampede for the buffet tables. An army may march on its stomach, but it's never as desperate for food as a room full of people who have just gone through the process of forming a committee.

To: Sam

From Cat

Subject: RE. Sheila's revenge

Date: Mon 20/6/2006

Dear Sheila,

Okay, let's do a deal. I'll stop calling you Sheila if you promise not to set me up with all the boys from my class in Friends Reunited! I'd forgotten what a cheeky git you are. Some sympathy would have been nice!

Thanks for the tips on holding a baby the right way up. Not sure I needed all that detail about the nappy contents though. I'll remember your descriptions the next time I've reached the 'point of almost no return' without a condom – it could be the perfect contraception method!

To answer your question, no I haven't gone off men. I just don't want to be in relationship with one. Both you and Kelly have told me that I need to get laid – perhaps the time is right for me to go through the promiscuous stage I somehow missed out at university? Perhaps I can sleep my way to the top at Sunshine and marry a rich SVP?

Seriously though, it's great having you on the end of email. I miss the way we used to talk about life, the universe, but mainly about men! Ah it all seemed so important back then, but the here and now still seems fairly difficult. I hope you don't mind if I run a few things by you in the future? Kelly's my sister and all that, but she's a rubbish listener and Mum, well she wanted to marry me off years ago. And who wants to discuss sex with your parents? She might start discussing their favourite positions or something. Yuck!

Have fun getting up in the night to feed little Bruce and pop a few shrimps on the Barbie for me.

G'day sport

Cat

Chapter 4

Cat (419) inwardly cursed the wayward leads belonging to her presentation equipment. Once more she unsuccessfully attempted to close the lid of the carry case that cleverly housed all manner of leads, adaptors and wossnames when it was brand new. She was in a double hurry, she was going to be late for Kelly's do and she wanted to get out of the venue before...

"So how's my Puss in Boots?" It was the General Manager (98) of the trendy London venue that Sunshine hired to try and impress medical consultants. It wasn't just a case of getting favourable rates, this creep regularly played golf with one of the powers-that-be at Sunshine. He tried to get as much added value out of his buddy status as possible.

His propensity to drool, while gawping at Cat's chest, had persuaded her to attend the event wearing a chaste outfit of a high necked jumper and a long skirt. However, his sharp lecherous eyes had spotted her boots at 20 paces.

Cat shuddered. "Don't be a dick." She retorted.

"Ha ha! That's my Cat," he cried, smoothing back his jet black curls of hair that constantly tumbled into his face. "Always quick off the mark."

Cat forced a fake smile on to her face as the creep took the opportunity to look her up and down lecherously, his fingers twitching involuntarily as his eyes lingered on the curve of her bum.

"Sorry about the equipment cock up," he said with a cheery laugh. "Shit happens eh?"

"Lucky for you I had my back up," Cat said as she hurriedly finished packing all the leads into the carry case. "You should have your own back up systems, we pay you enough for your services."

"I provide many personal services that you have yet to take up my proud little pussy cat." He responded with a leer.

"Just because you play golf with the head of my department, it doesn't give you licence to sexually harass me in the workplace."

"Now that's a good point," the creep conceded with a thoughtful look. "Perhaps we should make a move to the pub so we can do it off work premises?"

"In your dreams," Cat snarled. "I'm going home and you're staying here."

"Oh my dear pussy, I can assure you I have done quite enough work for today."

"Really? I hadn't noticed. However, I've got an important meeting to get to back home."

"Come, come, I don't think that can be true can it? It's nearly eight o'clock and not even my friends at Sunshine would try and keep you that long."

"It's a local business meeting, at my sister's pub."

"You're coming out to dinner with me," The creep said bluntly. I have booked a very romantic restaurant for us."

Cat finally managed to snap the case shut. "I really don't think that your wife is going to approve of that."

"Why should she approve of it? She's not going to know, and there is so much for you to gain."

"No." Cat said angrily. "I said no and now I'm going home." She picked up her belongings and went to push past him, but he grabbed hold of her wrist in a maliciously tight grip.

"I don't think you understand," he said in a pleasant voice that belied the pressure on her wrist. I have been watching you for some time, you have invaded my fantasies and I do intend to have you."

"Let me go!" Cat shouted angrily as she tried to twist her wrist free.

"Why the shouting Catherine?" he said soothingly. "We both know that there is no-one left here to hear you."

Cat tensed up, her heart thundering in her chest.

"Did you hear that?" He giggled. "I made a pun, here to hear you!"

Cat struggled again and raised the computer case menacingly.

"Now, now pussycat. I think you need to retract your claws. Because I know that you need me more than you think. And what's a little sexual favour between friends?"

"I don't need you for anything!" Cat snarled and changed her grip on the case so she could swing it more easily.

"But I think you do," he continued, still in his overly pleasant voice. "You missed something during your little event this afternoon. An announcement. The sun has gone down in Overchurch. Sunshine is pulling out, moving some jobs around, but 75 per cent are going, and one of them, my proud pussy, is you."

In her surprise Cat paused in her retaliation and stared at him as he pushed his errant curls back off his forehead.

"You see, I can be very, very useful to you. I have contacts, many contacts throughout the event management business. I can wave your CV under the nose of the people who really matter. I can get you another job, a much better job in fact, more money, more responsibility, less of this scrabbling around fighting fires in front of an expectant audience."

He eased the pressure on her wrist and gently slipped his hand into hers.

"It's not just one job; I have contacts with all the major players. They listen to me; I can pull strings, offer favours. I can set you up with your dream job."

Cat tried to slip her hand free but he quickly grasped her wrist again.

"I only want one thing in return Cat. Just one night. No strings. I've been watching you for such a long time Cat. I just can't wait to make you purr."

Cat swung the case at his head and he quickly released his grip and moved quickly away. He stayed just out of range of the case, smiling condescendingly as he looked her up and down.

"You stay away from me!" Cat seethed. "I have only ever been civil to you because of your contacts with Sunshine. It looks as though I don't have to bother any more." She backed away slowly, holding the case in front of her.

"Oh pussycat, pussycat, you're committing career suicide. Don't you know that if I can open any doors for you in the business, I can also shut and lock them in your face? We all know how easy it is to shut cats out for the night. Walk away now and you'll never work in this business again."

"I'd sign on rather than go anywhere near you," Cat snarled as she continued to back away. "And if you follow me I'll call the police."

"I'm disappointed Cat," he said holding up his hands. "Now, if you really *have* to go I'll cancel the restaurant and luxury hotel room *with* Champagne and spend the time black balling you in the industry."

"Have fun," Cat said dryly. "That's the closest you will ever get to screwing me." She sped out of the door and hurried to the street where she was very relieved to be able to hail a cab. She told the cabbie (79) to take her to the train station and slumped back into her seat.

"You alright love?" the cabbie asked as he swung out into the throng of slow moving traffic.

"Yes, yes, I'm fine," Cat replied automatically. "End of a busy day that's all."

"You and me both," the cabbie smiled before turning his attention to nudging his way into the correct lane.

Cat was far from fine. The unexpected display of concern from a stranger had made tears prickle in her eyes. She took a deep breath and looked at the brisk rush of the Londoners around her as they made their usual way home after another normal day. Did that really just happen? Had she just been made redundant and shunned by her industry all in the space of five minutes? Didn't she deserve just a tiny bit of luck after all she had been through?

The cabbie hit his horn in response to a driver who had the audacity to be dithering between two lanes. Cat jumped and made a big effort to slow her breathing with some yoga breathing exercises. She was just starting to breath from the depths of her stomach when her mobile rang, making her jump again. It was Kelly (160).

"Cat! Where are you?" She wailed. "The place is heaving! We haven't got enough food, we might not even have enough beer! When are you going to get here?"

Cat paused, fighting her impulse to scream down the phone about her own stressful news. "I'm still in London Kelly, calm down." She said in impressively measured tones.

"You what? Calm down? This was your idea and you promised you'd be back in time!"

"I know Kel," Cat sighed, "and I'm sorry, but I'm not exactly having a good time either."

"Yes, yes. We know about the closure. That's why everyone's here stupid! And they're still coming in the door! You've got to help us. What do we do?"

Cat took a deep breath and formed a mental picture of herself slapping Kelly's petulant face. "Right, have you called in *all* your bar staff?" She asked in a calm voice.

*

When Cat finally made it to the Dog and Bacon there only one lone drinker at the bar. A tired looking man (473) in his late thirties with prematurely grey hair who gave off the aura of someone who needed to be in the receiving end of some feminine love and attention. He was wearing a suit that needed pressing, a shirt that needed washing and shoes that needed shining. Somewhere under the forlorn exterior there was a rogue waiting to get out, but in the meantime he was fondling Ferrero's silky ears.

Cat's appearance was all it took to tear Ferrero from his new best friend. He bounded enthusiastically through the deserted bar area to greet his exhausted mistress.

She crouched down to greet him and to stop him from jumping up against her. If she had been alone she would have given him a very needy hug, but she had to make do with an affectionate pat. Ferrero tried unsuccessfully to lick her face and then changed tactics by launching himself onto his back and rolled around in ecstasy, his paws waving wildly in the air.

"When a beautiful woman enters the room the meek males roll at her feet," the man at the bar observed drunkenly.

"I beg your pardon?" Cat said curtly, standing up quickly.

"I am sorry, please don't take offence ma'am," the man replied, breaking eye contact. "It was merely a turn of phrase, and a weak one at that. Please forgive me. I am in an interesting mood. It has been a bad day."

Cat eyed him with distrust, a move that earned her a knowing smile from the lone bar fly.

"And I'll wager that you have endured one of those days that creep up behind one and scream boo! Before savaging one with sharp, pointed teeth?" He continued unabashed.

Cat was just trying to decide how to reply to this strange man when Kelly popped her head up from behind the bar.

"Man, you made it at last!" Kelly said walking wearily round the bar to hug her sister. "What's with the frumpy outfit? What happened to my glam big sis?"

"Oh thanks," Cat sighed. "A few hours ago I was Kelly's public enemy number one and now you criticise my fashion sense."

"Easy tiger," Kelly grinned. "I just didn't realise you were cultivating the over-the-hill middle-aged woman look."

"Well, on this occasion I was, although it still backfired."

"My dear," the drunken man cried effusively. "Pray, do not try to tease me over matters of female fashion. A subject of which I have very little knowledge or understanding. Is it now de rigueur for graceful ladies to dress badly on purpose?"

Cat's eyes swept over the tired appearance of his own attire and he quickly got the message.

"Yes, yes, I quite see your point," he said hurriedly. "I am not making a positive fashion statement, but have not had sufficient time to stop and freshen my attire since very early this morning."

"What I think my big sis was saying was that she was trying not to attract unwanted male attention," Kelly pointed out with a mischievous grin.

"Quite so, quite so," the man agreed. "I find the tactic also stops all female attention, wanted or otherwise."

Cat frowned and turned to Kelly. "Can I have a drink?" She asked. "A large one. What happened to everyone?"

"It's after hours Cat. Malc's gone to bed already. They practically drank us dry," Kelly grinned. "And they ate *everything*. You're a genius. We made more profit tonight than we did in the whole of last week."

"God, is it that late?" Cat exclaimed. "I can't believe I've missed last orders. I'm so sorry about missing your do."

"Forget last orders. It's time for a lock in. Tim, you want to go home?"

"Not if I have the opportunity to buy you two ladies a drink."

"You can have a drink on the house," Kelly said as she locked the door.

"I had better perform a watery portrait on the porcelain first," Tim muttered and staggered off towards the toilets.

Cat raised her eyes with disbelief at Kelly. "If you're trying to set me up then you're so dead!"

"Oh relax," Kelly sighed. "He's a funny guy, a wedding photographer. Apparently he gets all poncy when he's had a few, and he's certainly done well on that score. Are you alright chick?"

By the time Tim returned the girls were seated comfortably on a couple of the softer chairs in the pub, surrounded by a sea of empty glasses that Kelly didn't have the strength to start cleaning. He took his seat just as Cat was finishing telling Kelly about her terrible experience.

"So there it is," Cat concluded. "Apparently I will never work in the events industry ever again."

"And which ghastly apparition told you that?" Tim asked theatrically as he sat down clumsily. He raised his glass to Kelly. "Chin chin."

"Some loser tried to bribe my lovely sister to sleep with him." Kelly said angrily.

"Methinks that his brains are in his balls, his thoughts stuck in a rancid gutter and that his ego far exceeds the size of his manhood." Tim declared, finally earning a smile from Cat.

"But he does have contacts with all the big players," she sighed.

"In my experience Cat, the people who actually have the power to exclude someone from the magic circle do not try and force you to dance to their tune; they just quietly turn off the music leaving you in the dark," Tim announced. "People who claim to have the power are usually notorious exaggerators. And who wants to make merry with people who have so little respect for their compatriots anyway?"

"So you wouldn't be worried if someone threatened to tell everyone that you did a really bad job of their wedding photos?" Cat asked.

"Of course I would be concerned," Tim agreed, "I rely on word of mouth for my business, but just one person making heinous, and unfounded, accusations is quickly over-ruled by your own network of contacts. I know from experience."

"What experience?" Kelly probed.

"Alas, I was apprehended by my intended in a hotel room with a gorgeous fashion model." Tim sighed.

The girls looked at each other in shock.

"Well go on man!" Kelly laughed. "What happened?"

"I was covering an international bridal fair in London and was working with a woman who was so divine that even the women sighed in appreciation when she glided past them."

"And she fell for you?" Kelly asked somewhat dubiously.

"If only you had the depth of character and insight that my intended had, my wild-haired hostess," Tim mused. "The truth of the matter is that this model was full of physical beauty, but hard as a stone inside. I could no more fall in love with her than I could with root canal work. However, she was a damsel in distress so how could a gentleman like myself refuse to help her? A group of lads had followed her back to her room and had scared her poisonous little soul.

"She escaped to my room. It had twin beds. We were professional adults. My intended arrived unexpectedly to surprise me with some pre-nuptial romancing. Instead she discovered a vision of beauty clad only in a hotel dressing gown, emerging from wisps of steam in the bathroom. My intended failed to believe that I could be in the close vicinity of such a goddess without succumbing to her seduction. The cold hearted model was stunned that anyone could believe that she would lie with someone of my appearance. My intended turned bitter and tried to besmirch my professional reputation."

"What happened?" Cat asked eagerly, drawn into the dramatic story.

"The photos from the shoot were immensely popular and

everyone who knew of me found it so amusing that I was being accused of seducing one of the top models in the business that it only served to enhance my working reputation. Cat, if you are good at your job and you have a solid network of contacts, there is nothing that a jumped up bully can do to destroy you. Besides I may have a job for you."

He reached into his pocket and pulled out his business card and handed it to her courteously. "A group of us are trying to organise a local bridal fair. Dresses, photographers, stationery, florists, caterers, venues, marquees – the lot. An over abundance of cooks intent on spoiling broths. We need someone to organise us. Email me tomorrow and I'll introduce you to the loop."

He drained his glass, got to his feet and summoning as much dignity as is possible for someone who discovers that the floor has just started to wobble, he waved them good night.

"Farewell, my glamorous drinking companions," he said grandly before turning towards the door, tripping over a snoozing Ferrero and falling full length on the floor.

The House of Fun Blog

Diary of a mad house
Date 21st June 2006

A new beginning

VIKING - Some things happen faster than you expect, or want them to. You can plan for big events, face the inevitable but they can still pop up early and threaten to give your arse a good kicking.
The House of Fun is shortly to double up as the workplace of fun as I go freelance and try to earn an honest wage from the confines of a flat that is disarmingly close to distractions like pubs, takeways and the corner shop with the foxy sales assistant I have fancied ever since I arrived here.
So stay tuned to find out what it's like to work and live from home and whether the Viking can sail the high seas of employment by himself.

SPANIARD - You're not exactly sailing alone off into the sunset you Nordic poof.

CELT - Who cares about the sailing? I want to know more about the sexy shop assistant. You never mentioned her to me!!

GUEST - CapnJack: What's this? Jealousy in the House of Lurve?

SPANIARD - Who says the sales assistant is a senora? I bet it's the big bearded hombre with the turban.

CELT – That can't be right because I fancy him! So, Viking, you asked this babe out yet? If you don't ask you don't get!

SPANIARD – He would if he could but she's spoken for and knows all about the Viking's subscription for Babes in Boots Monthly.

VIKING – I am truly a tortured artist amongst barbarians… BTW, does that mag exist?!

GUEST – Ute: What line of work U in Viking?

VIKING – Probably best not to say here, but it involves writing and web design.

GUEST – Ute: Hard to get work when you're anonymous! ;)

SPANIARD – Who is this Ute? I thought this was supposed to be a blog about us???

Chapter 5

Jonny (80) was not so much snoozing, as closing his eyes to keep out the harsh light while he waited for his brain to shrink enough to fit his skull without pulsing. He tried pretending that he was relishing the fact that he didn't have to commute into work, and that today was the day when he was going to start work on his new business.

It didn't work. The reality was that he was still in bed at nine o'clock. He had been invaded by a relentless hangover and he had a nagging suspicion that he had missed out on a number of golden opportunities to capture his first customers in the haze of last night.

He turned over and forced his eyes open. Despite the shrouded gloom of his bedroom, he could see through a chink in the curtains that it was a bright sunny day. The perfect start to a new day. He mentally cringed as he realised that, even after Antonio's verbal kick up the arse, he had actually spent the rest of the evening with the few people he already knew.

He remembered joking with the silver haired woman about the impossibility of carrying a drink and a paper plate of food while introducing yourself, shaking hands *and* exchanging business cards. It had been easier to wait until later to mingle and here he was with three business cards on his bedside table when he should have thirty.

He took a deep breath as through the fuzz in his toxic brain he remembered that he needed to finish designing his web site and needed to order some business cards. He swung his legs over the bed, waited for his brain to catch up with his skull and stumbled towards the shower.

Twenty minutes later he was padding into the kitchen in his socks, tracksuit trousers and an un-ironed T-shirt. He felt clean and almost refreshed. Working from home was starting to look up. He set up his lap top on the kitchen table, brewed a killer strength coffee and fired up his email, trying to ignore the steady drip-dripping sound from the leaking kitchen tap.

He was surprised to see an email from the Carrot Lady. She had written up the minutes from the meeting and emailed them out before he had even managed to get vertical. He flicked through a few paragraphs of fighting talk, an over-verbose version of 'all for one and one for all'. She was determined to make people come to the town and use its services if it killed her.

Despite the enthusiastic rhetoric, he was more captivated by the list of attendees included at the end. Antonio was right. He had been standing amongst his potential customers all evening and all he had done was try to chat up a married barmaid and spend beer money he couldn't afford. Richard Branson he certainly wasn't.

He scanned the list. There was everything from an organic vegetable box delivery scheme to a masseuse via travel agents and a micro brewery – the same brewery that produced his favourite pint. How did he miss talking to them? Jonny gradually forgot his hangover as the excitement of the potential of his new business mingled with the energy rush from the caffeine.

The Carrot Lady's list was full of people who needed to promote their products or services to a potentially dwindling number of customers. Not to mention all the people Sunshine had 'let go' who may be trying their hand at going freelance. They would need web sites, ezines and press releases. He needed to make sure that people knew that he was *the* person to come to in the local area.

His mind raced as he devised new ideas. He could create a town 'newspaper' on-line and charge companies to advertise in it. Then there were banner ads and affiliate links for online retailers like Amazon. He grinned as he thought about including a review section on local restaurants, pubs and clubs. That could lead to all sorts of freebies!

His train of thought was distracted by the steady – and irritating – sound of the dripping kitchen tap. This slight disturbance was enough to allow reality to reassert itself and his excitement abruptly fizzled out when he realised that any sort of venture would need investment. He had no capital. He sat back. Come to think of it, he was going to struggle to pay the rent. After next month, the only income he would have was from the monthly ezine he had been editing for a friend of his dad's since his university days.

He needed to think smaller. He could specialise in helping small businesses promote themselves. He could write those lift pitches for them for free. Then show them the advantages of a well designed web site with informative, eye-catching copy. Then again, he needed to write his own lift pitch first.

He mused on this for a while and filled a page with different versions before he was happy with it. He celebrated his achievement by getting up to grab himself a pint of water to try and rehydrate himself. He turned the tap off hard to try and stop the monotonous dripping and his world was suddenly soaked by a jet of cold water as the tap came away in his hand.

"Shit!" He exclaimed as he jumped back in shock, dropping his glass that shattered around his feet. The water fountain burst unhindered into the room nearly reaching his laptop. He moved back towards the tap to try and stop the water, but trod on a shard of glass and leapt back again. He looked around him, grabbed a tea towel and threw it over the tap, deflecting the water flow.

He balanced on one foot and surveyed the scene. His foot was starting to bleed copiously, forming a patch of scarlet on his white sports socks that was starting to drip onto the water on the floor. The water was still managing to squirt out from under the tea towel that was not thick enough to redirect the flow to the sink. He checked behind him and it seemed clear of glass. He hopped backwards carefully, grabbed a broom out of the cupboard and balancing on one foot he swept the glass out of the way.

He opened the cupboard under the sink and gingerly knelt down on the floor, wincing as small jets of cold water splashed onto his back. He yanked the contents of the cupboard out on to the sopping wet floor and fumbled for the stopcock. After some struggling and copious swearing he managed to turn it off and sighed with relief as the water finally stopped soaking his T-shirt.

He pulled himself up on one foot and surveyed the scene of destruction. The floor was covered with assorted items of cleaning equipment and washing up gloves, nestled in water that was tinted rosé in places from his blood.

He examined the sole of his foot. There was a piece of glass embedded in it. He took a deep breath and pulled it out releasing another spurt of blood into the flotsam on the floor.

Half an hour later Jonny had cleared up the glass and most of the water and was sitting with his bandaged foot propped on a chair as he tried plumber after plumber from the Yellow Pages. Apparently he didn't qualify for an emergency as by turning off the stopcock he had averted a flood. It appeared that rather than setting himself up as a web designer, he should retrain as a plumber and wait for the work to come to him.

He flung the phone down on the table in disgust and his eyes were drawn to the list of attendees from last night's meeting. He noticed that one of them was a plumber and quickly phoned the number. The plumber George (356) was busy, but in the area and within an hour he was surveying the damage in Jonny's kitchen.

"This tap's older than the hills, not to mention cheap crap," George complained as he ran his work-roughened fingers along the broken metal. "Surprised it didn't go years ago. I can seal it off for you so you can at least turn the water back on, but I can't come and put a new 'un in for you for a couple of days."

"That's fine," Jonny said gratefully. "I'll get my flatmate to splash out on some new taps."

"Splash out eh?" George grinned. "Still in the mood for jokes I see."

"Not really," Jonny said with a rueful smile and pointed to table where a pile of papers surrounded his lap top. "It's not exactly the ideal way to launch a business."

"Another one joining the work from home brigade eh? They'll

be a few more now Sunshine's closing down."

"That's exactly why I was trying to get ahead. I was trying to get my foot in the door."

They both laughed at the pun.

"I'm a web designer and copy writer. I don't suppose you know anyone who needs a new web site do you?"

"Well you seem to have a way with words mate." He looked down at Jonny's crudely bandaged foot that was just starting to turn pink at the bottom. "You better get that looked at. And after that you can do worse than having a chat with the people at Business Link. It's a government run thingy, helps as you start up a new business. Reckon they'll be dead busy around here soon. They helped me out a year or so ago and now I don't have a bloody minute to meself. I certainly don't need no web site. I only went to that do last night to see how I can support my customers. I don't want this place turning into a ghost town."

To: Sam
From Cat
Subject: RE. Sheila's revenge
Date: Tues 21/6/2006

Dear Sheila, sorry Sam,

Thanks sooo much for the delightful photos of darling Bruce. I can now see that you were not exaggerating about the contents of his nappies. Why anyone would take, let alone send, a photo of that is beyond me, you need to get help. However, Bruce looks very cute when he's clean and you're not looking so bad yourself.

I do realise that you have decided to call your little sprog by a name other than Bruce, but as far as I'm concerned, all Ozzie blokes are called Bruce and all Ozzie sheilas are called She…

Yes, as you have guessed I have completely embraced promiscuity and am struggling to write this as I have three strapping men in my bed who are all clamouring to please me in very special ways, but you come first babe (no pun intended). Seriously though, I did have someone trying to bribe me to sleep with him recently, which was horrible, but apart from that there is still nothing on the man front. My rude bits are demanding a full annual service but my heart and brain really aren't interested.

I hope little Bruce starts to sleep better soon, it's weird, when you're getting up in the night to deal with him, I'm out and about, working through my day.

G'day sport

Cat

Chapter 6

Cat (420) was enjoying having a minute to herself. Her face was flushed and she was panting, focusing on achieving her objective - finishing the final kilometre on the rowing machine.

She was not someone to internalise stress, she sweated it out, and if she ever entered the gym with a heavy heart, she made it work so hard that it was relieved when it could slow down again. A good workout always made her feel good; her smile wasn't absent for too long.

She completed her target distance with just over a minute to spare. As she continued to row at half speed she slowly became more aware of her surroundings and the other people who were paying for the privilege of torturing their muscles.

While Cat may have been in a world of her own there was someone on an exercise bike (474) who was having considerable trouble averting his eyes from her perspiring form. In fact the more his eyes looked, the slower his legs seemed to go round. He was making a reasonable effort both to avert his eyes and to boost his speed. It was just that Cat seemed to draw his eyes.

She looked in his direction as she unfurled herself from the rowing machine, a little less gracefully than she planned; as her aching muscles made her legs uncooperative. She executed a neat double-take as she recognised Tim. He was looking both smarter and more dishevelled from the last time she saw him. His T-shirt and tracksuit trousers looked new and if not clean, then at least clean on today. He was flushed and sweating and the damage from the previous night's alcohol was evident in the bags under his eyes.

"Hi," She said a little self-consciously. "Sorry, I didn't see you there."

"I may be biased," Tim puffed, his legs suddenly whirring much faster than a few seconds earlier. "But if you didn't win gold after that effort there should be a steward's enquiry."

Cat smiled as she grabbed the spray and a paper towel to wipe down the rowing machine. "I get a bit carried away in here when the stress levels build up."

"If only I could follow your example," Tim wheezed. "Exercise and I have a love hate relationship. If I truly love myself I should exercise, but I truly hate doing it."

Cat found herself laughing as she swung her leg over the saddle of the exercise bike next to him. She normally preferred to stay in her own bubble in the gym, but seeing the state of Tim made her feel better about herself. She may have had her career sunk, but at least she could still hold her own in the gym.

"I'm impressed that you're in here at all today. You must have made a hefty boost to my sister's profits last night."

"Please do not venture too near me," Tim sighed as he gave up the pretence of being a high speed cyclist. "I fear that my sweat is about 90% proof."

"You're probably right," Cat grinned as she set the bike controls and started pedalling, noticeably faster than Tim.

"I hope I wasn't too unspeakable last night. I'm afraid I don't venture forth into the outside world as much as I should do. Always the wedding photographer, never the party animal."

"You were okay," Cat assured him. "Very helpful in fact, it was good to know that there's life outside the corporate world. That there are people I can turn to for help."

"From corporate to network," Tim observed, his feet pedalling just fast enough to show willing, while still leaving him enough oxygen to speak with. "A chance to revert to normal conversations that do not evolve around the fuel economy of the company car you may just get on your next promotion."

"Oh very clever. I take it you're a regular at those events?"

"I try to mingle with the best of them. It keeps me active. The intriguing aspect of networking is that you never know which individual is going to be your holy grail - the person who is going to open the door to your next big contract. In my experience it never seems to be the individual you converse with, it is always one of their contacts."

"All sounds a bit optimistic to me," Cat said between taking gulps of air as she started to find her cycling rhythm.

"An analogy. Pretend, if you will, that you were trying to match make your delightful sister with a suitable gentleman."

"But Kelly's married!"

"I realise that. It is simply an analogy. Have a look round here and see if you can see the type of fellow that Kelly would find attractive."

Cat scanned the room. It was no contest really. There was a scary looking army-type man in his late thirties who was straining to lift substantial free weights while staring directly at her; a very fit runner effortlessly tramping a treadmill at high speed and a lacklustre man in his forties who was fooling himself if he thought his half-hearted efforts were going to shrink his impressive beer gut.

"I'm predicting that she would prefer the lithe individual on the treadmill, but let's say that he is married, or gay even, to spice up our little scenario. Who would you choose now?"

Cat had another surreptitious look around the room. "I don't mean to be rude, but I wouldn't choose anyone."

"Fair enough, and I fear I would agree with your opinion, but what if you made the effort to have a conversation with one of the others and you discovered that one of his acquaintances was a perfect match for your sister? You would be glad that you talked to him and his acquaintance would definitely be pleased with the introduction.

"This is my very point. Everyone is potentially useful to you and you to them. You might meet an individual who is worthless to you in a business sense, but they might play golf with a fellow who is your ideal customer. It is in the interests of the person who does the introduction as he now has two people who are likely to want to return his favour."

"It just all sounds so random."

"But is it?" Tim asked as he gave up the pretence of continuing to exercise and turned to face Cat who was still cycling steadily. "I'm presuming that you haven't read the Celestine Prophecy?"

"No, but it sounds ominous."

Tim laughed. "It's perfectly harmless. It's a rather curious little novel that examines some basic, but often overlooked aspects of our spirituality."

"You're not going to get all new age and hippy on me like Kelly, are you?"

"Don't worry, your karma is safe with me," Tim smiled. "However, it might make you contemplate a little bit more about some of life's unanswered questions. The underlying premise of the book is that everything happens for a reason, therefore there are no accidents or coincidences. The author argues that we should be open to new experiences and the people that cross our paths. I know it sounds rather loopy but thinking in this manner can open your perspectives and enable you to make the most of new opportunities."

"I think the exercise has got the booze back into your bloodstream. A coincidence is a coincidence." Cat said and she started to increase her cycling speed again.

"Fair enough, perhaps we should return to our analogy on romance? Perhaps I could be so bold as to enquire where you met your current boyfriend?"

"I don't have a current boyfriend," Cat replied a little more harshly than she intended.

"Again, fair enough," Tim replied reassuringly, although he was unable to stop a pleased little smile appearing on his face. "But perhaps you could tell me where you met your previous boyfriend? What I am asking is whether or not it was a chance encounter."

"Not really, I met him in a pub, nothing special."

"But was it a planned event? Was this trip to the pub planned and written on your calendar?"

"Not at all. A group of us decided to meet up and get drunk."

"And what about your ex-boyfriend?"

"No, he just..." Cat stopped pedalling. "Oh I see, very clever. You're claiming that me meeting my ex was a coincidence. But everyone has to meet by coincidence unless you live on the same street, or work in the same place, or...where do I stop?"

Tim laughed. "One step ahead of me as usual Cat! So if everything happens by coincidences, is it not a good idea to be more aware of them and the potential good fortune they can bring you?

"You can take this further by discovering the manner in which your parents met, how their parents met, and their parents and so on. You can be certain that a number of coincidences will be involved and even if they did grow up in the same village you have to ask yourself what coincidences were involved in bringing them to the village, in keeping them alive through hard times."

"I get your point Tim."

"But it goes even further than that," Tim protested. "Your lineage goes back thousands of years, all those chance encounters, all your ancestors surviving in times of low life expectancy. Then, on one wonderful night, one particular sperm from your Father fuses with your Mother's egg to make you, not someone similar to you, but *you*. They made the most of that coincidence and they created you."

"Okay," Cat conceded. "That is rather freaky and perhaps slightly too much biological detail than I really needed, but life is still random."

"My point is that we can make use of the randomness, shape it slightly for our own means. People looking for love can go to a singles bar where they know that the other drinkers are also looking to form a relationship."

"Are you implying that I'm desperate for a man?" Cat snapped.

"Not at all my dear," Tim replied hurriedly. "If we return to the networking scenario we can go to networking events, where we can meet like-minded individuals. My original point, that seems to have got lost in my ramblings; is that by being open to coincidences, as you call them, we can improve on our handouts from Lady Luck. For example, last night I was going to go home just before you arrived, but I got a strong urge to stay."

"You also had a strong urge to pee." Cat pointed out with a grin.

"But I stayed for a bit longer," Tim continued, determined not to be put off his stride, "and was delighted to meet you and to hopefully pass some business your way. Now we have met again, and I think we will in the future. If you had ignored me last night, assumed that I was just an inebriated fool, then you would have missed out on a potential business lead and I would have missed out on the undoubted pleasure of your company. If I walked into this gym there is no way I would strike up a conversation with a woman so beautiful and athletic as you. I would try and be as inconspicuous as possible."

"That's ridiculous!"

"Not really, no man likes to be shown up in a gym. Especially by a woman. A glamorous, intelligent woman at that."

Cat blushed with all the flattery; she had let her guard down with this harmless looking man. She wanted to keep the relationship at a level where Tim was happy to provide support, hopefully with no other agenda.

She was pleased when her exercise bike bleeped at her to say that her time was up. She stepped onto the nearest treadmill and was soon lost in her own world of exercise concentration.

Tim realised that he would be too mesmerised by her bouncing form to concentrate on any more exercise and made a polite exit in the direction of the changing room. A cold shower suddenly seemed to be a good idea.

Cat heard him go and started to relax into her workout. Her feet thumping out a steady rhythm, her body cleansing her build up of stress. But, while her sweat released alcohol by-products, maybe even a few sex pheromones, it couldn't disperse the big problems that Cat was keeping locked away.

The House of Fun Blog

Diary of a mad house

Date 22nd June 2006

One step forward, two steps back

VIKING – It has been a busy day and there is more than a whiff of legal threats in the air. Despite numerous requests about a dripping kitchen tap my glorious Spanish landlord has failed to ensure that our basic safety has been met.
Whilst engaged in the simple task of getting myself a drink of water, the tap broke ending in a soaked kitchen and me needing four stitches in my foot. This, on the first day of my new business venture, means that I am now without transport and am relying on the kindness of the Celt to get me to a local networking breakfast meeting. As auspicious starts go this is a non-starter.

SPANIARD – Only the Viking could manage to break a tap and cut his foot open at the same time. Send the ambulance chasers if you like, you're not getting a Euro off me. We all know that the Viking is having trouble pulling, he probably pulled this stunt to give himself a chance of chatting up some nurses.

VIKING – Forget the nurses. How can I run a business without a car?

GUEST – Ute: Who needs to meet people nowadays? Isn't it all done via the internet?

SPANIARD – Get real! You can't sell services to people without a face to face meeting.

GUEST – CapnJack: I bet you could sell anything with the MySpace wenches!

CELT –Pack it in you lot. I'm the one who has to get up at a stupid hour to ferry the Viking to his posh breakfast…

GUEST – Ute: Hope foot gets better soon Viking.

VIKING – Thanks Ute. Nice to see that someone cares…

Chapter 7

Heather (179) stopped her car with a lurch, directly in front of the main entrance to the hotel. "Are you sure you dinnae want me to help you intae the hotel?" she asked, handing Jonny (80) his crutch.

"No please, that's fine, I'll be fine from here," Jonny said hoping that no-one could see him. "This is already feeling far too much like being dropped off for my first day of school."

Heather laughed, kissed him on his forehead and ruffled his hair that he had spent ages trying to sweep back of his face in a suitably arty and creative style. "Dinnae let anyone steal your dinner money," she giggled as she jumped back in her car and roared off down the drive.

Jonny quickly turned his back and headed up the stairs as quickly as possible. He pushed open the door of the function room with his crutch and put his worst foot forward into the Business Link breakfast meeting.

"Oh hello, you must be Jonny!" A kindly looking lady (593) with short, black, trendy hair and a myriad of necklaces said as she moved forward quickly to help him. "You poor thing!" She said. Her expression of mothering pity was so intense that Jonny half expected her to spit on a tissue and wipe a bit of grime off his cheek. "I'm Jenny, welcome to Business Link."

"Thank you, and it's really not that bad," Jonny insisted, embarrassed by the way the other people hovering around the coffee percolators had all turned to watch him come in. "It's only a few stitches, it doesn't really hurt, I just have to try and keep the weight off it."

"Well, needless to say, I can tell that we're going to have to look after you," Jenny insisted. She pulled up a bar stool and put it against the wall next to the coffee drinkers. "There now, you pop yourself there. I'll bring you a cup of coffee and your name badge, and I'll make sure that people come to you. We can't have you hopping around with a cup of hot coffee in your hand now, can we?"

Within five minutes Jonny found himself sipping hot coffee, wearing a pre-printed plastic name badge and recounting the story of his accident to an accountant (368); a solicitor (412); a landscape gardener (102); a graphic designer (328); a florist (367); a printer (205); a financial advisor (94); a photographer (479); a life coach (137); Mr Wills (481) and a copywriter (315). Jonny noticed that the copywriter, a chubby man in his mid-forties, did not look pleased to meet Jonny at all, despite his friendly words.

Jonny was just forming the opinion that this networking lark wasn't so bad after all when the topic of conversation turned to the topic of his previous failure.

"So you attended the crisis meeting?" Tim, the photographer asked. "That's most peculiar. I don't remember seeing you there."

"Well, there were quite a lot of us there," Jonny reasoned, mentally kicking himself for not circulating when he had two good feet to move around on. "And to be honest, I think that I overdid the Dutch courage and talked for too long to too few people. Perhaps I should have brought this crutch as a prop, it's certainly been useful here for breaking the ice."

"Indeed yes," Tim replied. "To be honest I was also overambitious on the old booze front. Ended up falling at the feet of a most wonderful woman at the end of the evening. Then I met her in the gym, of all places, the next day. I do believe that Lady Luck and Cupid have teamed up to help me out."

Their conversation was interrupted by the arrival of a stern looking lady (212) who ran a company that cleaned mattresses.

"Hello Tim," she said, shaking his hand. "How's your wife? Has she got over that 'flu now?"

"Yes, yes!" Tim breezed. "Right as rain now. Just needed a bit of the old R'n'R."

Jonny smirked at the ease that Tim slipped between his two public faces, but it was soon all change and he found himself being sat at the end of a long table while everyone helped themselves to a buffet cooked breakfast. He started to rue his networking prop as while he had been seated at the end of the table for his convenience, the other networkers had naturally gravitated to the centre of the table.

Jenny arrived with a huge plate of fried food for him and she stroked his shoulder reassuringly as she put the plate down.

"There you go. I hope you like everything. Now, you must excuse me as we've just had a rather late, and I must say, glamorous networker arrive."

Jonny noticed Tim's head spin round just as he sat down to claim his spot in the centre of the table. Jonny smiled as Tim paused to consider changing position, but the seats around him were promptly filled leaving the only empty space opposite Jonny.

Jenny soon returned alone. "It looks like we have another brave soul from Sunshine who is venturing on a start up venture. Now, if everyone is sorted I'll get some food and come and join you."

Jonny tucked into his food before anyone could ask him a question. He was just looking up after putting a large slice of herby sausage in his mouth when he saw the latecomer walking towards him with a tray of food. His surprise nearly transformed the humble slice of meat by-products into a projectile missile. It was Sarah (762), the snotty-totty whose nose had come violently into contact with the security gates. She was even wearing his favourite skirt and boots combo.

She smiled at everyone with no trace of nerves.

"Hello, my name's Sarah," she said before sitting down opposite Jonny. Her nose had recovered well and was straight, if a little swollen. However, gone was the majestical Cleopatra look. She was now sporting some serious eighties-style eye shadow to camouflage the remains of the bruising.

She looked up at Jonny, seeing him properly for the first time.

"Oh!" She said quietly, dropping her knife onto the table with a clatter.

"Do you two know each other?" The host asked as she walked past them with her own tray of food.

"Erm, yes," Jonny replied slowly. "We, er, bumped into each other at Sunshine."

Sarah gave a surprised little laugh, but made no comment. They both tucked into their food.

"I can't believe how hungry I am," Jonny said the moment he had finished his mouthful. "Then again, I suppose I have been up since before six."

"Not an early bird then?" Sarah asked with just a touch of disdain. "I always get up at six. It's the only way to get everything into the day."

Jonny started to say something, but changed his tack. "I'm *so* sorry about what happened before!" Jonny said quietly as their neighbours started their own conversations. "I've been having nightmares about it. My toes curl just thinking about it."

"I hated you," Sarah admitted flashing him a cold glare. "Especially at work the next day. It looked as if my boyfriend had been battering me."

Jonny winced. "I bet he wasn't too impressed."

"No boyfriend to impress," she replied impassively, carving out another mouthful of her scrambled eggs on toast. "After the takeover news hit I started looking at it in a different way. It was a disaster for my career and I started pulling in a few favours from my contacts. I had already mentally sold my house and moved back to London.

"But sod that. I don't want to move. I loved my job, but that's gone. So what next? I thought about the accident and how you could be so stupid."

"Well..." Jonny started fishing for the right thing to say.

"Don't bother. It was a good lesson. I was too fixed on my short term goals. I needed to slow down and re-evaluate. Why put all my eggs into one project?" She asked as she scrutinised his face.

Jonny soon lost his monopoly on Sarah as the other networkers asked about her progress as a management consultant and, after the breakfasts were demolished, they moved into a meeting room to hear the two presentations of the day.

The first presentation intrigued Jonny. It was all about working with competitors and a very earnest man (812) with the type of well-established goatee beard that Antonio could only dream of, was urging them to forge alliances with their competitors. The idea was to work together to be able to bid for big contracts with the multinationals. Jonny liked the concept, especially as the other copywriter in the group gave the second presentation.

He gave some very solid tips for good business writing; avoiding clichés, using short, punchy paragraphs for the Internet, and getting other people to check the final copy for spelling and grammatical errors. It was a very professional presentation, apart from the egg and ketchup stains on his shirt, but Jonny was left wondering why his competitor had gone to such lengths to reveal all the trade secrets to his potential customers.

Jenny thanked the speakers and spent some minutes talking about how it made sense to delegate your admin tasks to other businesses, claiming that the average sole trader cannot make a decent profit if they are spending large amounts of their time doing things that can be done much faster by specialists.

"For example," she said. "We have two experts in copywriting and web design in the room. Now I know a lot of people have the basic skills to set up their own web site, but you have to ask yourselves; how long will it take me away from earning money, and will the end result be as professional as their work?"

Jonny approved of the logic where it involved him picking up work, but he didn't currently have the resources to pay other people for their specialised services. He needed money to pay for those life essentials. He decided to ignore this potential setback in the hostess' theory and set about trying to drum up some sales.

He approached the financial advisor who was already walking towards him offering Jonny his business card.

"Hi," Jonny said as he accepted the business card. "So do you spend too much time on your web design or copywriting? As our speakers said, it certainly makes sense to save time to concentrate on earning a living rather than struggling with the things you are not an expert in."

"Erm no," the financial advisor said. "I already have a marketing strategy, thank you." He smiled at Jonny politely and moved to the next person without taking Jonny's business card.

Jonny's embarrassed silence was broken by the arrival of a very cheerful looking accountant who was looking very dapper in a razor sharp suit and a bright purple tie.

"I won't bore you with the details," the accountant smiled. "After all, everyone knows what an accountant does, they save you money, but we do it with a smile on our face." He handed a business card to Jonny.

"Thanks," Jonny said taking the card and offering his own card in return. "I'll bear it in mind. Now how can I help you with your marketing? I can design a very cheerful web site or liven up your copy for you."

"Oh, well," the accountant said as he looked around the room and played for time. "You see, we've just updated our site, so you're a little late."

"But I really can make words work for you," Jonny insisted.

"No really. I'm not interested," the accountant said politely before quickly moving away.

Jonny was just deciding on whether to try and pitch his wares to someone else or to try and have another chat with Sarah, when his friend 'Mr Wills' took him to one side.

"You seem to have obtained the wrong end of the stick, should we say?" he said quietly. "The golden rule of networking is not to bludgeon your peers with your services. You see, me, myself, I tell people what I do and I ask what they do. Very occasionally I might need their services, but it is more likely that I know someone else who needs their particular talents. That is the true value of networking."

"But I need business now," Jonny said.

"Absolutely, and we all know how that feels Jonny, but networking is not a quick fix. You can't attend a networking meeting and expect to come away with a handful of contracts. It's about helping each other. I have my mental list of the members of my BNI Chapter and I refer people to them when the opportunity arises. The other members do the same for me. It takes time, but it works Jonny. Why don't you come to a meeting and find out?"

"Thank you," Jonny said. His mind starting to whirl. "I'll have a think about it and get back to you."

The meeting began to break up. Jenny reminded everyone to return their name badges. The people with pressing appointments quickly slipped away, but the new starters and dedicated networkers continued their networking discussions and card swapping. Jonny pocketed the stash of business cards he had collected, grabbed his crutch and headed for the exit. He realised that not only had he not picked up any business; he hadn't got Sarah's business card.

He turned the corner and nearly collided with Sarah as she sped out of the toilets.

"Look out!" She laughed before leaning in conspiratorially. "Thought I was never going to get away back there; absolutely dying for the loo! Not really something you can say to someone who is asking if I know anyone in extruded plastics is it?"

"I suppose not," Jonny agreed. "Did you get anything out of the meeting?"

"Always useful to meet people. You never know who may be useful further down the line and I wanted to apply for all the help I can from Business Link. Everything helps eh?"

Jonny was just about to agree again when Sarah interrupted. "Look, do you have to go? Got time for a coffee?" She pointed towards the coffee shop. "I'd like to pick your brains."

"A coffee would be great," Jonny said, trying to conceal his surprise. "As long as you promise to carry my cup back to the table for me."

Sarah laughed. "It's a deal."

Twenty minutes later Sarah was grilling him about his old job in Sunshine. It was some time before she came up for air. Sarah talked as fast as she walked.

When he was able to sneak a word in he expressed his concerns about the lack of short term results from networking.

"It's no quick fix," she argued. "People do business with people they like. It's all about building a relationship, which then leads on to a sale."

"Oh don't, I live with an estate agent!"

"Perfect!" Sarah laughed. "A salesman makes sure you like them, it means you're more likely to part with your money. With networking it's all about finding something in common with the other person as quickly as possible.

"Some people have a list of words that describe them on the back of their business cards. The person who receives it looks at it, notices that say, you have a dog so they say 'Hey! I have a dog too' and you're off. They call it accelerated networking."

"Sounds like some weird type of speed dating to me."

"Good analogy!" Sarah laughed. "You wouldn't dream of walking up to someone you fancy and asking them to sleep with you. You start flirting to create a bond."

Jonny tried to think of a witty response, but he'd suddenly realised that he was on a pseudo-date with his ideal woman. And she had just mentioned the concept of casual sex! The resulting silence was long enough for them both to blush and for Sarah to change the subject in a hurry.

"Do you think you have what it takes to become a self-made

millionaire then?" She asked.

"I'm not sure that I'm aiming that high," Jonny admitted. "I just want to have fun; to enjoy my working life and to be able to enjoy my home life as well. I don't need to make millions of pounds."

"Why not?" Sarah asked with a smile. "If you enjoy your work and you're good at it, then why not be successful?"

"I hardly think that I'm going to join the millionaire club through copywriting and web design."

"Not with that attitude," she scolded. "You've got to believe in yourself Jonny. I back myself to the last and put the maximum amount of effort into *everything*. I'm not going to be successful if I spend my evenings watching crap TV programmes. Some people turn their brains off after work. They get home at 6.30 and waste away until they go to bed. Then they complain about not having enough time."

"I thought you said that you were going to take it easy, to rediscover yourself?"

Sarah laughed. "You so don't know me Jonny! There's an upper level out there and it's full of opportunities."

"I'll take your word for it." Jonny smiled. "I'm finding it hard enough just starting out on my own."

"You'll be fine," Sarah assured him. "You're doing the right things, networking, getting your name about the place. You heard of Ecademy?"

"What academy?"

"No, E-cademy. It's a huge online network of people, all looking to do business with other small companies." She took out a business card, wrote down a URL on the back and handed it to Jonny. "Take a look at it and don't be scared off by the sheer scale of it. There's business out there. You have to find it and win it."

Jonny took the card and winced as he shifted his leg in order to get one of his own business cards out of his pocket and handed it to Sarah.

"How are you getting home?" Sarah asked. "I take it you can't drive with a gammy foot?"

"No, I'm getting the bus, there's a stop just down the road."

"You need to think about your image," Sarah laughed. "Come on, I'll give you a lift."

Jonny was in sensory overload as Sarah zipped through the busy streets on the way to his house. Sitting in a flash car being expertly driven by a babe he had fancied for ages, breathing in the delicate, feminine fragrance of her perfume was proving almost too much for his reality sensors. He was currently forcing his eyes not to drift down to her legs where her knee-length skirt had moved up to reveal slightly more of her thigh than he thought he ought to be seeing.

In defence he was desperately trying to project an alluring image of raw sexuality while grasping a crutch and clinging on to the door handle every time Sarah threw the car into a bend.

"How did you get to the event?" Sarah asked as she braked hard to stop at a pedestrian crossing while a huddled old lady (38) bumbled across with her shopping trolley.

"My flatmate's girlfriend gave me a lift," Jonny replied keeping his eyes on the road in front.

"Oh dear, 'my flatmate's girlfriend'", Sarah laughed. "Sounds like a porn film."

"Her name's Heather." Jonny replied with a grin.

"And you like her?" Sarah asked innocently as she sped away from the crossing.

"Not in that sort of way," Jonny said, starting to wonder where this conversation was leading. "She's a nice looking girl, but, anyway, she's going out with my best mate."

"No! I don't mean that!" Sarah laughed. "Lots of people have difficulties with their flatmate's other halves, it can cause bad karma. Of course, I hear that all men fancy their mate's birds as well."

Jonny started to feel defensive, but noticed that Sarah was giggling away to herself.

"Have you ever noticed the way that women always refer to men's girlfriend's as birds and then get arsy when men use the term?" He asked with a grin.

"Touché!" Sarah laughed. "But you haven't answered my question."

Jonny paused, wondering how much to say. "The truth is that it's difficult. It's only a two bed flat and Heather has practically moved in. There's no room for three of us and my flatmate owns the flat."

"Doesn't sound good."

"I get on really well with her. She's a good laugh, but, well, there's just not enough room."

"Sounds like you're going to be moving on," Sarah observed as she pulled up outside the flat. "See you around Jonny and don't forget to believe in yourself!"

Jonny eased himself out of the low slung car with as much grace as he could muster. Once out onto the pavement, he balanced on his crutch and turned back towards the car to see Sarah grinning at him. "I'll see you around Sarah, but next time, try not to wear so much eye make-up eh!"

Sarah gasped in shock and then laughed as she sped away with a toot of her horn leaving Jonny still breathing in the smell of the perfume.

You have an instant message from SAM:

SAM: G'day Sport!

CAT: G'day? Must be the middle of the night for you!

SAM: 2am and pitch black.

CAT: Ouch! Is Bruce bellyaching again?

SAM: HIS NAME IS MARK!

CAT: That's what I said. Isn't that spelt B-R-U-C-E?

SAM: Ohh, sooo funny! I contact you for some adult conversation in the small hours and this is what I get?

CAT: Adult conversation? There are special web sites for that type of thing you know?

CAT: Anyway, doesn't having an insomniac baby soothe those sort of urges?

SAM: There was me being clever and using fancy technology so we could chat across the world in real time and you just want to talk about sex.

SAM: Your sister is right. You definitely need to get laid.

CAT: And you need some sleep Sheila!

SAM: I'll ignore that. So tell me about your love life.

SAM: Don't worry, I haven't got long, I'm knackered. ☺

CAT: Huh, ye of little faith. There may be a man on the scene actually…

SAM: Wow! Is he tall dark and handsome?

CAT: Erm, no.

SAM: Rich?

CAT: Nope?

SAM: A toy boy!

CAT: Certainly not!

SAM: Oh dear, he's a bit ropey with a GSOH

CAT: GSOH?

SAM: Good Sense Of Humour...

CAT: Hmm, you sure you're living on the other side of the world? OK so he's not really an oil painting but he is funny, he's passionate and

SAM: You've slept with him already?!

CAT: No! I'm not even sure that I fancy him. I was going to say that he has strong beliefs!

SAM: I'm sure he does sweetheart. Now let me guess, he also looks as if he needs a little bit of looking after? A bit scruffy round the edges? A bit of a project?

CAT: What are you on about?

SAM: You forget how well I know you. I know all about your mothering instinct.

CAT: Excuse me! You're the one with a baby Brucie!

SAM: You're bipolar when it comes to men. It's either confident, successful leaders or neglected puppy dogs who need some TLC.

SAM: This bloke needs some TLC doesn't he?

CAT: I've got to go now, I'm going to be late for a networking meeting.

SAM: You know I'm right!

CAT: Give Bruce a burping from me

SAM: Give your man in need a kiss from me. I take it he will be at the meeting?

CAT: Yes, yes, yes.

CAT: He does have the hurt puppy look and yes he invited me to the meeting.

SAM: They do say that the desperate ones are better in bed as they are so keen to please.

CAT: You're a nightmare! And you say that I'm the one who needs to get laid? Must dash. Have fun being smug and not sleeping!

SAM: Don't do anything I wouldn't do…

Cat has logged out.

Chapter 8

Cat (425) hurried into the hotel car park, worried that she was going to be late. She reversed into a vacant space and went to open her car door only to have it blocked by the occupant of the next car who was trying to get out at the same time. The other car driver (121) smiled and motioned for her to get out first.

When they were both out of their cars, she found herself shaking hands with a man who very much reminded her of a mole. He had fine black hair, cut short to the same length all over his head, a long pointed nose and seemed to have a uniformed roundness to his physique, not helped by the way he had pulled his trousers up too high. Fortunately for him, his eyes did not show any myopic tendencies, and were actually the most active part of him.

"Hello," he giggled. "My name's Simon. Sorry, didn't notice you arrive. I was a bit early and was waiting for the right time to go in."

"Oh, I was worried about being late," Cat smiled.

"Well, yes, there is a danger of that. No-one likes going into a room of strangers do they?" He said as they started walking together towards the hotel.

"It's never much fun." Cat agreed, "But isn't that just what we're here to do?"

The man nodded. "It's just no good living inside your comfort zone is it?"

Cat was just about to introduce herself when they arrived at the meeting where Jenny, the kindly hostess (603) who looked after Jonny earlier in the day, was delighted to see another new face. Simon said a brisk hello to Jenny, picked up his name badge from the desk and with a deep breath entered the melee of people grouped, as ever, around the coffee percolators.

"Hello," Cat said, appreciating the warm expression on Jenny's face. "My name is Cat Forsythe, we spoke on the phone earlier?"

"Yes, yes, Cat, welcome!" Jenny beamed. "Lovely to have you here and thank you for taking the time off work to come and visit us. It must be a very trying time for you at the moment at Sunshine. Our numbers have certainly swelled since the announcement, we were almost overflowing this morning. One poor man even came in on crutches!"

"He must have been keen," Cat laughed and then turned to look at the babbling throng behind them. Well, life's not that bad for me, but it looks like I'm not alone in trying to get a head start on the competition."

The host laughed. "I think you'll find that we're all on the same side here Cat."

"I realise that," Cat smiled. "To be honest, I was more worried about being late."

"Well, you got here just in time. Although I often think that most of the real business gets done while people are waiting for the event to start."

Cat was just about to mention her conversation with Simon, the man she met in the car park, when she was enveloped in the warm welcome of Tim (489). He shook her warmly by the hand and then proceeded to walk her round the room and introduce her to everyone in glowing terms. Although she was a little embarrassed by his enthusiasm, she was grateful for him paving the way for her to meet a group of strangers. Especially when she noticed Simon hovering with uncertainty around the edge of the group.

It was hard to remember everyone's names and business, but one person grabbed her attention by the sheer power of her smile and enthusiasm. Tim introduced her as Gladys (371) a local florist and left them to talk while he fetched Cat some refreshments. She was in her early fifties and was tall and chunky in many of the wrong places, quite the opposite of the delicate produce that she sold. However, in tune with her cheerful products, she appeared to be blessed with a permanent smile.

"When I was little I always wanted to be a florist," Cat said.

"But then I discovered boys and my interest changed to receiving flowers from them."

"Oh, I absolutely adore my job!" Gladys gushed. "I start my day at the flower markets, while most people are still asleep, chatting with the stall holders surrounded by the most beautiful and colourful creations in the world. Oh the smell of it Cat! In the winter it is like coming out of the night and into the middle of a dream. Inside this dumpy old body is a delicate flower that is dying to bob daintily on the breeze."

Cat laughed. "But don't you have to get up terribly early?"

"About 4:30," Gladys admitted. "But not every morning and I love the thrill of being up and about before the rest of the world has caught up with itself. And then I get back to my little shop and transform it with the colours and the smells of the market. Are you telling me that there are no early starts in event management?"

"Occasionally," Cat agreed. "But I get caught up with it. Each event has a reason, something that will change people's lives in some way, even if they are only going to be persuaded to buy something. Without me being there I know that the event will not be as good. There's a definite end point to each gig."

"It's the same with me Cat. Many people find it strange, but I love doing funerals. Oh don't get me wrong. Funerals are ghastly, heartbreaking events, but what gives people the most comfort? The flowers! People will comment on how much the deceased would have loved the flowers and when they remember the funeral, they will remember the number of people who came and how beautiful the flowers looked. I make it my mission to provide the best funeral flowers and I love doing it."

"I never thought about it like that," Cat said thoughtfully. "So what about weddings?"

"Weddings are a different kettle of fish," Gladys carried on enthusiastically. "My job then is to match everything to the theme of the event and to make sure that no matter how beautiful my flowers are, they *never* overshadow the bride."

Cat laughed. "You really do love your job, don't you?"

"It's my secret weapon," Gladys smiled. "All those entrepreneur self-help books, and I've read a few, tell you to do something that you're passionate about. I've found my vocation. I used to be a PA and believe me it is much easier getting up at four am on a Monday morning to visit the flower markets than struggling out of bed at seven knowing that the most exciting thing I was going to do was buy my bosses' wife an anniversary present."

"You didn't buy her flowers then?"

Gladys laughed. "I can tell that I'm going to get on with you Cat! In fact I'll let you into a little secret. I used to feel stupid about telling people how much I adore my job, but now I know it helps to bring me business. If people realise that you are genuinely enthusiastic about what you are selling it makes them much more likely to invest time and money in your product."

"It's a risk though, surely, if you look too enthusiastic you'll sound like a greasy salesman."

"Or woman," Gladys agreed with a chortle. "The other trick is to see if you can help people. It is the best feeling in the world when someone starts sending business your way after you have made the effort to do them a favour."

"I must admit to being a little wary of the networking scene," Cat admitted. "I don't mean to sound callous, but all this helping each other must have its limits. We are all chasing a limited amount of work, it's a business world, only the best will survive. There's just so much scope for someone to abuse the system."

"Of course there is Cat. It's all about building and maintaining trust. In networking circles you will probably find a large proportion of people who are happy to help and guide and you, but a lot of these people are business or life coaches. It's in their interest to show how they can help you. The whole ethos of networking is to try and help other people without looking for a reward oneself. You will hear this bandied about a lot in these sort of networking circles. You'll also hear quite a few mentions of that silly book *The Celestine Prophecy*, not that I..."

"Are you mocking my favourite book?" Tim quipped as he arrived with a coffee and an enormous Danish pastry for Cat.

"Doubtless you are checking out our auras now Tim?" Gladys remarked with just a hint of sarcasm.

"Do I detect a tiny thorn in the demeanour of our English rose?" Tim sighed theatrically as he handed the Danish pastry to Cat.

"I can't eat all that!" Cat exclaimed. "It's enormous!"

"I am sure you can manage Cat," Gladys said with a smile. "Anyway, I have already scoffed one so I will feel dreadful if you abstain."

Cat took a bite out of the pastry making a mental note to subtly leave the majority of it behind as soon as people started moving on from the coffee area.

"And as for our doubting flower here," Tim continued. "I simply pay attention to coincidences. I had the pleasure of meeting Cat because I had an urge not to leave a meeting when everyone else did."

"So it was nothing to do with the opportunity of a lock-in then?" Cat asked around a mouthful of sticky pastry.

"You may jest Cat, but I would normally run a mile from the chance of extra late night drinking on a school night. That night I listened to my urges and met you."

"And managed to trip over my 30 kilo Labrador!"

"He's brown and so was the carpet!" Tim objected with a huge smile on his face. "But the plot thickens, as I then inexplicably had an urge to go to the gym the next morning when I should have been nursing a very bad hangover. Lo and behold, you were there again. Out of these meetings we have created some potential business opportunities and now you have met the English Rose here. If I had not followed those two urges, you would not be here today."

"The Lord Coincidence moves in mysterious ways," Gladys smirked at Cat as they followed the rest of the group through

113

into the meeting room, with Cat discreetly leaving her half-eaten pastry on the coffee cart.

If Cat thought that she was going to spend the next hour or so relaxing she was very much mistaken. There were no presentations at this meeting, instead, the group split into pairs where the object was to find out as much about the other person as possible and then present the findings to the rest of the group. Cat wasn't too surprised to be quickly grabbed by Tim and she spent the next five minutes being grilled about all and sundry, but it was noticeable that there was more of a focus on her personal life than her business attributes. Cat didn't mind this too much as she was able to do some digging of her own when her time came. Although he seemed reluctant to reveal too much about his private life she did find out enough to present Tim's life to the group.

"Tim describes himself as a hopeless romantic, although he refused to be drawn on exactly what part of romancing he is hopeless at. He believes that he is a long way away from finding and interacting fully with his true soul mate and says that he is always looking for that moment of true togetherness. Quite frankly Tim needs to get out more as he spends so much of his time working that he doesn't really have time for hobbies, although he does occasionally make it to the gym where he is known to theorise on the true nature of coincidences to people he barely knows.

"Tim sees a world through a lens, some might say it is a rose-tinted lens, but he is the sort of person that stops at nothing to ensure that everything about your photo shoot is perfect and shows you in the best possible light. He is looking for any couples who have recently got engaged, so if you know of anyone who has recently taken the first step to marital bliss can you send him their details?"

Whilst the majority of the audience laughed in all the right places, it was noticeable that a number of the women present were looking at Tim with a particularly cold expression.

The House of Fun Blog

Diary of a mad house
Date Sat 26th June 2006

No-one knows you when you're down

VIKING – Ever noticed that when you're spoken for, you meet lots of women who seem to fancy you? Then when things change and you're single again, those interested women disappear.

It's just the same as starting your own business. All those people who were interested in discussing your work as an interesting side project disappear when you actually tout for business.

SPANIARD – Welcome to the real world hombre!

CELT – You'll get there Viking. We believe in you! xxx

GUEST – Ute: Get there with a little help from your friends eh? xx

SPANIARD – He's got friends here, all this blog love is getting out of hand. What do you know about Viking anyway?

GUEST – Ute: He's blond, wears glasses, he's sensitive, would like to be a ladies man, and probably could be with a bit of luck. He was having the time of his life with the Spaniard, then the Celt arrives and he's struggling to adjust to the change in the status quo. How's that for starters?

GUEST – CapnJack: Now that is what I call a conversation killer!

Chapter 9

Jonny (97) sighed and tried to shift his weight more comfortably in his bed. He rubbed his eyes and refocused them on the bright screen of his laptop, propped on his duvet covered legs. The screen was filled with a distracting array of text, photos and hyperlinks that made up the Ecademy home page.

His foot ached and his tired brain was struggling to cope with the fact that it was in bed early on a Saturday morning and not dozing happily. However, his one nagging thought was the paradoxical question that if this web site was offering to introduce him to thousands of people, why was he feeling so alone?

He pushed his fingers through his sleep-tangled hair and tried to return his attention to the busy screen in front of him. He had parted with some of his, now precious, funds to get membership and now he was wondering if it was a good investment. He could see a row of photos of smiling faces, all people who apparently wanted to do business with him. Below that were blog titles ranging from self promotion to the inane, nestling against listings for a huge range of services, mixed with strange claims and attention grabbing headlines. Jonny was depressed to notice that these services already included copywriters and web designers.

He flicked through the Frequently Asked Questions and started reading about how to network virtually, rather than his current situation of virtually getting round to networking. He was advised to list 50 words about himself, which seemed a bit of a tricky task, but he went to his profile page and started his word list.

freelance, copywriter, web design, sales, innovative, dynamic, boost profile, improve profits, small companies, buy local, beer, pubs, films, cinema, sore foot, tired, stuck inside, practically unemployed, broke, single, lonely, randy, desperate!

He sighed again and returned to the help section to see what was next. He was told to fill in his profile text with information about himself, concentrating on him as a person rather than his business.

"Who cares about me?" He grumbled, "I just want people to pay me to improve their business. Swapping emails about the weather isn't going to pay the rent." He returned to his profile page and started typing.

Hello everyone. It is good to be able to virtually meet people from across the world and to discover more about different cultures and viewpoints. I am a freelance copywriter and web designer escaping from the corporate world so that I can make a difference for small companies.

So what can I tell you about me? Well, I like socialising, like most people, although this often happens in the pub, although I am not a total boozer - I am a regular cinema goer, and that doesn't involve alcohol, or much socialising I suppose. Although I have been known to complain about the films afterwards – how do some of them make it to the big screen?!

Anyway, back to the beer. I like real ale, in fact I can't believe that people would be content to drink the other mass produced muck – long shelf life, no taste. You have to serve it extra cold and leave it to the marketing people to persuade people that it is a quality product.

This just shows the power of marketing and this is something that I can tap into with my copywriting and innovative web site design, I can make your brand look like a world beater even if you have a modest budget.

Perhaps I should point out that I don't have a beer belly or a beard. These are not essential characteristics of a real ale drinker. Of course there is nothing wrong with beer bellies and beards, especially if the owners want to pay for my services. I have even seen some very attractive women drinking real ale. Before you ask, this observation was not made after eight pints and a curry!

Hmm, this telling people about yourself lark is easier than I thought. I am writing this in bed, nothing kinky, but I cut my foot open recently and it helps to keep it up – helps to stop it aching. It's strange working in bed. Perhaps it gives me an insight into the world of prostitution? ;O) Although I'm afraid that it has been so long since I made the two-backed beast that I've probably forgotten how to do it!

Obviously, this is not a perfect situation, especially as I went to bed early last night so I would feel refreshed today, only to be kept awake by my housemate having vigorous sex with his ridiculously attractive girlfriend. She appears to have moved into our flat and while she is a babe, there is not enough room for three of us, so I will have to make a fuss or move out, but I don't have enough money for my own gaff.

I should get up and get some breakfast, my stomach is grumbling like a female rhino on heat, but my flatmates will soon be turning the kitchen into their post-shag fuel stop. She will be flouncing around in nothing more than a T-shirt and a rosy, flushed face – not a good sight for an unwilling celibate.

Uh-oh, I can hear them moving about now. They'll probably start shagging on the sofa in front of Saturday morning TV. I caught them doing that a few weeks ago. It didn't leave much to imagination. I have now developed a very noisy way of entering the lounge –well I'm noisy going everywhere at the moment as I can't get far without my crutch. Still, it wasn't a very pleasant experience sitting on the sofa after that. I should…

Jonny was interrupted in his typing by Heather (179) breezing into his room carrying a steaming mug of tea. As he predicted she was wearing only Antonio's Spanish football shirt. She still looked half-asleep and obviously had not yet found the hair brush, her tousled hair was pushed back behind her ears.

Jonny went to quickly shut his lap top, but caught his hand in it so it took him two attempts.

"Hey Hop-along," Heather said sleepily. "Thought you might like a cuppa…" She paused as her brain belatedly took in Jonny's swift response to her entrance. "OhmiGod! Were you looking at porn?" She covered her mouth and nose with her hand so quickly that she almost poked herself in the eye. "Oh, I'm sorry! I dinnae ken! I just barged straight in and you were…"

"No! You've got it wrong!" Jonny objected. "I was online networking."

"It's nae big deal Jonny," Heather said with a smirk as she put the mug down on his bedside table. "It's good tae know you're active as it were, I worry about you sometimes. I'm just a wee bit surprised, you ken?" She gave him a little wink.

"I wasn't… I was writing my profile. Look." He gingerly opened the lap top slightly so she could see the Ecademy page, but not read what he had typed. But the page had changed. His hand must have hit the return button when it was trapped in the laptop and the site had saved his data. The words that he had typed before were now part of his profile and visible to anyone who happened to click on his link.

"Shit!" He exclaimed, opening up the lap top fully. "It's saved it!"

Heather craned her neck to have a look and started to read aloud. "Hello everyone. It is good to be able to virtually meet people from across the world and to…"

"Sorry Heather, but can you leave me to get on with this? I was er, just writing stuff off the top of my head and it's all been saved. That's really bad, I'm trying to sell my writing ability."

Heather gave him a knowing smirk and winked seductively before nipping out of the room. Jonny clicked on an edit button next to his profile and was relieved when the previous screen returned. He highlighted his '50 word' list and deleted it and was just highlighting the flippant sections of his profile text when his email pinged. He hit delete and then checked his email.

Ecademy Networking message from Julius Mortimer

He opened the email only to be told that Julius Mortimer had left him a private message. He clicked on the URL link in the email to find a message next to a passport sized photo of a thin man (627) with thick, long black hair, smoking a cigarette and wearing hip looking sunglasses as he brandished a hefty TV film camera.

Wow! Now that is what I call an honest profile! ;)

Good to see you on Ecademy Jonny, but you might want to think about toning down your prose a bit. That off the top of the head stuff is very amusing, but it is going to make the female members run a mile!

Cheers

Julius

Jonny smacked his forehead with his palm, cursing himself for being so stupid. It didn't help that he could hear Heather whispering and giggling in the next room. He saw the box above the message and realised it was the space for him to write a reply.

Hello Julius,

Thanks for your message. I was messing about on the system and pressed the wrong button by mistake, well to tell the truth my mate's girlfriend who I was blathering about walked in the room!

I have deleted all the text and will now write a proper one in Word and cut and paste it in.

Thanks for being understanding. I hope no one else saw it!

Jonny

Jonny tried to return his attention to writing his profile, but kept being distracted by the whispers and giggles from the next room. He took a sip of his tea and winced as the whispers changed to a slow, rhythmic creaking sound.

"Oh yes baby that feels soooo good!" Heather murmured theatrically.

"Network me baby!" Antonio (1,241) groaned before they both burst into giggles.

Jonny was relieved when his computer pinged him a new email message.

Ecademy Networking message from Sarah Lewis

Hey Jonny,

Saw you online.

Nice profile!

S.

Johnny cringed. First he breaks the woman's nose and now he shows her the innermost rants of his mind. His email pinged again making him jump.

Ecademy Networking message from Sarah Lewis

OK, sarcasm doesn't work on-line. Where's your profile?!! You won't get anywhere until you fill that in.

Hope your foot is healing as fast as my nose. There's probably been a dive in the cosmetics stock market prices as I no longer need to slap on the war paint with a trowel to avoid looking like a boxer!

Good to see you on ecad, get your profile up quick and include a pic!

I'm a happy camper as I've got some work with one of my contacts from Sunshine, it's only for a few weeks, but it's a start!

Let me know how you get on.

S.

Jonny couldn't reply quickly enough.

Hi Sarah,

Thanks for your message, great to hear from a friendly face, even if your pic was taken *before* you head-butted a security gate.

I'm currently writing up my profile in bed and no, please don't make any sarky comments as my flatmate's girlfriend has already walked in and accused me of surfing for porn!

Well done on getting some work already! Is it in the local area? I'm jealous.

I had better get back to my profile. Lovely to hear from you.

Take care

Jonny

His computer pinged again before he had chance to finish and he discovered that he had another message from Julius.

Jonny,

Writing your profile in Word sounds a plan mate!

By the way, you mentioned that the cinema is full of crap films, that's because the cinemas are run by the distributors. Ever noticed how few of the films are from anywhere other than the US? About 80% of the film screenings in this country are showing a US film – means that it's practically impossible for UK indie companies to get our films shown.

Don't mean to rant. It's my pet topic so I won't bang on about it, but if you're interested in this sort of thing you should join the Bohemian Revolution Club here on Ecademy. It's an online forum just on this topic.

Happy profile writing and give us a shout if I can be of any help.

Cheers

Julius

Ping!

Re. Ecademy Networking message from Sarah Lewis

And what was your 'flatmate's girlfriend' doing walking into your room!? ;)

Nope, the work's in London, but worth commuting in for a couple of weeks.

You'll get some work, but probably not immediately from networking. It's slow burn stuff. I've been doing it for a few years – just for when something like this happens! Get your web site finished and your profile done and start making some sales calls – don't wait for work to come to you!

Have fun in bed!

S.

Re. Ecademy Networking message from Sarah Lewis

What is it with you women and dirty minds?

Sales calls? Not sure that I'm up to doing them, but I'll certainly up my web presence.

Someone has just invited me to an Ecademy club. What's all that about?

You're jealous because you're not in bed!

Jonny

Re. Ecademy Networking message from Sarah Lewis

You flirting with me Jonny? I'm not sure that's suitable behaviour for a business networking site!

Getting into clubs already eh? Just follow the link from their email and you'll find out what the club's all about. You can take part in their forum where you can post messages on the theme of the club and many of them also have face-to-face meetings. It's a good way to get to know people.

Have fun. Must dash. Off to meet another potential client on a golf course – I punch my weight with the big boys! However, a lady doesn't ask a man out for a date so call that number on my business card soon and suggest somewhere nice…

S.

Jonny read the last message with his chin on his lap. He had never been instructed to ask someone out before! He decided to go and spread the good news, but stopped himself. He couldn't wait to tell Antonio and Heather, but he still hadn't written his profile. This would be the perfect incentive to make him write up his profile faster. He decided to tell them after he had finished setting up his Ecademy profile – he would also have proof to show Heather what he was really doing.

It was late afternoon before Jonny bothered to get dressed. He had perfected his profile and now had 12 people in his Ecademy network. He had written his first blog, joined the Writer's Club, the Web Designer's Club and the Sad Football Fans Club as well as the Bohemian Revolution Club. He had received a warm welcome everywhere, but there was still not a whiff of work. He hobbled his way into the kitchen, grateful that Heather wasn't hanging round the flat waiting for Antonio to come home.

He made himself a coffee and called Sarah for the third time, only to be greeted by her answer phone message yet again.

"Hi, you've reached the phone of Sarah Lewis but I'm a busy bunny right now so I'll call you back as soon as I possibly can."

He swore under his breath, it was no use bragging to the others about his date if he couldn't actually close the deal. He turned on the television to check on the football scores and powered up his laptop, determined to make his networking investment pay.

Ecademy networking message from Julius Mortimer

Great blog mate! You've got a few comments already. You're a natural! Have you heard about the way to blog/blag your way up the Google rankings?

A mate of mine has bribed a cinema in London to show his film on Friday night. It would be fantastic if you could come along and tell all your mates about it. Obviously the more people we get to go the more chances it will have of being screened elsewhere.

Laters

Julius

Jonny opened the Ecademy front page to chart the progress of his first Ecademy blog.

The first networking cut is the deepest – 125 views – 4 comments

Some people may find that leaving the corporate world and setting up your own business is a painful process. Well it wasn't for me until I ended up with a gash in my foot that needed four stitches.
I was so excited about my new venture that I was too vigorous in my efforts to turn off the tap when I was getting myself a glass of water. The tap broke, shooting water in my face, I dropped my glass and well, you can imagine the rest…
The good news is that I managed to find a plumber to fix the Niagara Falls in my kitchen through networking contacts – all the ones in the local directory were too busy.
I'm looking forward to meeting people and getting to know this networking lark.
Jonny

Welcome Jonny!

Good to see you here and hope the foot gets better soon! :o)

Donna Jenkins

Do you need a Virtual PA?

Cut and thrust

Sorry to hear about your accident,
but perhaps I can advise you about
advertising on blogs? If you add a
link to your web site or to something
that you want to promote at the bottom
of your blog then people can follow
the link if they're interested. They
can follow the link to your profile
anyway.

Hope to hear more from you in the
future. ;)

George Wiseman

*Wiseman says only fools rush in - talk
to Wiseman Consulting first!*

Break a leg!

Enjoy putting your feet up mate!

Julius Mortimer

*Bringing your company to the small
screen and a big audience*

Think I need to re-train as a plumber!

```
It must be hard being a plumber –
always having more work than you can
cope with and always being served lots
of cups of tea…

Andy Collier
```

We take the pain out of IT

Jonny read the responses with a big grin on his face before replying to Julius.

Hi Julius,

Sorry, but I won't be able to make your premiere. I'm already booked up for Friday, there's a do down the local pub for my ex-work colleagues. I'm also not too mobile at the moment. Hope it goes well.

What's this about Google rankings?

Jonny

Ecademy networking message from Julius Mortimer

Beer before culture eh? Philistine! There is a kinky sex scene in the film you know? ;)

Put my name into Google and you will find me as the top answer. I also have a very good Alexa ranking (hard to explain in detail, but it's an acknowledged way of ranking web sites). It starts at no. 1 with Yahoo currently the best connected site and goes up from there. My ranking is about

302,000. That means there are only 302,000 sites that are better connected than me in the world. It puts me ahead of loads of big companies with huge marketing budgets! Part of the reason for my good ranking is that I write a regular blog that links back to my web site. I also blog on Ecademy as it is indexed by Google every night.

I know that people won't search for a film maker by putting 'Julius Mortimer' into Google, but if they do hear of me and 'Google' me, they will discover that I have a good web presence. I am also heading steadily up the rankings for the term 'film maker' – but I've got a way to go there!

The bad news is that you have to blog once a day to make it really effective…

Cheers

Julius

"Once a day," Jonny mumbled to himself. "I think I can do that." He returned to his profile on the off chance that anyone else had left him a message. He was not surprised to find an empty inbox. He found a list of members that are online and clicked on the name at the top of the list 'Cat Forsythe' and instantly grinned when he saw Cat's face smiling at him.

At last! Jonny is now able to contact Cat directly, no degrees of separation at all. Just an email away.

"Hellllo!" He said and then jumped as the phone rang right next to him. He closed Cat's profile and answered the phone.

"Jonny! Thanks for your messages. I'd love to go out with you. I can't believe how you got the idea I was interested!" Sarah (795) gushed without pausing for breath. "But work has literally gone mad! I'm schmoozing potential clients all this week and I'm talking to you as I'm getting changed to go out again now. No peeping! I'm naked at the moment!"

"Oh..." was all that Jonny managed to get in before Sarah continued.

"I'll give you a ring when I'm back in town and I'll try to have some clothes on by then!"

"Okaaay," Jonny said slowly, "but didn't you say before that you were trying to do less work and get your life back?"

"That's what so great! Before I was working all the hours for a corporate company, now it's all for me! I've never had so much energy! Now I must say ciao, I can't put my bra on one-handed. Ciao!"

Jonny put the phone down, not sure whether to be turned on or exhausted by the speed and candid nature of Sarah's delivery. He was saved from making a decision by the arrival of Antonio and Heather.

"Still 'online networking' I see Hombre," Antonio quipped as he and Heather appeared lugging heavy bags of supermarket shopping. "I think that makes us even."

"Even?"

"You know? For you walking in when we were doing the wild thing on the sofa?"

"What? One, I wasn't doing what Heather thought. Two, I was in my own bedroom, not on something we all sit on. And three, you were not with your Mum!"

Heather covered her face with her hand. "Oh dinnae!"

"And finally, when you walked in just now I was just in the process of arranging myself a date."

"Were you?" Heather exclaimed, rather too loudly. "Ma Jonny's got a girlfriend?"

"Yes." Jonny replied, stung by her reaction. "And I'm not actually *your* Jonny!"

"A date? Nice one," Antonio grinned, ignoring Jonny's last remark. "For tonight?"

"We haven't actually settled on the date yet. She's away on business at the moment." Jonny admitted.

"So it's a dateless date!" Antonio quipped. "I'm guessing she's snotty-totty, bit older than you and you've seen her in boots."

"Ye-es."

"You're so predicable!" Antonio grinned. "Is she keen?"

"She seems to be, she was bragging about being naked while talking to me on the phone."

"Jonny!" Heather exclaimed. "You dinnae meet her through..." she looked meaningfully at his laptop.

"No! She used to work at Sunshine."

"Ohh," Heather breathed out with relief. "Well I think it's just the best news!" She gave Jonny a big kiss on the cheek and hugged him. "We can double date!"

You have an Instant Message from SAM:

SAM: G'day Sport. How is it in Pommie Land? Is it afternoon?

CAT: G'day Sheila, little Bruce still keeping you nocturnal?

SAM: He certainly is. I'm thinking of reporting him to Health and Safety for noise pollution. Perhaps they'll take him away then.

CAT: I bet you had a belting set of lungs when you were in nappies yourself!

SAM: Doesn't mean I should pay for it now! So cmon, I want more details from Cat's daily diary of the re-awakening of her sex life!

CAT: I get the feeling that I'm not the only one who needs to get laid here…

SAM: Don't change the subject! How's your funny ugly man coming along?

CAT: I'm still not too sure about it, but I had the surreal experience of interviewing him and then telling a group of strangers about him.

SAM: You didn't go to an alcoholics meeting by mistake did you?

CAT: Don't be cheeky!

SAM: So! Did he pass the interview?

CAT: I think so, he was a bit vague about personal details, but then it was going to be revealed to the whole room.

SAM: What sort of details? Like the size of his w....allet! ☺

CAT: No! Like whether he has a significant other, has been married, that sort of thing.

SAM: Oooh dear, watch out. You could turn into a bunny boiler. The 'other woman' never gets a look in you know?

CAT: Oh behave! I'm sure he's not spoken for, it's just strange that he doesn't talk about it, he's not exactly shy when it comes to talking about himself.

SAM: Show me a man who is love! ☺ I don't mean to be rude but why are we talking about this bloke as a potential love interest?

CAT: It's not me, you are!

SAM: He's not great looking, he needs looking after yet likes talking about himself, he appears to have baggage. Tell me something positive.

CAT: He is the perfect gentleman.

SAM: Uh-oh 'gentlemen' are nearly always 'complete cads'.

SAM: U still there?

CAT: Sorry was thinking. I think it's all about the gentleman bit. It makes a nice change.

SAM: So it's not about you looking after him – it's the other way round?

CAT: S'pose so. That sounds weird. It didn't start off that way.

SAM: Not to me Sweetheart. You're always looking after

everyone else, why not want someone to look after you?

SAM: Is there anyone else on the scene that could fill the role?

CAT: Well there is someone called Jonny Philips and he lives in the area.

SAM: You've kept quiet about him!

CAT: I haven't met him yet. He just checked out my profile.

SAM: He what!

CAT: He looked at my profile on Ecademy, it's a networking site that someone recommended.

CAT: You take far too long to reply.

SAM: You mean to say that you're not giving me your full attention?

CAT: You know me, short attention span...

CAT: I'm just checking out his profile now.

SAM: Is he fit?

CAT: Hmm, he looks alright, very blonde hair, blue eyes.

SAM: Box him up and send him to me

CAT: Easy Sheila!

SAM: So if you found out that he could fulfil your caring role would you prefer him to the FUM?

CAT: FUM?

SAM: Funny Ugly Man, keep up woman!

CAT: Oh… yes I suppose.

SAM: Yes you suppose 'cos anything's better than FUM or because you fancy him?

CAT: I wouldn't say I fancy him as such. He wouldn't make me go weak at the knees or anything.

SAM: But if he offered to buy you a drink you'd say?

CAT: Yes please, G'n'T with lime not lemon.

SAM: And if he was charming and asked lots of nice questions about you?

CAT: I'd be charming and ask nice questions back.

SAM: And would you kiss on a first date?

CAT: If he didn't have bad breath.

SAM: Would you shag on a first date?!

CAT: Depends how drunk I was.

SAM: Liar! You're far too moral!

CAT: I might let him have a bit of a grope, though.

SAM: ;o)

SAM: So, how are you going to meet him?

CAT: I suppose I had better send him an email.

SAM: What!!!!!!

SAM: You're going to ask him out just like that! :o0

CAT: No! It's networking. You just say hello and work out if you can help each other in a business way.

SAM: So why didn't he send you a message when he looked at your profile?

CAT: Thanks Sheila, now you've got me feeling self-conscious.

SAM: No worries mate. Sorry, but Bruce has just started bellyaching again. Have to go. I'll compete your psychoanalysis at some other time.

CAT: You called him Bruce!

SAM: *&%$!!!! Byeee.

SAM has logged out.

Chapter 10

Cat (437) was staring at Jonny's profile on the screen, unsure as to whether to send him a message. Was she intrigued by his profile because he was local or did she just like the look of him?

"What do you think mutt?" She asked Ferrero who was in his ultimate relaxation position of lying on his back with his feet in the air. "I mean, I could do with someone to write me a web site, but how do I know he's any good? If I contact him will he assume that I'm going to give him the job? And he is *very* local. What if I don't get on with him?"

Ferrero waggled his rear end gently from side-to-side. She stared at the screen for a few seconds. "I could just send him a message saying 'hello', but he might think I'm coming on to him or something." She looked at Ferrero whose feet were swaying slightly as he started to doze off. "Men are like that you know? Thinking about it rationally I would definitely contact him if he was a woman. Am I reading too much into this?" Ferrero gently slumped onto one side as his snooze took hold.

"Oi mutt! Wake up! I'm asking you a question!"

Ferrero wriggled to his feet and turned to look at her.

"Do I contact this bloke or not?"

Ferrero yawned and stretched, releasing a small, yet distinctly audible fart in the process.

"Oh yuck! Get out you mangy mutt!" Cat groaned. Ferrero trudged sadly out into the kitchen and Cat returned her attention to the laptop screen. "I'm sorry Jonny Philips, you might be the perfect networking contact, but not according to my dog." She closed Jonny's profile and saw that she had received a networking message from someone called Dennis Bartholemew (8,482). He was in his mid-forties and sported a carefully groomed moustache that unfortunately had denser hair than most of his head.

Dear Cat,

I noticed you on-line and thought I would drop you a note to see how you are getting on here at Ecademy – it can be very big and daunting when you first join can't it?

Firstly I would like to stress that I am not selling anything – I know telesales people always start by saying that, but I won't even mention my own products in this mail. :o) I'm simply interested in whether you want to join my network. I have boosted my business through networking and while you can probably see that I have over 2,000 people in my Ecademy network I have many more contacts in places like LinkedIn, BNI, BRE, Ryze and my local Chamber of Commerce. In fact I have nearly 8,500 contacts!

What do I do with all these people? Well, I try to help them. I believe in givers gain. I enjoy helping people connect with the very person or business they need whether they want to sell or buy.

So how can I help you? Tell me the one thing you need at the moment and I'll see what I can do to sort it for you. Don't forget that if I don't know someone I know nearly 8,500 people who probably do!

I hope you enjoy your time on Ecademy and do let me know if I can help you in anyway.

Best regards

Dennis

Cat whistled softly to herself. 8,500! How is it possible to know so many people? She wondered whether she had been missing out on something or if this network building was just one big waste of time?

She re-read the message, tutted and closed it, but stopped short of moving onto her next task. She had just admitted to Sam that she would like someone to help her for a change and here was someone offering no strings assistance and she didn't even have to meet him. She thought back to the words of her florist friend and decided that Dennis deserved a reply at the very least.

Dear Dennis,

Thanks for your warm and welcoming message. At the moment I am just adjusting to working for myself rather than a big corporate company, so I'm really only interested in people in Hampshire or London who want to organise an event. Sorry this is a bit vague, but I haven't worked out my new focus yet. I'm still getting my head around the givers-gain principle too.

Warm regards

Cat

Cat left her computer and went to make peace with her smelly pooch and to brew a cup of tea. She was idly watching the tea bag bob around in the hot water when she had a thought that made her cringe. She shuddered and scooped the tea bag out of the mug and deftly sent it flying into the sink.

"No, I couldn't!" she muttered to herself. "That would be the epitome of sad behaviour." She looked back across at her lap on the table. "Oh bollocks!" she exclaimed crossly and marched over to her laptop. She entered a name into the search facility on the Ecademy site and hit return.

She gasped as the name returned an exact match, but quickly sighed with relief as she saw that the man was based in San Francisco. She opened up the profile to reveal a grey haired man with a ruddy complexion and a cheery grin. She laughed at herself before turning to Ferrero.

"That's what you get for looking up your ex on networking sites," she said with a self admonishing shake of the head. "Now what are these other sites that Dennis chap was on about?" She went to the LinkedIn web site and after filling in the registration form she was given the opportunity to invite the people already in her Outlook contacts list to join her network. She clicked her mouse and looked on in surprise at all the people she knew who were already members.

"Why doesn't anyone tell me about these things?" She asked no-one in particular. Then she yelped and sat back in her seat. Someone with a surname she had almost taken as her own appeared on the screen. "What is that bastard still doing in my contacts file?" She asked crossly. She opened her ex-boyfriend's profile and saw all the puffery that he had used in order to make himself look more important. She looked through his connections and her mouth fell open as she realised that a number of her friends, which she hadn't heard from for ages, were amongst the list.

"They were *my* friends!" She exclaimed. "So why are they in contact with him and not me?" She selected all her friends and old work contacts, ignored her ex and clicked the button to send the invites. Then she set about filling her profile with all the companies she had worked for in the hope that old colleagues would now think of using her now she was working freelance. She was just looking at the screen with defiant satisfaction when she was distracted by an instant messenger prompt.

You have an instant message from: KELLY

Kelly: Hey Top Cat. Thanks for passing this on. This software is dead cool. I've been catching up with my mates from all over the place. How's things with you?

Cat: Hi Kel

Cat: Hmm, not sure really. I'm trying to get in contact with some old colleagues and avoiding others.

Kelly: Avoiding people?

Cat: You don't want to know. Oh yes, and the dog's got the farts again.

Kelly: Still living the high life eh? We've got some news this end.

Cat: You're not pregnant already!

Kelly: Nope, but we're having great fun trying.

Kelly: It's amazing, it's just as if lying on your back with bum propped up and your legs in the air while your hubby pounds away is the most beautiful and natural thing, rather than being a bit kinky. Apparently it's the perfect way to conceive,

Cat: That's about 100% more info than I needed

Cat: You're supposed to keep things short and sweet on IM.

Kelly: Short and sweet is definitely the way to go

Kelly: Means there's more chance of a second go before we go to sleep!

Cat: Stop it now!

Cat: I've got my fingers in my ears!

Kelly: You'll never get pregnant like that!

Cat: I'll sign off!

Kelly: Ok, ok!

Kelly: Don't suppose you could lend us your brain this evening? We've had no interest in the flat and business is totally crap. We're barely making anything after staff costs and we're down to a skeleton staff.

Cat: No problem, I'll bring the little stinker with me.

Kelly: That'll bring the punters flocking in.

Cat: Sounds like you need to do some promotions or something.

Kelly: Malc's organising something but he won't tell me what it is yet.

Cat: Let's discuss this later, I'll try and think of something.

Kelly: Ooh, what're you up to? You got a hot date with that Tim guy or something?

Cat: I'm just busy that's all, and yes, I'm going out with Tim tomorrow.

Cat: Go on, do your worst!

Cat: I think you're supposed to take the piss at this point.

Kelly: There's something about him I don't like.

Cat: You were the one who told me that he was okay!

Kelly: He was here in the pub last night – how can I put it?

Kelly: He's a bit of a letch. If he could have plucked out one of his eyeballs and stuffed down the barmaid's cleavage he would have.

Cat: Did she have her tits on display?

Kelly: She was wearing a padded bra

Cat: How do you know?

Kelly: I asked her to. I told you business was bad!

Cat: I was joking about that!

Kelly: It's doubled our trade, we had 6 sad loser blokes instead of 3.

Cat: Right, conversation over. I'll see you later and Kel?

Kelly: What?

Cat: Put some clothes on!

Cat has signed out.

The House of Fun Blog

Diary of a mad house
Date Sat 25th June 2006

Viking's pulled!

SPANIARD – Sound the bells! Bring out the Champagne! The Viking has pulled! However, we think he may have met her through a dodgy sex web site as she's always naked when she calls him. We'll update everyone when we have more information!

GUEST – Ute: How could you Viking? Gutted. ;)

CELT – Can you 'pull' someone without actually meeting them?

GUEST – Ute: If you can run a business online then surely you can steal a girl's heart as well?

VIKING – Thanks flatmates I think this is several steps too far in terms of releasing personal information. For any readers who are really interested, I met this 'mystery woman' through work and not through any dodgy porn sites. I'm sure the readers also don't want to know this but the Spaniard's idea of foreplay is shouting 'Come ride the bull, senora!'

Chapter 11

Jonny (131) was sitting at the kitchen table in front of his laptop with his head in his hands. He had spent all Sunday morning looking for work and was beginning to have serious worries about his lack of business leads. He had just made a decision to design and print some flyers to post to local businesses when his mobile rang. It was Sarah. (820) launching in with her usual enthusiasm.

"Jonny! Me again. Just telling you that I'm not here again."

"I presume you've got some clothes on this time?"

"Watch it you! Yup, suited and booted. Off to start my stint in London. I'm staying there with an old school friend. Just met someone from the local BNI, I'm in there now. I did ask about you, but they've just accepted a copy writer and web designer."

"Shit! I was going to get hold of them tomorrow."

"Sorry, the area is awash with new businesses now Sunshine has closed."

"That's exactly what I don't want to hear," Jonny sighed before realising that he didn't want to sound weak and sorry for himself. "So are you going to take me up on my offer of a date some time this year?"

"How about Monday week? I'm going to the Beermat event in London, you can sign up via Ecademy. It's a laid back networking event in a bar so you can mingle with a pint in your hand. Just your cup of tea."

"Or pint of beer?"

"Absolutely. So you'll come?"

"Of course."

"Great. Sign yourself up and I'll see you there!"

Jonny sighed and checked the latest blog he had written to showcase his talents. There were a number of new comments added beneath his carefully crafted words.

```
Good points Jonny
Anyone wanting to know more about keeping
people's attention and making them contact
you can see my free e-book here.
Keith Stevens
The New Wave of Web Design

Don't forget that some people prefer to
listen
You can lose potential customers if you
don't have an auditory element to your web
site. There's more information on the audio
message on my profile.
Toni Williams
Bring your website to life with sound!
```

Jonny was just venting his frustration with the way that his blog had been hijacked when a new text box appeared on his screen.

You have a Skype message from JULIUS

JULIUS: Good to see you on Skype. Got yourself a headset yet?

JONNY: What's going on? I thought this SKYPE thingy was all about being able to talk over the Internet.

JULIUS: Keep up matey! It does both. You can talk and send docs etc at the same time.

JONNY: Oh, ordered headset today…

JULIUS: Nice one. We can talk for free then. How's the foot?

JONNY: Foot's getting better. Work situation isn't. I've spent hours on Ecademy this weekend and I've got nothing. Some bastards have even trumped my blog!

JULIUS: Eh? Hang on I'll have a peek....

JONNY: I spent ages crafting that.

JONNY: I'm less than impressed. What's the point of me making the effort if other people sabotage it?

JULIUS: What do you expect? If you're going to blog advertorial then other people, especially those of us who've been here for much longer than you, are going to join in. Your blogs have got to show people what you're like and allude to what you do, not be a blatant ad.

JONNY: What!!!!

JULIUS: Think about what advice you can give away for free, something useful to other people.

JONNY: Yeah, yeah, but if I tell people all the juicy stuff, they'll be able to do it themselves.

JULIUS: That's the gamble. They could steal your ideas OR think that you obviously know what you're talking about so decide to hire you.

JULIUS: Just think of those fluffy bunnies from Watership Down!

JONNY: You what?

JULIUS: Philistine! Sometimes I think I live in a different world to everyone else. It's the quote from the film when they make the point that practically everything wants to eat rabbits.

JULIUS: Hang on. I'll google it…

JONNY: This had better be good!

JULIUS: Here it is. *All the world will be your enemy, Prince of a Thousand enemies. And when they catch you, they will kill you. But first they must catch you; digger, listener, runner, Prince with a swift warren. Be cunning, and full of tricks, and your people will never be destroyed.*

JONNY: Bloody Hell Julius. That's being a bit strong isn't it?

JULIUS: ☺ You know what I mean! You're a sole trader and everyone is your competitor or wants to steal your inspiration.

JONNY: Oh, whatever. I'm concentrating on the local market now, designing some flyers.

JULIUS: A cunning plan. Networking is anything but a quick fix. Have you seen the posts in the Bohemian Club? Do us a favour and back me up, this is important to me. ;)

JONNY: I'll have a look now.

JULIUS: You're a gent!

Jonny opened up the forum in the Bohemian Club to find Julius' post.

Title: Why can't we make a British film for British people?

Started by: Julius Mortimer

Messages: 10

I was told today by a potential investor that my film script was too British, that he didn't think it would sell overseas, that he really liked it, but that it would go over the heads of the US audience.

I don't care about the US audience! It's a cracking ultra-low budget film that applies to life in London right now. Why should it apply to American audiences? We have a huge cinema industry in the UK and how many people live in London? About 8 million? That's quite a few bums on seats.

Julius
Julius Mortimer
Bringing your company to the big screen

Comments:

If the UK market is huge, just think of the US market!

Why should he invest in your film with a target market of say 40 million when he could invest in one with a target market of say 200 million?

It's finance Julius – deal with it!

Gemma Wilkins
For PR by the hour

Hah!

Whatever happened to Love, Beauty, Freedom and Truth, Gemma! We're bohemians it's our duty to complain about the killjoys who pull the purse strings. ;)

Julius Mortimer
Bringing your company to the big screen

Get real!

Remember sparkling Satin in Moulin Rouge –
'if you can't pay then you won't play!'
Alice Pond
Pond Legal Advice

But we can pay!

Typical lawyer's comment. ;)
Brits love going to the cinema. Why can't we
have films that they want to watch?
Julius Mortimer
Bringing your company to the big screen

Get off your soapbox Julius Caesar!

Rome wasn't built in a day and it took lots
of slave labour, we need to prove that we
can make decent films that people will want
to see –preferably ones that don't involve
Hugh Grant, or people taking their clothes
off.
Gemma Wilkins
For PR by the hour

Yes please!

Now I would pay to see Hugh Grant taking his
clothes off! ☺
Alice Pond
Pond Legal Advice

Blame the farmer in Ohio!

Apparently it's all due to a farmer in

Ohio. Rumour has it that films have to be understood by the average farmer in Ohio to gain funding. It's a yardstick for the average American and an indication of its possible popularity in the land of the American Dream.
Danny West
Fancy trying a podcast but not sure where to start? Let us show you the way!

Find me a farmer!

Where do you find one? And don't say Ohio!
Julius Mortimer
Bringing your company to the big screen

Leave us Yanks alone!

Change the record guys! Just face it that your sarcastic sense of humor and fondness for 'clever' word play don't travel well. Why should we struggle through a movie when we have plenty of home-grown talent? Some of your regional accents and dialect are completely unintelligible to us! We say tomato and you say, well, tomato…
PS When is the naked Hugh Grant flick coming out Stateside?
Cindy Maltoser
Your first stop for Real Estate

Sorry Julius

I have to agree with Cindy. Make a mainstream film, get it shown and then write your clever masterpiece and cast some foxy American stars in it (and persuade Hugh

Grant to flash his arse)
Jonny Philips for sublime web design in half the time

Jonny was distracted from his work by an overloud knock on the kitchen door that made him jump. Antonio (1244) stomped in making exaggeratedly loud footsteps.

"Just checking you weren't otherwise engaged hombre," he quipped with a smirk.

"Oh leave it out!" Jonny snapped. "Stop treating me like a bloody teenager! It used to be fun living here. Now it's just one long piss take."

"Easy hombre, I warned you about the perils of being a sole trader."

"Forget work! You should try living with a loved-up couple who advertise the fact that they're having more sex than you at every given opportunity."

"No, we…"

"Of course you bloody do!" Jonny interrupted. "And then there's the fact that Heather is wearing less and less in the house. I know it's summer, but it's not a beach."

"What are you saying hombre?"

"I'm saying that I don't need her rubbing my face in her sexuality."

"Is that your fantasy or something?"

"My fantasy? Sometimes I think it might be hers. She's always flirting, especially when you're not here."

"Hey!" Antonio moved menacingly towards Jonny. "Are you saying that my girlfriend is making moves on you behind my back?"

Jonny looked at Antonio's hostile impression and sighed. "That's not what I'm saying at all Antonio. I just don't think she should be so familiar with me."

"Are you saying that you fancy her?"

"No!"

"Are you sure?"

"Of course I'm sure! She's a very sexy lady, but she's going out with you and well, she's not my type. I just don't need her in my face all the time, that's all."

"I didn't realise I was *in your face*."

Jonny turned to see Heather (179) standing in the doorway. She was doing a very good impression of a fashion model being innocent, hurt and sorrowful while apparently wearing nothing but a man's collared shirt.

Jonny looked from one to the other taking in their hurt expressions.

"I can't handle this!" He exclaimed and pushed past Heather, out of the room.

You have an instant message from SAM:

SAM: G'day Sport!

CAT: You again? Don't you ever get to sleep?

SAM: Not at the moment and the old man's away on business at the moment so there's only me to get up to see what the little darling wants.

CAT: Doesn't sound fun. How are you coping?

SAM: Coping sums it up. I must admit life isn't much fun.

SAM: I wouldn't change little Mark for anything, but

CAT: Go on, don't be shy with me!

CAT: Sam? You there?

SAM: Sorry, afraid I was just having a little boo. No big deal, it's just that sometimes I feel like I'm in the middle of nowhere, a long way away from home, cooped up in the house with a screaming baby.

CAT: You poor thing! I can quite understand. And there's me continually going on about my insignificant problems…

SAM: Shut up you. Your problems are always funny! ☺

CAT: Watch it! So haven't you been able to make any friends over there yet?

SAM: Yeah, a few, but none really on the baby circuit and there's a limit to how much people without babies want to hear about my darling little Mark.

CAT: You didn't send them the photos of his dirty nappies, did you?

SAM: They were for your eyes only.

SAM: Just thought you ought to know what it's like. ☺

CAT: Thanks…

CAT: Aren't there any mother and baby groups where you are?

SAM: Not as such. It's pretty isolated here. Hey, perhaps I can join your dating, sorry networking site! You chatted up that Jonny bloke yet?

CAT: I haven't chatted up anyone – cheeky cow!

SAM: Why not? What was wrong with Jonny?

CAT: Nothing. Anyway, this isn't about me, it's about you. You should join. There's a lot of socialising as well as business schmoozing.

CAT: I bet there's a mother and baby club you can join.

SAM: Great. I'll check it out. Now, tell me, how's your love life?

CAT: I'm just about to go out on a date with FUM – I'll tell you about it when I get back! ☺

SAM: Oi! More details please!

Cat has logged out.

Chapter 12

While Ferrero wasn't bothered who came with him on a walk as long as it got him out of the house, Cat (449) was having second thoughts about her walking companion (494). This was a shame because behind the scenes of her laidback, pretty appearance achieved with a light, summer dress, trainers and sunglasses, she had put a lot of effort into this date.

She knew that Tim wanted to wine, dine and do something rude with her, and part of her wanted to play that game just for the hell of it. But if she was going to play it was going to be according to her rules. Tim had made it clear that he didn't approve of her choice of venue for their first date, but Cat had stuck to her guns to show him that she was the ones wearing the trousers, even if she was wearing her best knickers underneath.

Tim looked distinctly uncomfortable as he walked awkwardly around anything that squidged underfoot in his polished shoes, smartly ironed slacks and a long-sleeved shirt. It was a far better look than his crumpled first impression, but it was not suited to the blazing hot day. He occasionally shot a look in Cat's direction that very obviously said 'can we go back yet?' but his eyes lingered on Cat's tanned body until he missed his footing yet again.

Ferrero was also giving Cat meaningful looks that probably meant something along the lines of – 'please let me off the lead so I can sniff that dog's bottom!'

"Go on then," Cat said as she slipped off his lead. "But behave yourself!"

Ferrero sped off down the lane to sample the other dogs' delightful aromas, seemingly oblivious to the other sounds, scents and the bright sunshine that contributed to the gorgeous summer day.

Tim watched him go and narrowly avoided stepping on a foul smelling dog offering that Ferrero had sniffed seconds earlier.

"I must say that this unworldly stench does not make the best backdrop for romance," he observed, wrinkling his nose as they walked past a steaming manure heap in a nearby field.

Cat laughed. "Just walk on a few paces and take a deep breath of the countryside air!" She insisted.

"I can't say that I share your enthusiasm," Tim sighed. "Hay fever. Always curtailed my enjoyment of the great outdoors. And the sight of your canine companion with his nose up another dog's tail is not a sight to get my heart beating."

"We'll keep away from grass," Cat promised. "We get into woodlands soon. Nice and cool and low in pollen."

"Sounds definitely more promising," Tim agreed, visibly perking up. "With the added bonus of privacy and seclusion."

"Watch it you," Cat said without smiling as she wondered if Tim was going to demonstrate that he was interested in anything else other than sex. "I've brought my chaperone with me."

"He seems to be succumbing to lustful thoughts of his own," Tim laughed as Ferrero decided that the bottom sniffing foreplay was over and it was time for some hopeful humping.

"Ferrero! No!" Cat shouted as she ran after him and shooed him away from the object of his lust, before showering apologies on the other dog's owner. Ferrero was subsequently restrained on his lead until they reached the woods where he sped off in search of badgers and rabbits.

"Isn't this beautiful?" Cat said as she span around in a clearing be-speckled with yellow and green light. Her dress swirled around her knees and when she looked back at Tim she noticed that his attention was firmly focused on her. She smiled. "You're supposed to looking at the trees."

"As the Bard said, thou art more lovely than a summer's day." Tim replied, holding out his arms to her, intent on pulling her into an embrace.

Cat deftly grabbed one of his hands and placed it in her own. "I believe that quote ends with 'and more temperate', in other words

I practise self restraint." She smiled as she started to walk him down the woodland track. "I don't know much about you," she said. "I know that you would rather have a candlelit dinner than a dog walk in the countryside, but very little else."

"But you must know that I have strong feelings for you," Tim declared. "In fact, without being overdramatic, I can't remember the last time I had such intense feelings about someone in such a short time."

"Trust me, I've got the message that you like me," Cat said with a smile, "but I know so little about you and…"

"And?"

"And I've been hurt before. Recently. I'm a little short of trust."

"Well, I am just going to have to be fortunate man who fills up your trust fund then," Tim declared. "You want to know more about me? You already know that I'm a hopeless romantic, totally hopeless. Everyone thinks that a wedding is the bride's day, but when I'm taking endless photos of nauseatingly happy couples, I only have eyes for the grooms. The way that they hold their shoulders back, puff their chests out, the pride in the way they receive everyone's compliments about their new wife. I know they will have someone to embrace and entwine with at night. Someone to wake up with, someone to complain about the lack of anything decent on television. If I travel anywhere by train there's no-one giving me a tearful hug at the station to see me off. I am a lonely romantic in the worst possible job. That's who I am."

"Wow, that's quite a speech." Cat said and they continued to walk together for some time in silence.

"I'm sorry if I came on a bit headstrong Cat," Tim said, stroking her hand with his thumb. "It's just that you asked what makes me tick, and I expressed what is whirring around in my head. And no, this is not my ideal date and I would prefer a candlelit dinner, but I'm here with you and enjoying your company and, well, your beauty."

"How can you not see the beauty in this place?" Cat asked as she looked around her once again. "There are a million different greens, let alone all the other colours. You can smell that it rained last night. You would never get that sort of fragrance out of an air freshener. Then there's the sound of the wind stirring the leaves. It's the most romantic place in the world."

"Apart from the mud squelching underneath my feet," Tim laughed. "Are you sure you haven't read the Celestine Prophecy? There is a lot of talk of tapping into the natural energy from the world around us. I never really understood what they meant until now."

"So you can see how beautiful this place is now?" Cat grinned.

"Obviously not in the same way that you do," Tim smiled at her, "but I do now see how people can pick up energy from the environment. You looked ravishing before we got here, but now you are almost glowing from head to toe."

"Oh come on Tim, you're laying it on a bit thick now!"

"Bear with me Cat. The theory goes that we all have a certain amount of energy and that we are looking to boost our own energy supplies by taking them from other people. For example, if you have an argument with someone you could look at the exchange of words and actions in terms of an exchange of energy. If you win the argument you are boosted by their energy that you have stolen. To take the analogy further, if you have a domineering boss they are constantly taking your energy.

"Looking at you now I can see that you are absorbing energy from your surroundings here. It is making you feel good and I can almost see the energy emanating out of you."

Tim walked up to Cat and put his palms out as if he was feeling the energy he was talking about. He moved his palms around her head always staying a set distance away and then moved his hands down over her shoulders and across to her chest. She gently pushed his hands away with a smirk.

"I can see where the energy is coming from you and it's certainly heading this way," she said.

Tim returned his hands to her face, this time gently cupping her cheeks in his hands. "My energy is drawn to you like a magnet," he said softly and quickly moved in to kiss her lightly on the lips.

Cat started back slightly, she was determined that this date was going to be on her terms. However, Tim stepped forward and added another soft kiss and Cat's lips started to respond. Tim kissed her more forcefully and she slid her tongue inside his mouth. He took her in his arms and pulled her tight against him so her soft stomach pressed against him. Cat was not expecting him to be such an expert kisser, she felt her body leaning into his regardless of her reservations.

Suddenly they both jumped apart as Ferrero barked loudly right beside them. Cat giggled and smoothed her dress down as she stepped away slightly, enjoying the sensation of feeling her heart beating hard in her chest. "Saved by my chaperone," she smiled and gently took Tim's hand and guided him back to the path, the way they had come.

For a moment Tim looked lost for words, but he managed to recover his composure. "I never liked chaperones," he quipped in a light tone that was at odds with the fierce frown he sent towards Ferrero. "I tell you what. Why don't we celebrate the end of the bridal fair, that you are going to make a huge success of, with a romantic evening in the country? There's a lovely old castle not far from the venue. They've got an amazing restaurant with fabulous wines and I can get us one of their best rooms. I've sent quite a lot of business their way."

"Sounds great, as long as we have separate rooms," Cat laughed.

"I wouldn't have it any other way," Tim smiled. "Just as long as the dog doesn't come too. Let's get back to that pub and I'll buy you lunch."

*

A couple of hours later and Cat was breezing into the Dog and Bacon with a big smile on her face that faltered slightly when she registered how empty it was. Ferrero didn't mind the lack of customers and sprinted across the room towards Kelly (180) the moment Cat let him off the lead.

"Hey Top Cat!" Kelly beamed. "Oh don't you look the gorgeous lady wot does summer walks for first dates! Have a good time? Turn round."

"How many questions are you going to ask?" Cat laughed.

"Lots, just turn round!"

Cat did as she told with a bemused expression on her face.

"No grass stains on your dress or twigs in your hair. It can't have been *that* good a date!"

"Kelly! You can't make insinuating comments about me like that in public," Cat complained.

Kelly laughed. "By the state of our rubbish Sunday trade I would hardly call this a public place."

Cat had another look around the pub that was empty except for a middle aged couple staring listlessly at each over their empty glasses in the far corner. "You've got a point," she conceded. "but, you could still be a bit more circumspect when you're talking about my love life."

"Ah c'mon Top Cat! You know I didn't mean any harm. I knew you wouldn't put out on a first date. You're far too straight for that."

"Huh, don't think you know everything about me little sister," Cat said, trying not to show how disgruntled she was by Kelly's comment.

"Well, I've got something you don't know about me," Kelly beamed. "One is in charge!"

"In charge of what?"

"In charge, charge! Malc was sounding out some people about

having a local folk festival here and one thing led to another and now he's organising a huge open air event at some castle in Scotland. He's getting paid a fortune for it."

"Please tell me you're joking!" Cat exclaimed. "How is he expecting you to run this place by yourself? You've only just got here."

"Oh untwist your tummy hugger knickers," Kelly sighed. "Business is slow anyway and he's only going to be away for a month. The extra money he earns will pay for all our investment in the flat. You told us not to borrow money unless we could help it."

"But what about the extra staff costs? You can't run this place all on your own."

"We've run the figures. It will work, and anyway, it will be a cool adventure for me."

"I will never understand you Kelly."

"Good, just the way I want it." Kelly grinned. "So you were saying that I don't know everything about you? I bet I do."

"You don't know who I bumped into on the way here."

"Ah, now that is a tricky one, erm Brad Pitt?"

"Nope. The woman who destroyed my life."

"Not the slimy, vile, shit bag of an assistant who stole your boyfriend!"

"Language Kelly! No wonder you haven't got any customers, but yes, you're right."

"Hope you decked her!"

"Well, I thought I would, but she put me off guard by saying that she had split up with that pillock and then she had the nerve to ask if she could come to my leaving do!"

"What leaving do?"

"The one that's here tomorrow night. That's not the point."

"Yes it is! It's totally the point. We've got no customers. How many are coming?"

"About 20, but…"

"20! I love you Top Cat!"

"If you love me let me finish!"

"Sorry, so the evil harlot asked to come to your party and you said?"

"I asked her if she was bringing a partner or leaving with someone else's."

"People are bringing partners! Does that mean that 40 people are coming?"

"Kelly!"

"Sorry, killer put down by the way. What did she say?"

"She said it depends if there are any men who are bored with their sex life!"

"No! She didn't! What a cow! So is it really going to be 40?"

"It might be."

"What did you say back?"

"Nothing. I couldn't think of anything! But she looked really depressed and upset anyway so I just walked off. It made me feel better about the situation if anything."

"It's the best way Top Cat, leave it be. He was a shit; she did you a favour, showed his true colours."

"You see, you don't know everything about me," Cat pointed out.

"Hmm," Kelly paused. "If I tell you a secret? Promise you won't get mad?"

"Whaaat?"

"Your toady ex phoned Mum a few weeks ago. He got bored with your young assistant and wanted to get back with you."

"What!"

"We told him to..." Kelly looked across at the middle-aged couple who were now staring over each other's shoulders. "... bleep off, said you'd rather sleep with George Bush."

"What did he say?"

"Not much but he's only just stopped ringing. He was very keen."

"Why didn't you tell me!"

"We didn't want to upset you all over again."

"It might have been nice to have the option."

"You didn't need the option babe."

Cat didn't respond and quietly took a seat on one of the bar stools while Kelly fixed her a large gin and tonic with lime with a worried look on her face.

"Are you okay Cat?"

"It would be nice to be kept up to date with my own love life. Why am I the last to know everything? I'm not a little girl. In fact I seem to be the only grown up in our entire family."

"Oh don't be like that Cat," Kelly sighed. "We're only trying to do the right thing for you. Besides," she gave a little wink. "You're just miffed that I know all your secrets, just like when we were little."

"Oh yes?" Cat said archly. "I've got another surprise for you."

"You did shag Tim!"

"No! I've found you a tenant for the flat."

"Kelly ran round from behind the bar and launched herself on her sister, giving her a huge hug. "You really are the bestest sister in the whole world! I love you!"

"Calm down woman!" Cat laughed as she struggled her way free. He'll be in the pub tomorrow night so give him a warm welcome eh?"

The House of Fun Blog

Diary of a mad house
Date Mon 27th June 2006

A change is as good as a rest?

VIKING – As anyone who has worked from home will know; there can be serious difficulties involved in separating work and home life. It is easy for the mind to stray into home activities (even the washing up can become tempting) during work hours and it can he hard to switch off from work in the evening. If and when I get my business on the road I will try and find an office somewhere that does not have to double up as a small home for three people.

GUEST – Ute: You can do my washing up Viking! ;)

CELT – Easy pal! I only asked you to clear the kitchen table of your papers so we could cook the dinner.

SPANIARD – Come on amigos, play nicely…

Chapter 13

Jonny (149) was very surprised by the warm welcome he got when he walked into The Dog and Bacon that evening. One minute he was trying to convince his conscience that he could afford to spend his dwindling savings on beer and the next his favourite landlady was rushing up to him and embracing him tightly against her decidedly prominent breasts.

"I'm so glad it's you!" Kelly (180) beamed. "Antonio was trying to explain who you were, and then I remembered. The cool guy who helped me out when the bottle opener broke!"

"Erm, it's lovely to have such a warm welcome," Jonny said as Kelly released her grip. "But I'm not really sure what I've supposed to have done."

"Sorry," Kelly laughed. "Always too enthusiastic. The flat! Antonio put down the deposit and all that on your behalf. It's great to know that there's going to be someone nice in there. Well to be honest, it's great to have anyone in there, but…" Kelly noticed Jonny's shocked expression. "Are you alright?"

Jonny was struggling to form a response when he saw Antonio (1247) and Heather (180) entering the pub.

"Here's the hombre!" Antonio cried. "Young, free and single, but not for long!" His cheerful expression froze when he noticed Jonny's hostile expression.

"I've just been welcoming him to the gang," Kelly beamed.

"Oh shit," Antonio murmured. "Heather, can you get some drinks in?" He took Jonny to one side. "It isn't what it looks likes Hombre. We're not trying to get rid of you; we're doing you a favour. I've negotiated you a good deal. It's hardly any more than you pay me at the moment. And I've paid your first two months so you've got time to get your new business on its feet."

"For God's sake Antonio. I know that I lost my temper the other day, but I've been living with you for two years!"

"It's not like that hombre! It's just that it was just like you said. The flat is not big enough for the three of us, and you were right. We were being a bit, as you English describe it, 'out of order.'"

"You really did want to get rid of me didn't you? Paying my rent and everything." Jonny observed, surprised to find that he was close to tears.

"No Jonny, I want you close by me. It's just that things change. Me and Heather, well I could never have predicted it. It's the L word hombre and you don't want to be stuck in a tiny flat with us, always fighting to get to the bathroom. No room on the sofa."

"Don't mention the sofa."

"That was a nightmare wasn't it?"

Jonny and Antonio looked at each other awkwardly for a few moments. Jonny felt an urge to plead with Antonio not to chuck him out. He really didn't want to be on his own again. However, he allowed his pride to re-assert itself and responded in less desperate terms.

"I just feel, like a, like a charity case," he said. "And yes, to be honest I feel squeezed out. I really enjoyed living with you, we had a laugh, it's been the best stage of my life."

"I know Hombre," Antonio said sadly and gripped him by the shoulder. "It's been good, but life moves on, and you've got yourself a flat in a pub! We can meet up for some big drinking sessions like we used to, without Heather. I bet I'll be gagging for some male bonding binge drinking."

"So when's Heather moving the rest of her stuff in?"

"She's not, I've found someone who is looking for a flat just like ours and I've got my eye on a pad in the posh end of town that needs major renovation. We're going to buy together."

"Jesus! You're heading for the altar!"

Antonio saw Heather coming back with a tray of drinks. "Don't you go putting ideas in her head, hombre."

"As if they're not there already."

"Pals?" Heather asked flashing her best girly smile.

"Of course," Jonny managed a smile and kissed her on the cheek, but had difficulty looking her in the eye.

"So!" Antonio declared. "Welcome to your new office! The perfect place to entertain your clients, not to mention your senora. Have you booked that date yet?"

"She might be popping in tonight, but she's really busy. As usual," Jonny sighed.

"She had better sort her priorities out," Antonio declared. "A man cannot wait for ever eh? Have you met Kelly's sister yet? She's the one who told me about the flat. She could be born for you hombre. Slightly older, well groomed, muy bueno figure." Antonio traced Cat's probable outline with his hands.

"EO!" Heather objected, whipping her hair back over her shoulder with a slight display of petulance.

"I'm just describing how perfect this senora is for Jonny. And guess what hombre? When we negotiated the flat deal she was wearing boots! Just... just like her!"

Jonny turned round to see Sarah (823) striding confidently into the pub wearing a long skirt with a split up to her thigh and shiny, black boots. She had ditched the eighties style make up and her Cleopatra style make up accentuated her eyes, rather than hid them.

"Hey Jonny," she beamed before planting a forceful kiss on his cheek. "I made it!"

"So you have," Jonny said, slightly nonplussed by her sudden appearance. "Antonio, Heather, this is Sarah who I told you about."

"And I've heard loads about you two!" Sarah declared giving Antonio an impish smile and aiming a significantly colder smile at Heather.

"We've heard that you are hard to track down," Antonio replied returning her smile.

"Busy, busy, busy," Sarah agreed. "So you're an estate agent?"

Two rounds later and it was obvious that Antonio and Sarah had a lot in common besides Jonny. They spent a lot of time discussing sales tactics and Jonny found it hard to get a look in.

He was also struggling to think of a conversation topic to help make the peace with Heather. He knew the recent events were nothing personal, but it was hard not to think of Heather as a sultry interloper who had seduced his mate and coyly wriggled between them.

"So," he said hesitantly. "You looking forward to being able to get into the bathroom in the mornings?"

Heather just smiled at him and twiddled with the ends of hair.

"Has the new flat got a window in the bathroom?" He asked desperately trying to get some conversation going.

"I dinnae know," she replied. Her hand not leaving her ponytail. "I havenae seen it yet."

"At least there won't be any shaving foam on all your toiletries," Jonny pointed out.

"I dinnae have that much stuff," Heather objected.

Jonny gave up making conversation and they just looked at Antonio and Sarah who were quickly bonding in a quick fire work-related conversation.

The silence between Heather and himself grew ever more ponderous and Jonny started to feel angry. Why should he be the one to build the bridges and make conversation when he was the one that was losing out?

If Sarah wasn't there he could have just slipped away and left everyone to be smug and happy at how well the situation had been resolved. Then again, what was the point of Sarah being there if she was spending the whole time talking to Antonio? He derailed his negative thought process and downed the remaining half of his pint before offering to get a round in.

He approached the bar to find Kelly serving and made a mental note to avoid the temptation of flashing a look at her prominent cleavage. He had better behave himself if she was going to double up as his pub and flat landlady, as well as new neighbour. He was going to need all the friends he could get. He fixed his gaze on her eyes instead.

"Hello new neighbour," he said as put his empty glass on the bar.

"Hi. Look, sorry about before. Was there something weird going on there?"

"No I'm sorry; it was a surprise. For me!" Jonny made a good effort at looking happy about the situation. "I suppose I'm lucky to have friends that care about me."

"Cool." Kelly grinned as she served his drinks. "You'll have to meet my sister Cat. Don't tell anyone but she's the brains behind this business and I only pay her in gin!"

"Now that is weird. You're the second person inside 10 minutes who's said I have to meet your sister."

"*Everyone* should meet my big sis," Kelly declared. "These are on the house."

"Wow! Thank you." Jonny beamed with his first genuine smile of the evening.

"Don't get used to it," Kelly warned with a grin.

*

By time they had finished the free drinks Sarah was heading towards the door.

"Hey, sorry I have to go, but it's been great spending time with you." She said brushing an errant lock of hair back from Jonny's face.

"You spent most of it with Antonio," Jonny pointed out.

"He is a bit of a talker isn't he?" she laughed. "Hey, I'll see you on Monday at the Beermat do in London. I promise that at the end of the evening you'll have me all to yourself!" She raised herself on tiptoe and kissed him mischievously on the lips. When Jonny didn't follow up on her camouflaged intention she slipped her hand around the back of his neck and pulled his head down and into a passionate kiss, allowing him to taste hints of the house red wine she had been drinking. She held him there for over a minute, forcing people to walk around them to enter the pub.

"Yum, that feels much better," she smiled. "See you later Blondie!"

She strode off, casting a single, mischievous look over her shoulder. Jonny stood and watched her go. He had been struggling to find work, been kicked out of his flat in the nicest possible way and now he had enjoyed a passionate kiss that definitely left him wanting more. It had certainly been a strange day.

He turned round and pushed the door of the pub open. He was met with the blast of boisterous noise that accompanies people enjoying their Friday night out. He decided that he didn't feel like being sociable at all. He let the door close and walked off down the street towards the flat that would soon no longer be his home.

Messages: Sam Clarke

New message: This will add them to your network

Dear Sheila,

Nothing from you via IM so far today so I hope that Bruce has finally managed to get through the night without waking you. Great to see you have joined Ecademy and I see you have joined the New Parents Club! Hope you have fun swapping all those nappy content photos…

I'm sorry you've been having a bad time. I feel really guilty that I've been babbling away about my problems while you were stuck out there in the bush with only Skippy the kangaroo and a few wombats to talk to. Strewth mate! You must tell me how things are going in your next communication, in whatever form it comes!

News from my end is that my date went well although Mr FUM is not an outdoors man. You should have seen him tiptoeing around any bits of mud! However, he is an expert kisser and if he had his way we would have done it up against the nearest tree! He nearly did but darling Ferrero did his chaperone duties by making a fuss when our kissing was just starting to heat up. You should have seen Mr FUM's face. It was an absolute picture. If he had a gun I think poor Ferrero would have been sent to the big kennel in the sky!

I must admit though, it felt VERY good to feel a bit of passion – I almost got carried away! But mustn't do for a man to think that I'm a sure thing though even if I was wearing my fancy undies. ;o)

Well, it's my last day of work today so I'm just about to

disappear to Kelly's pub for a bit of binge drinking to prepare myself for my new life as an entrepreneur. Wish me luck!

Give Bruce a kiss for me.

Cat

Chapter 14

While Jonny was letting one door of the pub close, Cat (452) was opening another and she was delighted to see how full the pub was as she checked around for her friends. She noticed Antonio and went over to grab him.

"Hi Antonio! Is our new tenant here yet?"

"Hi Cat, yeah he's around. I think he's just saying goodbye to someone at the moment."

"Sounds mysterious."

Antonio laughed. "There's nothing mysterious about Jonny. He's as straight as they come."

"Sounds like the perfect tenant."

"Oh, he will be. I guarantee it. So, how was your last day at Sunshine?"

"Not very spectacular. Let's just say that I'm glad to be out."

"And how's that Bridal Fair going?"

"Oh don't! I'm trying not to think of that tonight. It all seems to be going well so far, but there are bound to be some last minute hitches somewhere. Anyway, I had better touch base with Kelly, can you give me a shout when our new tenant turns up? I'll buy him a drink."

"I think that will make his day," Antonio said seriously.

Cat quickly made her way to the bar to find Kelly red faced and flustered, trying to cope with the sudden demand for drinks.

"Oh Top Cat! What have you done to me!" Kelly wailed. "We've gone from famine to feast again! How come you've got so many friends all of a sudden?"

Cat looked round the bar and noticed that quite a few of the familiar faces were not from Sunshine. "I emailed the list from the local business group and said that a few people were celebrating or commiserating their departure from Sunshine here tonight. Looks like they don't need too much of a push to do their liquid networking here."

"Congratulations Cat, you are now officially a free woman!"

Cat span round to see Tim (495) standing behind her. He looked smart and contented, a different person to the one who was tiptoeing around mud in the woods. She smiled and went to kiss him on the lips, but he turned his cheek and went for the continental kiss on each cheek greeting.

"Top Cat!" Kelly wailed. "Sorry to break you lovers up, but could you give us a hand here please? You've invited all these people and they're still walking in the door!"

Cat rolled her eyes good-naturedly and nipped behind the bar. "Sorry Tim, duty calls. Right Kel, you call the drinks out and I'll pour 'em. You can do the pints. I'm not spilling beer down my work stuff. Is that why you work in your underwear?"

"Watch it! Large G'n'T with ice and lime!"

"That'll be mine then." Cat observed as she poured the drink and took a gulp.

"Large glass house red! So did you sort out that cow who stole your boyfriend?"

"No, I let it go, but…"

"Two Smirnoff Ice!"

"… I did give her a friendly smile when I left. I think that frightened her more than anything I could say."

"Dry white wine spritzer! No ice. Did you meet my new tenant?"

"No, Antonio said he had just popped out."

"You'll like him Top Cat, just your type."

"Shhh! Tim is right there you know?"

"Three bottles of cider…ice in the cider! Well, he's doesn't seem overjoyed to see you. I've seen Ferrero show more passion to that barstool than Tim did to you. Three G'n'T's, ice and slice of lemon, *not* lime!"

"That dog's humping everything at the moment. I think the vet may have to relieve him of his happy sack."

"You heartless woman!" Kelly laughed before the humour fell from her face. She stopped her manic drink serving and froze.

"What's up Kel?"

"I'm sure I just heard someone asking Tim about his wife!"

"You're making this up!"

Kelly turned to look at Tim who was pontificating at Gladys the florist (379).

"Am I? Make sure you ask him tonight," Kelly instructed, giving her sister a meaningful stare. She kissed her on the cheek. "Thanks you're a star, we've caught up now."

Cat made her way to the other side of the bar and approached Tim who was still talking to Gladys.

"I've got a question for you Tim," she said after smiling a hello to Gladys.

"Questions, always questions!" Tim chuckled. "We were just talking about the big do on Sunday and how much you have got us in line."

"Yes, it's amazing Cat!" Gladys gushed. "It has just all come together and everyone seems to be talking about it. I can see now why *you* love your job; it must be such a buzz for you."

"It's only a buzz when it works," Cat laughed. "It's pretty much a case of raw fear until it all comes together on the day."

"Well, I am sure it will be problem free," Gladys declared.

"I can guarantee there will be problems," Cat assured her, that's what all the contingency plans are for."

"That sounds far too daunting for me," Gladys said. "I will just stick to flowers. Buy them fresh and sell them quick! I'll see you on Sunday."

Cat used the opportunity of Gladys walking away to take a sly look at Tim and noticed that he was standing at sociable distance away from her. She quietly moved closer to him.

"Right you," she said quietly. "I said that I have a question for you."

Tim smiled easily at her, but took a small step back.

"Anyone would think you don't want to be seen with me," Cat said, moving closer to him, invading his personal space.

"It's just that I don't really like PDA's in pubs."

"PDA's?"

"I would have thought that you would be more up to date on the female vernacular Cat. PDA's are public displays of affection."

"But you said that you dreamed of tearful farewells on train stations!" Cat objected wondering why he was suddenly playing hard to get.

"That's a bit different to being over tactile in a pub," Tim argued, taking a half step back again. "I believe the youngsters say 'get a room!'"

Cat laughed. "You really are a mix of contradictions aren't you? However, I do still have that question for you. You see, someone has overheard someone asking you after the health of your wife."

"Oh Cat that's just so funny!" Tim wheezed. "Do you think that I can have my clients think that I'm not married? It tends to add unnecessary complications to my sales patter when I try to assure people that I know exactly what they want and what they're going through. My 'wife' as you call her, just happens to be very susceptible to colds and flu and never seems to be present at big events. She is blonde, from a bottle I fear, not natural. She works as a secretary and she is always having to watch her weight, poor thing.

"However, I will admit to having one sordid little secret. I was once forced to hire the services of an actress when my little white lies caught me out."

"You mean you hired an escort?"

"Shh! Keep your voice down!" Tim hushed. "It was nothing at all like that, she was a professional actress, we played husband and wife for the evening and then I drove her home. It was very strange if you must know, very unsettling to let a stranger into your personal space in public."

"Let me guess. She was six foot tall, fake blonde and busty?"

Tim laughed. "Far from it. She was very average looking. The sort of person that people wouldn't look twice at, just what I was looking for. To be honest Cat, I don't think that people would believe that I would be involved with a woman like you. I keep having to pinch myself. Now, shouldn't we mingle? It looks as if you have managed to attract a fair amount of potential business here tonight."

Cat smirked as she went to talk to the nearest person that she recognised and started to tell herself that it was about time she started to trust people again.

The House of Fun Blog

Diary of a mad house
Date Tue 28th June 2006

All change as the House of Fun reduces to two

VIKING - The end of an era or the start of a brave new world? The House of Fun has been a strange place over the last few days as the trio is going to be reduced to a couple. The flat has slowly changed from a bachelor pad of testosterone to a love nest as I am moving on to pastures new. A flat above a pub no less.

Re-reading this blog brings up many happy memories, of good times and bad hangovers. When two lads got up to mischief just because they could and because it was fun! When we chased a lot of women and even managed to catch some of them.

However, things change, people change and life moves on, sometimes going forwards, sometimes back.

Will, or can, this blog continue? Time will tell.

GUEST - Ute: End of an era eh? Shame, I've enjoyed this blog. Any plans to start a new one?

PS. Viking. I think you're better off without the Spaniard anyway.

SPANIARD – Who *is* this Ute woman?

Chapter 15

Jonny (161) roared his car back up the road towards the flat relishing the freedom that he had taken for granted before injuring his foot. Beside him on the passenger seat was a box full of leaflets advertising his services, not to mention a bag full of unhealthy bribes in the form of sweets that were going to see him through his impending work hunting session.

He pulled up to the flat and noticed that Heather's car was still parked, straddled across two spaces, as it was last night. He grumbled to himself as he reversed his Mazda up on to the pavement. He used to get annoyed about Heather stealing one of their parking spaces before. Now it was different, she was the tenant and he was the interloper. However, that didn't explain what she was doing at home during work hours.

He limped out of the car and balanced his bag of goodies on his box of leaflets and gripped them awkwardly with one arm while he unlocked the door to the flat. His precarious grasp on the box slipped as he tried to walk around the door and it tumbled to the ground, breaking open to scatter his precious leaflets in an untidy fan on the faded carpet. The contents of the goodie bag also distributed itself randomly across the floor in a spectacular fashion, with a selection of chocolate bars, crisps and Jonny's most potent bribe, a big box of Smarties.

"Bollocks!" Jonny exclaimed as he looked at the wreckage at his feet.

"Are you okay Hen?" Heather (180) appeared at the doorway of Antonio's room looking dishevelled in one of Antonio's old work shirts.

Jonny didn't bother to look up. "Yes, yes, I'm fine." He grumbled irritably. "I've just dropped everything on the floor that's all. Don't worry about me."

"Calm down pal," Heather said in a hurt tone. "I was just worried in case you had hurt yourself again."

"Yes, well, you're not my mother," Jonny muttered as he started to pile leaflets and confectionary into the same box.

"No Jonny, I'm your pal." Heather said petulantly, as she bent over to pick up some of Jonny's leaflets.

Jonny looked up as he started to make a sarky comment but was thrown off guard by the view he got through Heather's gaping shirt. He looked away quickly.

"If you're going to waltz around here during the day in Antonio's clothes can you at least wear some underwear?" He said, quickly switching his attention to clearing up his mess.

Heather gasped and pulled the shirt tight around herself and scuttled back into Antonio's bedroom.

It was over an hour before she reappeared in a pink tracksuit, the soft, fleecy type specifically designed for people who would not be wearing it outside the house for any sporting activity whatsoever. Jonny was busy filling envelopes with letters and leaflets and barely looked up when she came in.

Heather stopped and looked at him and searched for split ends in her hair for a while. When it became obvious that he wasn't going to acknowledge her presence she opened the 'fridge and stared at the mainly empty shelves. "Looks like we're even then," she said while still staring listlessly at the unappetising contents.

"What?" Jonny mumbled, making a big show of carrying on his envelope stuffing activities.

"You showed me yours and now I've shown you most of mine."

"Yes, very funny," Jonny replied without emotion. "Are you going to get anything from the fridge or do you just enjoy the way it lights up your face?"

Heather sighed and closed the fridge door without taking anything from it. "Actually I was trying to work out what I could eat that isn't likely to come shooting out of ma arse within half an hour. I've got food poisoning, hence the complete lack of underwear. Let's just say that I wasnae getting much warning earlier and as they say, every second counts. I strongly advise steering well clear of the bathroom for as long as possible. It smells as if the air freshener has mutated into a honeysuckle smelling sewage pit. The extractor fan seems to have passed out."

Jonny started to smile despite himself, but he continued his charade of being focused on his envelope filling.

"You haven't tried Antonio's Super Squits Cure then?"

"I havenae heard of that one."

"It's very similar to the Super Cold Cure, only you drink port and brandy instead of wine and don't eat anything for at least six hours."

"Port *and* brandy?"

"Old sailor's cure apparently, you drink it half and half." Jonny sealed an envelope with a flourish. "Don't forget that the Spanish sailors discovered the whole world."

"And have the best football team that for some reason never win anything." Heather added automatically. She took a closer look at Jonny's activities. He had set up neat piles of letters, envelopes and leaflets. He signed a letter, before addressing an envelope and filling it with the letter and a leaflet. However, there were numerous piles of each. In the middle of the piles of stationary there was a large pile of Smarties.

"I may not be a doctor," she said taking a closer look the table. "But those Smarties look like the ideal cure for food poisoning."

"That's a shame," Jonny replied quietly as he continued with his endeavours.

"Why?"

"Because you have to fill ten envelopes for you to earn one," he replied just as he stuffed the last envelope from the mini pile in front of him and popped a Smartie into his mouth.

"Sounds fair tae me," Heather agreed and she sat herself down, looked at a letter, signed in Jonny's name and started to address an envelope. They continued to work in silence for a minute or so.

"I'm sorry Jonny," Heather said as she licked the seal of another envelope.

"What? For flashing your beaver at me?" Jonny replied with a straight face.

"Jonny!" Heather laughed as she blushed at his response. "No! Well yes, but I meant about stealing EO away from you."

"He doesn't belong to me," Jonny pointed out.

"I know that, but you two had some really braw times here and well, I've put a stop to all that haven't I? I didn't mean to, you ken? It wasn't my plan or anything, we just, well, we fell in love and I ended up wanting to spend as much time as possible with the arrogant bastard."

"Oh, it's not arrogance," Jonny remarked with a smirk. "It's..."

"Self confidence!" Heather finished for him.

Jonny acknowledged her input by raising his eyebrows. "I don't mean to be arsey Heather, but you're right, me and Ant were having a good time together." He paused as he sealed another envelope. "And I'm not sure that I'm ready for this stage of my life to finish. I know you two have moved onto this special relationship, but I've - oh, I don't know! I suppose I've got nothing to move on to."

Heather placed her hand gently on his arm only for Jonny to unwittingly flinch and move his hand away. She gasped at his reaction.

"I'm sorry Heather; I didn't mean to do that. It's just that there's the..." He stopped himself and picked up another letter to sign.

"There's the what?" Heather asked.

"There's the fact that I feel like a complete charity case. Not only do I not feel ready to move on, I now cannot even afford to move myself on. It's very kind of Ant to set me up, but it just feels even worse that he has to do that in order for you two to be together."

Heather grabbed Jonny's hand more forcibly. "He did it because he wanted to, not because he felt guilty. You should have seen his face when he showed me the details of the flat he got for you. His best pal living in a pub, what better excuse to go and get pished in the middle of the week?"

"It still feels a bit…" Jonny was interrupted by a ping from his computer that announced the arrival of an email message. He spun his laptop round to look at the screen and smacked Heather's hand as she reached for a Smartie. "Ah, ah, I don't think you've done ten yet have you?"

Heather grinned. "But I'm ill!" She sighed theatrically, but returned to her envelope stuffing duties.

"Oh great!" Jonny moaned. "Listen to this. 'Dear Jonny. Just saw your profile on Ecademy and noticed that we both love Smarties…"

"Me too!" Heather chirped and quickly grabbed a Smartie from the pile.

"…so I thought I would get in touch. I am a life coach specialising in helping small business reach their full potential. Please do not hesitate to contact me if I can pass on any advice that will help you not only set challenging goals but surpass them.' I mean, what sort of crap is that?"

"Sounds like a sales pitch tae me," Heather reasoned.

"Exactly, just what you're not supposed to do. I contacted people and offered to help them with search engine optimisation and someone accused me of sending out spam."

"Well, without being funny hen, your life coach has sent his message to a potential customer. I mean you're not surpassing your goals at the moment are you?"

"But everyone's lining up to sell me advice," Jonny wailed. "I've got this virtual network of over 50 people and none of them have helped me towards any work. Even if they don't need my services they are supposed to have a network of people themselves. If they all have 50 contacts then I should have, what?" He paused as he did the mental arithmetic.

"2500?" Heather prompted.

"Wow! Is it that much?" Jonny exclaimed. "2,500 people who know about my services."

"But are you promoting their businesses to your network?"

"To an extent."

"That's nae answer. You used to complain about saying 'hello' every morning to people you hardly knew at Sunshine. Surely you need to make even more of an effort to get through to people you only know through a computer?"

Jonny reflected on Heather's comment. "I thought you were supposed to be ill," He pointed out, as he returned to his work.

"You seem to get on with, whatshisname, Julius?" Heather continued encouragingly.

"Yeah, he seems one of the few really decent people out there."

Heather finished her pile of envelopes, grabbed a small handful of Smarties with a flourish and popped them in her mouth. Jonny gave her a reproachful look, but her satisfied look soon changed to one of concern and she disappeared out of the kitchen and headed straight for the bathroom.

Jonny grinned, "Perhaps there is a God," he said to himself but he was soon distracted by the computerised ringing tone of a Skype call on his laptop. He saw that it was Julius calling him so he slipped on his headset and clicked the accept button to answer the call.

"Hello Mr Mortimer," he chimed in his best sing-song telephonist voice. "Don't worry I'm not selling anything, but if you were given the choice of one, two, three, four or five free windows for your house, how many would you choose?"

"Bugger off you tart!" Julius replied with a laugh. "Please tell me that you're not chasing a career in telesales!"

"I'm not having a career in much to be honest and I'm just about to be homeless."

"Homeless!"

"Yup, I went to the pub on Friday night for a few beers and discovered that I'm being ejected from the flat and into a one bed place above a pub."

"You what?"

"Yup, that's right, above a pub."

"No forget that bit, go back to the going to the pub on a Friday night bit. You said you couldn't make the premiere of that film because you were in too much pain to go out."

"But."

"They said that if we could fill that screen that they would show the film for the rest of the week. We were about 40 people short."

"So it didn't matter that I didn't make it then."

"You're not getting the point Jonny. If you had come and tried to persuade some of your network of friends to go then we could have had a full house, which would have led to another set of screenings and other cinemas may have given us a go. My friend has invested a lot of money on this film. You keep saying that networking is not bringing anything up for you, but you're not putting in the work mate. As, perhaps our finest British film exports, sang 'Nothing will come from nothing'. You've got to look on the bright side of life and make it happen."

Jonny finished the call more confused than ever, just before Heather reappeared looking pale and miserable.

"Looks like Smarties aren't the answer after all," she said holding her stomach as she sat down at the kitchen table. Jonny got up and poured her a glass of water.

"Drink this," he said. "You need to keep your fluid levels up."

"You've got tae be joking," Heather groaned. "It just keeps going straight through."

"Have you taken anything for it?"

"No, I don't dare leave the house."

"I'll go and get something for you," Jonny said and he turned off his laptop.

"Thanks hen, you're a lifesaver, as usual." She looked at him as she deftly tied her hair into a side plait. "I'm sorry if I've flirted with you in the past. I didnae mean to be a tease, it was just nice having you look after me. You ken?"

"Don't worry about it," Jonny said gruffly.

"Oh, and I probably shouldnae say this but, I had a chat with Sarah on Friday."

"That was more than I managed."

"You do know what you're getting yourself in for, you ken? I mean, well, I don't think that Sarah is the sort of girl who's into relationships."

Jonny stopped sorting out his laptop and turned to look at her. "What do you mean?"

"Well, she was asking about you, fairly normal sort of things, ken? Like if you had a girlfriend, stuff like that, and she said that she has always fancied men with blonde hair, but that she never has any time for men around work. I dinnae think it's an exaggeration to say that you're on a sure thing there, but I'm not sure she's the type to stick around for too long."

"Are you saying that she sleeps around?"

"I wouldnae know that, but let's just say that at the moment she is only after you for one thing."

Jonny frowned as he gathered up the prepared envelopes ready for posting, trying to get his head around the concept of being told that a foxy woman wanting to use him for sex was bad news.

"I hope I havenae said the wrong thing," Heather said. "I just thought you should ken the situation."

"No problem," Jonny said without making eye contact as he headed for the door. "I'll be back soon."

"Thanks Jonny, and I'll miss this."

"Miss what?" Jonny said as he turned round to see that Heather had returned to working on the pile of leaflets.

"Living with you two has been like living with the perfect boyfriend. Not that EO isnae perfect for me, but he doesnae automatically do the little things that you do. Dinnae think I dinnae appreciate the way you look after me Jonny. You're gonnae to make someone the perfect boyfriend one day."

You have a video email from Sam Clarke

A plump and cheerful woman appears wearing a stereotypical Australian wide-brimmed hat hung with corks and holding a bemused looking baby on her lap. The woman is sitting at a small desk and staring into the camera that was obviously positioned on top of her PC screen.

"G'day Sheila! How's this for technology eh?" She grinned. "Say hi to little Mark. Now you can see him for real you should be able to get rid of that horrible Bruce image.

"So here I am, all the way from Oz onto your PC screen wherever that may be and the technology costs me next to nothing. In fact I have signed up to be an agent to sell this system so I should be able to make a few bucks to pay for Mark's nappies!"

Mark gave a mighty yawn and stretched his arm out of the blanket he was snuggled in and promptly dozed off.

"There you go," Sam said proudly. "Dozing off the moment he sits down, just like his father. So tell me more about your hot alfresco date you little minx you. That sounds more like the mischievous Cat I used to get drunk with. I think you're getting too organised and boring for your own good. It's high time you had some fun. Just remember the old saying –' no rubber, no lover'! Otherwise you'll soon find that your front bottom becomes a two way street and believe me Sheila, that hurts!

"Don't you go worrying about me, Sheila! I'm just fine. Sorry about my little boo before, but hey, it's hard being a Mum, especially in a new country where the local cows bounce along on their back legs and tail!

"Right I'm off now, but if you want to help out an old mate you could consider joining this scheme. There's a link at the end of this message."

Sam blows a big kiss into the camera and the footage stops.

Chapter 16

It was the best of times, it was the worst of times. The brides and grooms to be were reacting to the nuptial cornucopia of the Bridal Fair in a variety of different ways. While there were a number of couples walking around arm in arm, wide-eyed with excitement, there were also a number of couples who were moving round the hall as separate entities, with invisible walls building up between them. There were some women who were pleased that their Mum had come along to help, while others wished they had left their meddling maternal influence behind.

There were also more than a few men who secretly wished that they had been left behind. Those who were caught in the act of letting their bored eyes wander towards the other brides-to-be were in for an even more difficult afternoon.

However, as Cat (468) surveyed the beautifully decorated hall and the marquees outside in the blazing July sun she simply saw it as a job well done. The event had been buzzing with people and the businesses were meeting their potential customers and gently persuading them to say 'I do' before signing on the dotted line.

Of course, it had not gone without a hitch, but her back up plans had worked well and nothing had been a serious problem in the end. It was now getting towards the end of the event and she was starting to relax and enjoy the atmosphere.

She felt a warm glow inside her. Not just because of the success of the event, but also because she knew there would have been a depressing edge without the knowledge that her overnight bag was sitting in the boot of Tim's car.

She was kitted out in her best underwear beneath her smart business suit on the off chance that Tim would manage to persuade her to forgo her separate room. She could look at those brides-to-be with that satisfied twinkle in their eye and relish the fact that while she looked like business as usual on the outside, she was dressed to thrill underneath.

Cat knew all about bridal events. She had attended one with her ex and the business-like feel of the occasion was the first reality check that really drove the point home that it was actually going to happen; that she was going to get married. Except that her fiancé decided to sleep around. A slight scowl passed across her face as she found herself wondering how many of the other couples would actually get to say their vows. And perhaps, more importantly, how many would keep them.

She shook off the negative thoughts and went for a stroll around the stalls saying 'hello' to the stallholders who recognised her. While she did feel in the mood for a bit of fun with Tim, she was certainly going to put him through his paces over dinner to make sure he was going to stick around. She decided that there was no room for one night stands in networking circles.

She jumped as someone tapped her on the shoulder. It was Gladys, (387) her florist friend and she was beaming with happiness.

"You Cat, are a complete star! We would never have achieved this without you. It just goes to show that it is worth bringing in the pros when there is something important to be done."

"Thank you," Cat smiled. "It's always much easier when you know exactly what people want and when everyone's stalls look so gorgeous!"

"You must take some of the flowers from my stall Cat. You know me, I only the sell the best and most of the flowers will be past their best after being under these hot lights all day. They'll still be good for a couple of days though."

"That's very kind of you, but I'm going on from here after the event," Cat smiled.

"Oh how mysterious," Gladys laughed and she scuttled back towards her stall as another couple paused to take a look at the blooms on offer.

Cat turned to see Tim (512) striding around the hall taking quick arty snaps of any woman who looked remotely as if she was a potential bride. He then chased after them to give them a ticket to allow them to claim a free photo in a few minutes time. He caught Cat's eye and let his gaze fall lecherously down her body. Cat felt herself blush and giggled quietly to herself as Tim zoomed his camera lens on her and snapped a quick fire series of photos. She decided that she would like to see those photos to see how well she was disguising her true feelings. Watching Tim flirting with all the women and knowing that he only had eyes for her gave her a flutter of excitement. She had the novel feeling of being both reckless and in control. She decided that, should she end up in Tim's room that night, she was definitely the one who was calling the shots.

Tim disappeared again, in hot pursuit of another young, nubile bride-to-be and Cat turned her attention to one of the stalls displaying wedding dresses. She was always fascinated by wedding dresses, an intriguing mix of the chaste and the sensuous. There was one bright scarlet Celtic design that caught her eye, matching the sense of rebelliousness in her current mood.

She was really interested in the stall hosted by the castle that Tim was taking her to tonight and she wanted to check it out without being noticed. It was one thing to have a classy night of daring passion, but it becomes much more daunting if it is run by someone on the local business scene. Unfortunately her feigned casual observations of the castle's stand were hampered by a dearth of potential customers visiting the stall. She returned her attention to the striking wedding dress, only to meet the Carrot lady (603) from the Overchurch Business Association. Her hair clashed horribly with the beautiful dress.

"I must say Catherine, that this is a most impressive event," She gushed at Cat over her half-moon glasses.

"It's Cat," Cat reminded her, "and thank you, it's very kind of you to say so."

"Well, I always believe in giving praise when praise is due," the Carrot lady breezed on, "and it has got the old grey matter working. Why can we not get this sort of exposure for all of our members? I mean, what have we here? A group of small, local, businesses who are teaming up for the common good, to attract customers into one area where we can hunt them down."

"I wouldn't have put it quite like that," Cat replied, "there is a special theme here. It's not as if you have a random selection of stalls. They are all here to advertise their wedding related services."

"Of course!" The lady beamed, "but if we put on something to appeal to our local residents can we not entice them into one area to see our wares? We seem to only do this sort of thing at Christmas, but people spend money all year round."

"A good point," Cat agreed, "and if my sister's pub is involved I would be happy to help out."

"That's just wonderful!" The Carrot lady gushed and set forth back into the main arena."

Cat took a deep breath and was just about to have another look at the castle stall when she heard Tim's voice. She looked up to see him talking with the man who was just starting to pack up his stall. She ducked back out of sight of them and moved closer so she could overhear their conversation.

"So how was business?" Tim asked.

"Oh not bad," the man (213) replied. "You know how it is. They take a brochure and make the right sort of noises, but don't sign on the line."

"Perhaps you need a special offer," Tim suggested.

"No way, we're top of the line and expect to keep it that way," the man laughed. "So I hear you have booked us for a special romantic rendezvous tonight."

Cat smiled as she pictured Tim blushing and looking uncomfortable.

"Yes indeed," Tim replied with no trace of embarrassment. "I've been working on this one for a while so she had better put out for me tonight."

Cat gasped and hurriedly covered her mouth to stop them hearing her.

"I can never believe how a washed-up looking bloke like you can manage a wife as well as a never ending stream of mistresses," the man laughed. "What's your secret?"

Cat nearly ended up kneeling on the floor as her knees suddenly gave way. She caught hold of a pole supporting the stand and steadied herself with tears brimming into her eyes.

"I'm still using that Celestine Prophecy bollocks," Tim replied. "It's amazing how susceptible women are to that chance meeting that *can't possibly* just be a coincidence. It's all in the technique. You just need to be attentive the first time you meet them. With this one I started chatting up her sister, alternative type, big tits, face full of piercings. Thought it might make a nice change from pseudo-business types, but she was a total non-starter. Fortunately she started talking about Cat, my current sexy little number, and about how she loved going to the gym. I met Cat and turned up to the gym at the appropriate time, job done. I just continue my over-verbose networking persona and file away all those important details for later use."

"You're kidding me?" the man exclaimed. "Not the fit bird that organised this event? Brunette, nice arse, great tits?

"The very same," Tim said smugly. "I made sure I had sex with the wife this morning, no good shagging this one on a loaded gun. A looker like that, I'd be finished in seconds!"

As the men laughed at their own witty banter Cat tried her best to mop up the tears flowing down her face. She had to get out somehow and that bastard had her stuff in his car.

"Are you okay love?" a concerned voice came from behind her. It was the dress shop owner (297).

"I'm sorry, no, I'm fine," Cat tried to reassure her quietly so Tim wouldn't hear her, but she couldn't stop the tears from rolling down her cheeks.

"There, there," the woman soothed. "You're not the first and I bet you won't be the last. Did he leave just when you had set your hopes on a long life together?"

"No, you really don't understand," Cat sobbed. "It's not what it looks like at all. I'm not engaged or anything. I've just er, heard some bad news. I'm really sorry about this, but can I just sneak through here?" She pointed to the back of the stall. "There's someone I really need to avoid."

"Whatever you need to do dear," the woman said kindly as she watched Cat disappear and looked around for the person she could have been hiding from.

After locking herself in a cubicle in the ladies and having a cry for the worst part of twenty minutes, Cat formulated a plan and was now attempting to tidy herself up in front of the mirror. She was just congratulating herself on a reasonable cover-up job when Jenny, the kindly host (649) from the Business Link meetings appeared, her short, black hair sporting a modern, sparkling tiara.

"Hello Cat!" She exclaimed in delight. "What do you think of this? I'm tying the knot myself soon and wondered if I could bring a bit of modern bling to altar."

Cat took a deep breath and turned round from the mirror. "Very funky," she said, managing a weak smile. "I'm afraid I must go. I'm late already."

"Are you alright Cat?" Jenny asked with a worried expression, her eyes scrutinising Cat's face.

"I'm fine," Cat said as she turned to leave. "I'm always fine. Don't worry about me."

"But I need to talk to you about this event..." Jenny started to say but Cat was gone.

Cat walked quickly through the hall keeping her head down so as not to make eye contact with anyone. She kept a surreptitious look out for Tim and made a beeline to Gladys' stall.

"Good Lord Cat!" she exclaimed. "What on earth has

happened?"

"You know that mystery date I was going on?" Cat said sadly. "It was with Tim, only I've just heard that he's married."

"With four children," Gladys added quietly. "I'm sorry Cat, I thought you were sharp enough to see through him." Cat's eyes brimmed with tears again. "Oh Lord, that didn't quite come out like it should have."

"I just heard him bragging to someone about how he had sex with his wife this morning and that he was going to screw me tonight!" Cat sobbed as her tears escaped from her eyes once more.

"I hope you have given him what for!"

"No, I just want to go, but he has got my overnight bag in his car and I've got no transport," Cat sobbed.

"Don't worry Cat, I'll go and get the keys for you and then I'll take you home, you poor thing."

"How will you get the keys?"

"Trust me Cat. Most people think I am an eccentric old bat anyway, I can get away with anything!"

*

Half an hour later Cat was putting the last of Gladys' things in her van when Gladys appeared dangling some car keys.

"How did you get them?" Cat asked.

"Easy as pie," Gladys smirked, "just used a bit of feminine guile. I said that you had spilt something down your top and that you wanted to change into something more comfortable. He couldn't get the keys out of his grubby little pocket fast enough!"

Cat managed a wry smile as she took the keys and unlocked the boot. She grabbed her bag and slammed the boot as hard as she could.

"I am sure you could do a bit better than that," Gladys observed with a wink. "Why not slip the keys down a drain?"

"But that's really vindictive."

"Cat! You're too full of morals. An eye for an eye and all that. You could always sleep with his wife!"

"You what?" Cat spun round, wide-eyed in astonishment.

"I was joking," Gladys smiled. "You can always count on me to add some drama to a crisis. Now, I think it is time for the old flat tyre trick."

She knelt down, unscrewed the cap and started letting air out of the rear tyre. She looked up at Cat, who was grinning at her. "Well, what are you waiting for?" She exclaimed. "What?" Cat asked in bewilderment.

"You may be a natural organiser, but you have no eye for detail. He has one spare tyre, if you let down two tyres he really is buggered."

Cat laughed and started work on the front tyre, relishing the blast of air and the sight of the car slowly sinking onto one side.

"What *are* you doing Cat?" A voice asked incredulously.

"Cat spun round to see Jenny standing behind her, still wearing her tiara, not to mention a shocked expression.

"Erm, I'm..." Cat mumbled, feeling her cheeks burn with embarrassment.

"Just providing a bit of constructive feedback," Gladys replied cheerfully. "Cat feels that she has been let down by someone. We're just letting him know about it."

"Hey!"

Cat spun round again to see Tim trying to run towards them, laden down with large photographic folders.

"Quick!" Gladys giggled. "Jump in the van!"

Cat grabbed her bag and scrambled into the van and Gladys

turned the ignition.

"Now this is what I call exciting!" Gladys panted. The engine managed a healthy cough and splutter, but quickly died and Tim was now only a few metres away. He handed his folders to Jenny who took them obediently and he reached out towards the passenger door.

"Lock the door, quick!" Gladys yelled. "It will start next time. I'm afraid it is long overdue for a service."

Cat scrambled for the lock on the door just as Tim grasped the exterior door handle. He yanked hard on the door, a fierce expression turning his usually soft and careworn face harsh and ugly. The lock engaged moments before he pulled the handle and to Cat's relief the door remained shut. Tim's face quickly transformed to a vulnerable puppy dog look.

"Cat! Where are you going? What are you doing?" He implored through the window.

Cat wound down the window a fraction. "Let's just say that a little 'coincidence' meant that I discovered some very useful information," she retorted, blinking back any remaining tears. Determined that he wouldn't know how upset she was.

Gladys got the engine to shudder into life at her third attempt.

"Whatever you heard, Cat," Tim wailed. "I'm, sure there's a rational explanation."

Gladys put the van in gear. "Silly question, but shall we put the pedal to the metal as my son would say?"

Cat nodded, she couldn't bring herself to look at Tim, to see the same person and remember those spiteful words he said about her.

Tim moved quickly round to the front of the car as Gladys slipped the van into gear.

"You can't go Cat, I beseech you!" He cried, putting his hands on the bonnet of the car.

"Now this is what is known in the gangster trade as a Mexican standoff," Gladys said calmly. "We can't drive off and he can't get to us. The moment he moves round to the side we can go, but until then he has to stand there."

"Just drive forward," Cat said keeping her eyes away from Tim's pathetic looking expression.

"What? Run the greasy scumbag over?" Gladys asked in surprise.

"No, just drive slowly, then he'll have to get out of the way."

Tim spread his legs wide and planted himself in the way.

"Now you're getting the hang of it," Gladys grinned as she gunned the engine and very slowly let up the clutch. The van moved forward very slowly, but at a consistent speed. Although Tim's eyes widened at the thought that they were going to try and push him out of the way, he stood his ground as the van moved centimetres closer to his knees.

"If you're going to go then you will have to run over me first!" He declared. "I just will not let you leave without clearing up this little misunderstanding."

The van touched his knees and then jolted forward, knocking him backwards on to the tarmac.

"Whoops!" Gladys giggled. "I told you that I needed a service."

Cat put her hand to her mouth as she giggled while Tim hobbled to one side, glaring at them as they rolled past, quickly gathering speed.

He limped manfully towards Jenny, reaching out his arms to retrieve his folders.

"It's not what it looks like," he breezed. "Just some silly misunderstanding, a few crossed lines.

"It's none of my business," Jenny said sweetly. "Now I must go and pay for this tiara or I'll get accused of stealing."

She left Tim wondering why his car now had *three* flat tyres.

The House of Fun Blog

Diary of a mad house
Date Fri 1st July 2006

Moving on, moving out, and the blog comes too

VIKING – Welcome to the calm after the storm. We've all managed to kiss and make up (don't even bother making a comment here Hornyboy!) and now the Spaniard and the Celt are on their way to setting up their own property investment empire.

The good news (hopefully) for the people who bother to read this blog is that I intend to continue. I have enjoyed the process too much to let it go and I will just have to try and find interesting things to discuss from my flat-for-one. I am sure that the others will add comments as and when they see fit.

So perhaps I need to turn my attention to how I am going to motivate myself to work when there is a pub full of food and booze and possibly foxy ladies below my feet. This blog could soon change to confessions of an alcoholic…

GUEST – CapnJack: We already assumed you were an alcoholic. Isn't it obligatory for writers?

GUEST – HornyBoy: Dream on Viking I dont even read your stupid blogs anymore its just a stupid tease.

GUEST – Ute: Eh? If you don't read the blogs
how have…? Oh never mind!

Chapter 17

Jonny's mind was in turmoil and he wasn't even awake yet. In his dream he was walking around the Sunshine offices asking everyone if they needed any work done. He knocked on an office door and entered, clutching a handful of leaflets to find a trendy woman in her late forties wearing a pin striped jacket typing manically at her computer. She was hidden behind in-boxes full of paper and her computer screen was covered in Post It notes.

"Good morning," he said in his best confident and friendly tone. "My name is Jonny Philips and I wondered if you would be interested in having your web site re-designed? I can provide a full service including the copy writing to ensure that you maximise the appeal of your brand."

"Yes, yes, that's all well and good," the woman snapped. "But can't you see that I'm so busy that I can hardly move?" She gestured at her overflowing in-boxes.

"Yes but..."

"Why on earth would I want your help to get me more work?" She demanded.

"I don't know," Jonny said feebly. "It's just that we've sent a few messages via Ecademy and..."

"Oh yes," the woman brightened. "You're that Jonny! Well it's very nice to see you. Have you had a chance to think over whether you would like your website redesigned yet?"

"But that's what I'm offering you!" Jonny wailed.

"Ah yes, but I can cut you a good deal," the woman smiled. "I have a lot useful contacts in my network."

"But I'm trying to sell to you!" Jonny shouted. He ran out of the office and in the corridor where he saw his old boss from Sunshine coming towards him.

"Ah Jonny!" His boss exclaimed. "I've got loads of work for you to do!"

Jonny ducked through a door and found himself in a stationary cupboard. He was not alone. There was a loud panting sound and he turned to see Sarah wearing nothing but a pair of kinky boots leaning over some cardboard boxes being taken from behind very vigorously by the CEO of Sunshine. He was sporting distastefully saggy buttocks and was grunting and puffing with the exertion. Sarah turned round to see him.

"Oh, hi Blondie," she said with no signs of being out breath. "I'll do you next. I've got a spare few minutes."

"Not until I've had my fill you won't," the CEO bellowed and he increased his thrusting.

Jonny escaped from the cupboard and ran into another room to find it empty except for a chair in the middle of the room. Sitting on the chair, wearing only a man's shirt open to her navel and big fluffy slippers was Heather.

"Hello hen," she smiled as she tousled her hair with one hand. "I'm here for the interview to be your girlfriend."

"But you're going out with Antonio!" Jonny cried, his frustration building with each stressful encounter.

"Yes and I feel that I have gained a lot of useful experience from this, but if I want to further my career with a viewpoint to marriage, I know that I need to step out of ma comfort zone and seek out a relationship that I feel will have more potential for a life long marriage." Heather replied, before adding a very girly giggle at the end.

"What so you're just going to dump him and move in with me?" Jonny shouted. "What sort of person are you?"

"We all deserve the chance to be happy Jonny," Heather reasoned and slowly unbuttoned the rest of the buttons on her shirt. She let it fall open, revealing her model's naked body. "I need someone tae look after me and you need someone tae look after you. It's very simple. We can be best mates and very kinky lovers!"

She got up from her chair, shrugged off the shirt and walked slowly towards Jonny. She took his face in her hand, pulled him towards her and kissed him.

Jonny (188) woke up with his head pressed against his pillow. He pushed it away with a shout and it collided with a glass of water beside his bed sending it to the floor where it smashed loudly. He was just looking blearily around the room when Antonio (1257) appeared at the door holding his pristine white dressing gown closed in front of him as he tried to focus his tired eyes into the room to see what was going on.

"What are you up to hombre?" He scowled as he took in the mess on the floor. "You have remembered that we've got people viewing the flat this morning?"

"Sorry," Jonny muttered. "I was having a nightmare."

"You're telling me. You've been shouting the place down. Typical, the one Saturday a year I get off work and you wake me up."

Heather (180) stuck her head around the door. "What were you dreaming about pal?"

"Believe me," Jonny said bluntly. "You just don't want to know."

*

If Antonio was unimpressed with Jonny first thing in the morning, Jonny was extremely impressed with Antonio's performance a few hours later. He watched as Antonio extolled to an excited young couple how perfect the cramped flat would be as that vital first rung on the property ladder. Jonny also appreciated how he paid extra attention to the pretty woman who spent most of the viewing holding a hand on her barely visible pregnancy bump.

Jonny heard how his room would make the perfect nursery for twins, especially as they would be able to hear the babies if anything was wrong in the night. In no time at all Antonio was showing them out the door, listening to their pleas not to show anyone else around until they had a chance to phone in with their offer. Jonny grinned to himself as he started to set up his 'office' in the kitchen as Antonio finally closed the door.

"That was so slick it was almost greasy," he quipped as Antonio sauntered in the room.

"I just say exactly what they want to hear hombre," Antonio smiled. "I get the feeling I'll be hearing from them very soon."

"Lucky you," Jonny sighed as he booted up his laptop.

"There's nothing lucky about it hombre. You need to know what you want and go and get it."

"Okay then, I want some business. I've been a good little networker and have been helping other people. I've sent out loads of leaflets and have got bugger all."

"Have you followed any of the leaflets up?"

"No, not yet." Jonny admitted.

"Why not? You can't just rely on people thinking that they need your services at the same moment that they read your fancy leaflet." Antonio looked at Jonny with frustration. "What planet do you live on?" They exchanged a long searching look. "Oh give me your mailing list. I presume you've got their phone numbers too?"

"But it's Saturday!"

"If they're not there they won't answer the phone will they? Are you free for meetings next week?

"Yes, except for Monday evening. I'm going to that Beermat thing but..."

Antonio took the mailing list and the phone and went in to the lounge leaving a sceptical Jonny to check his email.

*

An hour or so later and Antonio swaggered into the kitchen. "You had better iron your best shirt hombre. You've got three meetings on Monday with people who are interested in your services." He splatted a piece of paper with the names and appointment times onto the table.

"But that's amazing!" Jonny exclaimed.

"No, it's just business," Antonio said airily. "If you have a service you need to persuade other people that they need it now. You need to follow up and you need to find new leads." He brandished the local paper folded at the business pages. "Look, these companies have just received grants for innovation, you could get your hands on some of that. Check their web sites out and if you have something to offer ring them up on Monday to congratulate them and pitch your services. They'll either say yes or no, but at least you tried."

"But..."

"No 'buts', hombre. I know you're working at networking, but that takes time and you need work now. You have to develop a thick skin and a healthy dose of self-belief. You used to tell me all about how you had to charm and work your way round the secretaries at Sunshine. It's just the same with small businesses. You may not always get to talk to the person who makes the decisions on your service, you need to learn how to get past the gatekeeper."

"The what?"

"The people who decide who to let in to see the person in charge, the hombre with the money to spend. There are all sorts of techniques that people claim will work, but the best way is to be nice and that's you all over hombre. With all these weird dreams and stuff, you're forgetting what you're good at, why people like you.

"I know that you think I'm arrogant and that I'm only in it for the money, but I won't thrive unless people recommend my services. My sales banter today. I didn't tell that couple anything they didn't know and I didn't tell any lies. They need a starter home with twins on the way and I knew the sort of positive features they are looking for.

"Your Sarah chica, she's the same as me. She has a millionaire mentality. She's aiming for the top and will work as hard as it takes to get there."

"Excuse me, but I'm working bloody hard!" Jonny objected.

"I know hombre, but not necessarily in the right ways. Take Sarah, how many ways do you think she's tried at getting new business? I bet she's tried loads more techniques than you."

"But everyone's giving, or rather, trying to sell me advice," Jonny wailed. "It can't all work and I don't have time for it all. I could spend thousands on training and join countless groups and clubs and I still wouldn't necessarily get work."

Antonio laughed. "When you're right, you're right hombre. I wouldn't want to be in your position. Life seemed so easy working for a corporate didn't it?"

Jonny was just about to respond when the phone rang. Antonio picked it up, smiled and said. "That's perfect! I know you'll be very happy here," and put the phone down.

"Full asking price, no chain, mortgage agreed. I love it! You and me hombre, we're going out to get drunk."

"But I need to work!"

"No, you need a break and we need a lad's day out."

"Do you promise not to bombard me with advice?"

"Promise. It will be a work free zone."

"And it's just going to be us two?"

"Senors alone and on the town."

"You're not going to try and chat up some women, 'just to see if you've still got it' are you?"

"The thought never crossed my mind hombre."

"Bollocks!"

"Why do you ask stupido questions if you already know the answers?"

"One of these days you're going to get something wrong and fall flat on your face."

"That's very true hombre, but I'm lucky enough to have you to pick me back up!"

"That's what I was worried about."

To: Sam

From Cat

Subject: All men ARE bastards

Date:

Dear Sam,

Thanks for your lovely video email and of course I will join your scheme and send you video emails. However, I'm afraid that this time it's me that's having a good old cry as I've just discovered that the ugly, not at all funny bastard I was telling you about is married!

I've just got back from a bridal fair – don't ask… and heard him telling someone only a few feet away about his wife and kids and that he was having an affair with me! It was so embarrassing, because no-one else there knew we were 'together' so I couldn't really cause a scene, nor did I want to look unprofessional amongst fellow professionals – does that make sense?

What is it with me and men? I'm not asking for the world, just someone who tells the truth and respects me. Is that really asking too much? I know I have had a lucky escape as I found out before anything really happened, but I think I deserve a bit more luck on the romance side…

Anyway, sorry to dump all this on you. I'll send you a video mail when I've pulled myself together a bit. Little Bruce looks very cute, almost makes me feel clucky… And you look great, you foxy Sheila you! ☺

Take care

Cat

Chapter 18

Cat (468) was relieved by the relative anonymity of online networking the next day as she logged into her various accounts and checked for new messages. The thousands of people out there didn't need to know that she had very nearly been tricked into bed by a con artist she'd been attracted to more out of pity than anything else. Only Ferrero needed to know that it was the first time for months she was wearing clothes she would normally only wear while decorating or doing something equally messy.

To be honest Ferrero didn't give a stuff about what she was wearing, but he knew that she was upset and he made it his mission to stay as close to her as possible. He was currently achieving this by leaning against her leg and gazing up at her with his adoring amber eyes.

Cat grinned as she noticed a blog by Sam on the front page of Ecademy with the title 'New Mother's do it all night!' She was just about to read it when there was a knock at the door. She jumped so much that the laptop almost slid off her lap and on to the floor.

Ferrero hurtled towards the front door with a flurry of barking and Cat decided that she was not going to answer just it in case it was Tim. She had no desire to talk to him again – ever. Then she noticed that Ferrero's barking had turned into puppy-like whining frenzy, it must be someone he both knew and loved, and he never bonded with Tim.

Cat walked cautiously into the hall and smiled as she saw the big bushy outline of braided hair and the sun reflecting off Kelly's piercings. Kelly (182) took one look at her sister, handed her a bunch of flowers and gave her a big hug.

"Oh babe!" She said. "That bloke's such a loser, I'm sorry I ever introduced him to you."

Cat smiled. "It's not your fault, it was me who was naïve."

"If it helps there's been someone I keep trying to introduce to you, but you always seem to miss each other."

"No thanks, Kel," Cat managed a laugh. Much as she loved her sister, she knew from experience that she was very bad at listening, let alone giving helpful advice.

"But he is perfect for you and I can keep an eye on him 'cos he'll be living in the pub!"

"The chap who's renting your flat?" Cat laughed. "That sounds far too close to home to me. Anyway, how come you've been let out?"

"It's dead quiet," Kelly admitted. "And I'm never too busy to pop over and cheer my big sis up with a bunch of flowers." Kelly walked in to the living room to find the room just as cluttered and crowded as it was before Cat's big clean up. Every spare space had something with flowers sticking out of it. Vases, glasses, teapots and even saucepans were temporary homes to blooms in a rainbow of different colours.

"Well bugger me sideways!" Kelly exclaimed. "I should have brought choccies! Who's sent you all these flowers?"

"No-one." Cat laughed. "My friendly florist insisted on leaving all her surplus stock here to cheer me up."

"Bloody hell. It's a good job you don't have hay fever," Kelly remarked.

"No, but Tim does, so hopefully it will keep him far away," Cat sighed.

"He'll get a good slapping from me if he comes anywhere near you," Kelly declared. "Hey is that Sam?" She asked, spotting Sam's Ecademy profile on the screen. "She's put on weight!"

"Don't be so rude!" Cat exclaimed. "I expect you'll put on a few pounds yourself when you get to produce your little devil child."

"Devil child eh?" Kelly snorted. "I'll make sure it always plays up when you're around."

"That's what I mean," Cat laughed. "I remember what a monster you were when you were little."

Their playful bickering was interrupted by a loud electronic ring tone announcing that Cat had a Skype call.

"Who's that then?" Kelly asked.

"I'm not sure," Cat replied as she took a look at her laptop screen to see the photo displayed next to the Skype prompt. It showed a man with a carefully groomed moustache. "Oh yes, it's Dennis, we exchanged a few messages last week." She looked around for her headset and grabbed it, dodging Ferrero, who thought it was a great game.

"Oh yeah?" Kelly trilled. "Cat's got a secret lover! Cat's got a secret lover!"

"Shut up Kel," Cat said crossly as she fumbled at the back of her lap top to plug in her headphones. "Considering what has just happened that's hardly likely is it?"

Kelly slapped the side of her head to demonstrate that she had put her foot in it and watched with interest as Cat slipped the headphones on and accepted the call.

"Hello?" She said.

"Hi Cat!" A genial and relaxed male voice (18,517) replied. "Hope I haven't caught you at an inconvenient moment?"

"No, not at all," Cat reassured him hurriedly. "To tell you the truth I haven't used this Skype thing much. I was scrabbling around trying to plug the headphones in."

She was greeted with warm laughter at the other end. "I remember very well the first few times I used the system. I missed quite a few calls! I hope you don't mind me calling Cat, but you said earlier that you didn't really understand the givers gain principle and how it can benefit you. I thought it would be easier to have a quick chat rather than exchange a series of messages."

"You didn't need to go to all this trouble," Cat said. "I understand it. It's just that it doesn't sound like something that can thrive in a business environment. I mean we all get conned, or treated badly in business at some time," Cat exchanged a meaningful look with Kelly. "To be totally honest it sounds like something that is tripped out by organisations who want people to take out membership or something."

"That's a good point Cat. Very brave of you to put it so bluntly. If you don't mind I'll give you a run down of what got me interested in this subject. Have you got a few minutes?"

"Of course," Cat reassured him, making a yapping mouth movement with her hand towards Kelly, who rolled her eyes and returned her attention to Sam's profile on the screen.

"The problem with me is that I am a frustrated scientist," the man continued. "I did a brief stint in academia, but couldn't cope with the restricted world that they work in and jumped ship to business. I am now doing some research into networking on the side and it is bearing fruit."

Cat nodded her head in the way that we all do when listening to someone explain something on the phone, but her eyes widened as Kelly grew tired of trying to read around the Skype prompts on the screen and minimised them.

"The fun thing about networking is that it's the random contacts that really seem to work," the voice continued, unaffected by Kelly's antics. Kelly gave Cat a 'I knew it would be alright!' look and started to scroll through Sam's profile.

"For example, if you were looking for a job, your close friends and family may not be much help to you, but a cousin, or friend that moves in completely different circles may know of the perfect job that it is going begging. Have you heard of the book, the Celestine Prophecy?

"Oh don't!" Cat groaned. "If you're going to say that there is no such thing as coincidences then you can forget it."

Dennis laughed. "Aha, I can tell that you've been cornered by a Celestine Prophecy enthusiast! No, I think the coincidence part is irrelevant, but making the most of meetings with people is important. For example, our paths crossed online at Ecademy and we could have gone our separate ways, but I made the effort to call you as I'm sure I will be able to help you."

"But what are you selling?" Cat said suspiciously.

"Nothing," Dennis laughed. "All I am interested in is how I can help you."

"But why?"

"Why not? Because I can? And because I know that somewhere today someone will be doing something for me. Not because I asked them to, but because they will see something that will make them think of me and my services and will make a recommendation on my behalf. If not today, then tomorrow, or the next day."

"So if you do me a favour, then I owe you one?"

"You are very suspicious Cat! No-one owes me anything, but they know what I do and will be more likely to help me out when they can. As I said before in my email, I have a very large network and many of them will be both willing and able to help you."

"But how do remember all those people?"

"I have been gifted with a memory for people and I can also use the search tools in the networking platforms. For example, I may not remember your name the next time someone wants an event organiser, but a quick search will bring you up and I'll see your name and remember you, and can refer to the notes I will make. Also having a big network makes me attractive to other people. They are more likely to approach me than someone, say on Ecademy with twenty people in their network. The more people I can help the better my situation becomes."

Cat was just about to respond to this strange claim when she was nudged by Kelly who had pulled up the profile of the person who had called her.

"Have you heard of the six degrees of separation?" He enquired.

Kelly pulled a handful of her hair around to under her nose and held it between her nose and top lip while crossing her eyes.

"No," Cat managed before covering up her mouthpiece as she laughed.

"Well it has become very much oversimplified, but the gist of it is that you are only six people away from anyone in the world. I've been trying out lots of tests on this and we normally get there in three or four. An example, a woman makes designer lingerie and wanted to get her product in front of the lingerie buyer in Marks and Spencer. I sent off an email to some people I know that I thought might have the right contacts and one person knew someone whose son went to the same school as the buyer in question. The request came from trusted sources all along the line, in this case three degrees of separation. The woman was able to get a meeting with the buyer within a few weeks of her request coming to me."

Kelly started to jig her gurning face about in front of Cat who was still holding the mouthpiece to stop Dennis hearing her giggles. Ferrero also joined in the act by starting to bark excitedly at Kelly's antics.

"So you see how useful this giver's gain tool can be?" Dennis asked, a little bemused by the silence at the other end of the line.

"Yes, it sounds great," Cat replied waving at Kelly to stop it. "Sorry, I was just thinking about what you said. It's quite a lot to take in. A friend who is now living in Australia contacted me recently via Friends Re-United so I suppose it's all possible." Cat turned away from Kelly so she could continue her conversation. "But is it possible for me to get my business message in front of anyone. Anyone at all? Richard Branson? Bill Gates? Anita Roddick?"

Kelly was getting bored now she didn't have the attention of her sister so she started playing tug of war with Ferrero with one of his toys.

"In theory, yes," Dennis replied. "Of course the people you mention are going to have a lot of people trying the same tactics, so it might be more difficult, but there are plenty of other influential people. Perhaps more importantly, people can find you just as easily. There are theories going around that our current job market is going to change drastically over the next decades."

Kelly managed to grab the toy off Ferrero who responded to his loss with a loud bark.

"Go on," Cat said, wishing that her sister had decided to come around a bit later to cheer her up.

"With the advent of Internet technology we have the ability to work from where we like and many of us, you and me included, have taken advantage of this situation and are able to run a business from home. However, the technology is also available in developing countries like India and China and the hourly rates of pay are much, much lower, so they can easily undercut the developed countries. Some people are suggesting that instead of steadily increasing, our wages could soon be cut and our notion of having a steady job working for a large company could disappear."

Cat was just about to respond to this startling observation when there was a crash as Ferrero took a short cut over the sofa to beat Kelly to the toy, only to slip and bring Cat's trendy standard lamp crashing to the ground.

"Sorry for the noise in the background," Cat sighed. "My little sister has come round and my dog is going nuts."

"Aha, perhaps I will leave you to think about things a bit more then," Dennis laughed. "It certainly sounds interesting there."

"Oh it is, I assure you," Cat replied, now shooting daggers at both Kelly and Ferrero to behave themselves, but the ferocious look only caused Kelly to curl up on the floor laughing at Ferrero's mortified expression.

"Why don't you think about the most useful person that I can introduce you to? It helps to make it as specific as possible and we will see what we can get going for you. Also, are you going to the Beermat event on Monday? That's a great place to make random connections."

"Thanks, I've heard about that. I'll take a look at it," Cat assured him. "And thank you for taking the time to call me, it is most appreciated. Sorry if I sound a little distant."

"My pleasure," Dennis replied warmly and ended the call.

"Will you behave!" Cat exclaimed at Kelly who was rolling around on the floor laughing and trying to pull Ferrero's tail.

"Oh cool it Cat," Kelly giggled. "Don't be so bloody serious, he was only trying to sell you something."

"That's just it, he wasn't. He was trying to help me. I think it's about time you got back to your boozer before you cause me any more trouble."

"No way! I've come to cheer you up."

"I'm happy, alright?" Cat said with more than a touch of exasperation. "In fact I was probably happier before you arrived."

"Don't take this all out on me," Kelly said indignantly. "I've gone to a lot of trouble to come round and cheer you up. Even if you do have a house full of flowers and strange men with porno film moustaches who phone you up 'just to help you'. Anyway," Kelly said, as she got up off the floor and brushed dog hairs off herself. "I've had a bit of a 'eureka' while I was playing about on your PC. Why don't we hold a networking do in the pub? Get some people outside of the area in to drink some of my beer."

"The thought had crossed my mind," Cat admitted. "If you promise to go now and leave me in peace I'll have a think about it."

"You, Top Cat," Kelly said as she kissed her sister loudly on the cheek, "are a star!"

Suddenly there was an ear-splitting scream. Cat jumped and Ferrero ran round the house barking. Kelly just laughed and dug out her mobile phone from her pocket.

"Relax," she grinned. "It's just my phone. Cool ring tone eh? I've got a text message."

"Why on earth do you want that noise on your phone?"

"Cos it's funny," Kelly grinned. "It has to be loud so I can hear it in the pub." She looked at the message. "Yay! It's from Malc. She started to read it out. "Hey Babes. Sorry but got a few more days work here. It's mad! You would love it."

Kelly snapped the phone shut. "Oh great! So I'm left stuck at the pub while he parties hard in Scotland." She turned on her heel and stomped out the front door closing it loudly behind her.

Cat sighed with relief and checked her email. She saw a cluster of email responses from the invites she had sent to her old friends on the networking site LinkedIn. She smiled as she flicked through the replies that varied from reams of ecstatic text to the standard invitation acceptance text. She had a look at the stats on the site and saw that her 107 LinkedIn connections gives her access to a possible 32,100 connections. If she looked at the third degree connections, or as Cat preferred to think of it friends of friends of friends, she had a potential of 1,203,800 connections.

"Surely there's got to be some business amongst them for me," she said to herself. "If my ex boyfriend is out there, why shouldn't there be a few wealthy clients too? Not to mention a half-decent bloke who can keep his willy to himself."

Her email pinged and she gasped when she saw the email title from the LinkedIn site.

Luke Uppingham would like to connect

"Can he hear me or something!" she exclaimed. "Networking is not supposed to be about your ex being able to get back in contact with you." She cautiously opened the email wary of any reply receipt function.

Hi Cat,

I've missed you! I mean REALLY missed you! But I don't

expect you to come running back to me. How about starting the process by you joining my LinkedIn network?

Love, as always

Luke

"You can go and chop chips!" Cat exclaimed but she continued to look at the message for a surprisingly long time.

The House of Fun Blog

Diary of a mad house
Date Mon 4th July 2006

Two houses of fun?

VIKING - The boxes are nearly all packed and my room is looking bare and empty. Soon there will be no sign that I was ever here, except maybe the tooth marks on the toilet roll holder from when I was suffering the painful after effects of the Spaniard's so-called 'curry cure.'

This blog will now be split across two houses. Please keep your comments coming in you strange people who tune in every now and then. Without being melodramatic, it's nice to feel that I am not alone.

SPANIARD - I wondered what those marks were! We'll be round for beers as soon as you move in hombre.

CELT - Our Viking god alone? Not for long my wee pal. We've met your blonde bit of stuff and while she may be elusive, she still seems very keen to become an interesting part of your life!

GUEST - Ute: I'm still here Viking. ;)

GUEST - CapnJack: Less of this sad stuff, let's hear more about the blonde!

GUEST - HornyBoy: Don't bother asking you

```
wont get photos.
```

VIKING - I thought you weren't reading this anymore HornyBoy?

Chapter 19

Jonny (195) felt his heart rate steadily increase as he watched the scenery through the train window become steadily less green and more overcrowded. He had inflated the upcoming networking event into a do or die situation. He felt he had to make a good showing tonight; he had to drum up some business, not to mention grab a firm hold on the ever-elusive Sarah.

His mind switched from imaginary scenarios where he charmed a crowd of networkers with his wit and business knowledge and ended up licking Champagne off Sarah's naked body, to seeing himself outcast at the edge of a group of people who were exchanging banter and business contacts with aplomb.

His heart rate continued to rise as the speed of the train gradually decreased on its approach to central London. He decided to go and freshen up in the toilet so he would look his best when he arrived in London. As he walked unsteadily down the jolting corridor he overheard people introducing themselves.

"So you're off to the Beermat as well? What a coincidence!" A round faced, jovial man (523) laughed to a super fashionable Jamaican woman (712) who was sitting opposite him.

It was obvious that a small group of travellers had discovered that they were all going to the same networking event. He was worried about making a first impression at the meeting and there were people starting the meeting early on the train!

Jonny carried on walking past them, cursing himself for not stopping to join them. He opened the door of the toilet and promptly realised that this was not a place to freshen up in, so much as a place that makes you crave fresh air. Being careful not to touch anything he stared at himself in the mirror, willing himself to go out and include himself in their conversation.

He took a deep breath and strode out of the foul smelling toilet and sauntered down the corridor with fake bravado. However, the group were engrossed in conversation and he felt his borrowed confidence scurry away. He slowed down, hoping for a useful break where he could say something along the lines of 'Wow! Are you going to the Beermat do as well?' but it didn't materialise and he found himself walking past them again.

He tried to catch up with the group when the train stopped but he lost them in the busy underground system and he spent the rest of his journey fuming at himself and resolving to be a social whirlwind at the meeting.

However, his heart sank when he walked into the trendy pub to find it was practically empty apart from a few bored-looking drinkers who looked like they had popped in for a swift half after work. Then he saw the sign to the Beermat meeting upstairs and he was reminded of how he felt when he walked into the Overchurch local business meeting. Lost amongst a crowd of people. Walking up the stairs he resolved to try and think of it as the best sort of singles night. One where there was no pressure to pull, but with the opportunity to talk to as many people as possible.

He took a deep breath before entering the room and tried to swagger in with all the confidence he could muster. The room was already well populated with people talking animatedly in small groups. There were a few suits about, but mainly the occupants were casually, but smartly dressed and there was an edge of anticipation in the air. Some people were obviously meeting old friends and were enjoying a hearty chat and a laugh while others looked slightly overawed by the occasion.

He walked up to the bar to get himself a pint to lubricate his vocal chords and yanked his eyes back from the direction they were pulled by the sight of a tall, glamorous woman (497) with long dark hair, spliced with artful blonde streaks. She just happened to be wearing a knee length skirt with Jonny's favourite type of boots. He recognised her from his travels around Ecademy but there was no way he was going to repeat his mistakes at the Overchurch meeting by flirting rather than networking. Jonny and Cat were no longer separated by any degrees of separation, just by a few metres and Jonny's reluctance to approach her. He caught the barman's (167) eye, ordered his beer and turned to the person next to him.

"Hi, my name's Jonny," he said extending his hand towards the man (121) next to him at the bar. "Have you been to one of these type of events before?"

That was it, as easy as you like. He had a quick chat with the man who was starting up a mobile car washing business and had barely looked around before a cheerful looking woman with a mass of curls (835) stepped into his eye line.

"Hello, I'm Fiona," she smiled. "I haven't seen you here before, is this your first time?"

Jonny found himself alternatively in the company of experienced networkers who approached with ease and moved on with grace and with over eager amateurs who either blathered on about their products, or were reluctant to move on to the next person after they had found somewhere they felt safe. After about an hour of exchanging business cards, banter and pleasantries Jonny was starting to feel tired. The novel experience of meeting and getting to know so many people in such a short space of time made him crave a conversation with someone that lasted longer than ten minutes.

He scanned the room after swapping business cards with his latest contact and noticed that the room had filled up considerably since he had arrived. He made another Herculean effort not to let his gaze linger on Cat and looked around for Julius or Sarah. If there was one thing he had learned it was that people's photos on networking sites were often a lot more flattering than the people looked in real life, but he couldn't see anyone that resembled Julius with his long, thick, black hair. He was just about to move around the room when a tall, thin man (651) with artfully spiky, black short hair and very neat teeth that were a couple of sizes too large for his mouth, popped up in front of him.

"Hey! Jonny! Wow man! You look just like your photo!"

Jonny looked carefully at the man and suddenly realised who it was. "Julius! You look *nothing* like your photo!"

"Felt like a change, what can I say?" Julius smirked as they shook hands. "Nice to meet you at last mate. I was trying to grab you before, but you know what it's like? Always people popping up to say hi."

"Tell me about it. I'm knackered, all this meeting new people can't be good for your health."

"Hope you're not just collecting business cards matey. The aim of the game is to find a few people that you make a real connection with and then follow it up afterwards."

"Don't you go giving me new rules to follow, everyone keeps changing them as they go along! You can't sell, you can't harvest business cards, you can't make a beeline for attractive women."

"Don't take it all so personally mate," Julius smiled. "This is a cool way of developing people skills. When you get bored you can just pretend to be someone else."

"What?"

Julius laughed, flashing his impressive teeth. "It helps me develop characters for my scripts."

"But what happens when people realise you're faking it?"

"Relax man! It's just an extension of what we already do. Imagine you were waiting for a train or something and this place is a crowded waiting room. How many people would you like to strike up a conversation with?"

"Oh don't!" Jonny sighed. "I bottled out of talking to people on the train on the way here."

Julius laughed. "Don't be so hard on yourself matey. It's so much easier to read a book or stare into space. Maybe even eye up a foxy chick if there happened to be one in eyeshot?"

"Who wouldn't?" Jonny smirked.

"Exactly! But here it's totally different. People come here with the precise aim of talking to people. A lot of them will try to talk to as many people as possible. The aim is to be everyone's friend, but let's be real about it. You're not going to get on with everyone here. If someone looks as if they could be useful to you, you ignore their irritating aspects. You don't have to like someone to network or do business with them."

"The more advice you give me the less I understand," Jonny complained.

Julius laughed. "You've seen the film Fight Club yeah?" Well, like the main character, sometimes you can be Edward Norton, a bit shy and insecure, and other times you're Brad Pitt – confident and charming. Just think about how you talk to a woman and a man. Women like to find out about a person whereas men tend to prefer exchanging information. If you use a gentler approach with women you are more likely to build up a rapport, to gain mutual trust."

"You want me to be Brad Pitt?"

"No! You can be either Brad or Ed. You just display a different persona."

"Even though you're not being your true self?"

"Exactly!" Julius followed Jonny's line of sight back towards Cat. "Toot toot eh? Why not try a bit of random networking and see how Brad Pitt fares?"

"No way! I screwed up my first networking experience by flirting with a married woman."

Julius laughed. "What are you like? You're supposed to be bonding with them, not flirting."

"Yeah, but I noticed the babe in boots on the list of attendees and I fancied her. Her name's Cat, she's an events manager and she hasn't got a web site yet, but I don't feel comfortable approaching her because I'm not allowed to sell, not to mention flirt."

"Did someone mention flirting?"

Jonny turned round to receive a big kiss on the cheek from Sarah (897) who had appeared at his shoulder.

"Long time no see Blondie," she beamed. "Good to see you without your crutches. Are you going to introduce me?"

"Certainly," Jonny replied, desperately hoping that they wouldn't notice his blushes. "In my best Bridget Jones style; Sarah, this is Julius, the perfect man if you want a corporate video or even to hear random film quotes. Julius, this is Sarah, a business consultant whirlwind who never seems to stay in one place for more than five minutes."

"Corporate video!" Sarah exclaimed. "You could be just the person. Can I have your business card?"

"Certainly," Julius smiled as he passed her his card. "Anything in particular I can help you with?"

"I need to finalise the details, but one of my clients is interested in running a promotion via video email and needs someone to film it. Can you send me a quote if I email you the brief?"

"Certainly. I can also introduce you to some of my colleagues who can give you advice about free add-ons for your video email," Julius said, flashing his smile in a nonchalant Brad Pitt sort of way.

"Great!" Sarah smiled before turning to Jonny. "Right I'll catch up with you later. Don't leave without me! I need to go and see a man about hiring a limousine." She kissed Jonny on the cheek and disappeared off into the crowd.

"You're in there matey," Julius observed with a wink.

"Apparently so," Jonny sighed. "But it's not something that I have any control over. She turns up and then disappears just as quickly. Anyway, what's all this getting gigs right in front of my nose?"

Julius laughed. "You know what they say? Some people have it and others, well…"

"I certainly don't have it," Jonny moaned. "My housemate got me three bits of work on Saturday just by picking up the phone."

"Bit of cold calling eh? It's a good skill to have, and at least you've got some gigs now."

"Yes, thank God, I followed them up today and got most of the work in the bag, but I need to be able to get those leads myself."

"I can introduce you to someone who does cold calling training."

"But that costs money!" Jonny exclaimed crossly. "Why does everything I do have to cost so much money?"

Julius smiled sympathetically. "Your services cost money too matey. If everyone was scared of investment they would all use those crappy web site templates."

"Ah, bog off," Jonny said good naturedly. "I'm off to mingle and blag some more work."

"Go and introduce yourself to the babe in the boots mate," Julius grinned. "You've got nothing to lose, it's not as if you're trying to chat her up. That femme fatale Sarah will start boiling bunnies if you look as if you're getting anywhere."

"You need to watch less films!" Jonny sighed as he returned to his mingling.

You have a video email from Cat Forsythe

Cat is sitting on a chair and grinning at the camera. Her make up is immaculate and her hair is freshly straightened and glowing with health. She looks elegant and gorgeous.

"Well g'day there Sheila," she crows in a cheesy Australian accent. "It was just ripper to see you and little Brucie on video email the other day. As you can see I have joined the video email revolution and signed up to your package. Maybe I'm your first customer, but I bet I'm not going to be your last!

"I'm much better thanks. I think it was the shock at first. I knew there was something odd about him but then he was quite eccentric anyway and he spun a very good line about feeling alone in the world. You know that I'm a sucker for a sad story!

"Anyway I've sorted my head out now and done some retail therapy. Everything you see here is new today, right down to the boots!" Cat stands up and in one easy movement puts her foot on the arm of her chair. She is wearing a smart, black skirt and black knee high boots with a vertigo inducing high heel. "So you see, I still haven't grown out of wearing my kinky boots!

Cat settles back down in her chair. "I'm just about off to a big networking do in London and to be honest I don't care if Mr Ugly and not Funny is there. I'm making lots of new friends and I now feel great about myself and where I'm going with my life. It's good to see you trying out new things too. I've been telling people about the video email and directing them to your link so maybe you'll be able to buy yourself some of that Aussie Chardonnay that's saturating the market over here!

"Oh yes, remember that Jonny guy that you accused me of

checking out? Well I can check him out in the flesh tonight as he's on the list of attendees." Cat laughed at the camera. "I know! What am I like? But Sam, I've come to realise that life is so short and so what if I meet a bloke with half an eye on him as boyfriend material? From now on I'm going to be more impulsive and have some fun. Sounds like you're doing the same!"

"Right time to go. Say hi to your old man from me and give Brucie a big kiss!"

Cat blows a kiss at the camera and clicks the mouse to close down the recording.

Chapter 20

Cat was feeling as good as she looked. Gladys had very kindly spread the news far and wide about the success of the Bridal Fair and she had received a number of messages from people who wanted to meet her at this event. There is nothing better when you have to walk into a room full of strangers than to have someone walk over and introduce themselves, the moment you enter the room, to say how much they were looking forward to meeting you.

She had already collected a fair number of business cards in her Italian leather handbag and she had the feeling several of these would turn into useful leads. Now she was intent on enjoying herself and trying out the tips she had received from Dennis, her moustachioed networking guru. In short she was in full-on 'what can I do to help you?' mode. She finished one conversation and turned away to spot a shy woman (101) who was awkwardly standing on the outside of the throng, swirling the ice in her glass. She was in her forties and well dressed in a sharp trouser suit with a bright scarlet scarf draped across her shoulders. Cat walked over to her.

"Hi there," she said kindly. "You seem a little lost over here."

The woman laughed nervously. "Yes. Thank you. I've never really been good at this sort of thing. I think it's probably best if I leave, really."

"Oh no! Don't do that," Cat exclaimed. "There are some lovely people here and they're very easy to talk to. I'm Cat, what's your name."

The woman took another big gulp of her drink. "Sorry, I'm Mary – I told you I wasn't good at this. People may be nice, but the idea is to sell yourself, isn't it? And I can't even walk up to people and talk to them, which was exactly why I started the company in the first place." She stopped and took a deep breath. "Oh, I'm sorry, there I go wittering away like a nervous old bag."

"No you're not," Cat assured her. "So what is it you do?"

"That's the big joke! I help people meet people. I run a dating agency." Mary stopped and looked around the room as if she wanted nothing more than to run away.

"Go on," Cat encouraged.

"It's a dating agency for shy people. People like me. People who don't seem to be able to walk across a room and talk to the person they fancy. People who find themselves standing at the edges of groups reading the safety notices, or other people's staff rotas on the wall. Anything to avoid having to endlessly switch eye contact around the room."

Cat laughed. "That sounds brilliant! Let me guess, it's the sort of place where you know that everyone has been fretting about the event *all* day and who would actually much rather be sitting at home in front of the telly, except they really want to meet someone."

"That's exactly it!" Mary exclaimed in surprise. "You don't think it's silly?"

"Silly! It's inspired, even more so when people find out that it is run by someone just like them. That's a fab incentive for them to join."

"That's sort of what I thought. It's just that I don't know how to get the message across. I need a web site with some clever word play on it. That's sort of why I came here in the first place."

"I can't think of anyone offhand," Cat said thoughtfully, "but lets swap business cards and I'll let you know if I meet anyone that is suitable. I should also be able to give you some advice as I'm in event management so I might be able to help with venues and stuff like that."

"You'd do that for me?" Mary asked in surprise.

"Of course I will," Cat smiled. "And now let's introduce you to some people, and lets start with some of the shy ones around the edges. That could be the ideal hunting ground for potential customers!"

Twenty minutes later and Cat was feeling on top of the world and was seriously considering taking the Carrot Woman and Kelly up on their suggestions of starting a local networking group. Mary had discovered that socialising is not so difficult when everyone has gathered in one place with the sole reason of talking to each other.

Cat had also caught up with Gladys who assured her that there was, as yet, no sign of Tim attending the event. Of course, when anyone's positive feelings are running so high, it also means that they also have a long way to fall and Cat couldn't believe it when someone else edged their way into the group. It was the creep (107) from the London venue who had tried to blackmail her into having sex with him.

"Hello Cat," he said with false bonhomie. "Long time no see, eh?"

"What are you doing here?" Cat said through clenched teeth.

"There's the rub," he replied over cheerfully. "Sunshine was not the only company to get taken over this summer. We got gobbled up too and the bastards booted me out, so I'm in the market for a new job. Thought I'd check out the buzz here, see what was going down. Don't suppose you've got anything for me have you?"

Cat stared at him in disbelief. "So what happened to the contacts you had with all the 'major players'?"

"Oh come, come Cat," he laughed too enthusiastically. "We had a laugh didn't we? You didn't take my banter too seriously did you? You're an attractive woman, you can't blame a guy for trying."

Cat just stared at him. The other people in the group started to sense a vibe between them and fell silent.

"So!" The creep said, clapping his hands together. "Are you going to introduce me to everyone Cat?"

Cat paused before she responded as she weighed up her options. "No, I am not," she said firmly. "These people are my friends even though I have only known some of them for a short time and I hope they trust me to look out for them. With that in mind I do not want to introduce them to someone who habitually cheats on their wife and who is not beyond using blackmail to *try* to get what they want."

There was a sharp intake of breath as the rest of the group took in this information and the creep was met with a wall of stares. He laughed and tried to shake off his feelings of discomfort, but there was no avoiding the scornful gazes and he quickly turned and walked away. Cat felt the gazes turn towards her with an inquiring edge to them so she drained the last of her drink, made her excuses and quickly walked towards the bar. She felt a tap on her shoulder as she reached the counter and turned to see Mary.

"This drink is on me, Cat," she said forcefully. "And after that brave display, of course I trust you." As she busied about buying Cat's gin and tonic, unfortunately without the lime, Cat looked around the bar and noticed a man with long, white-blond hair and blue eyes who was sharing a joke with someone he was exchanging business cards with. She recognised him immediately as Jonny and she had to admit to herself that she liked the look of him. He looked across and their eyes met briefly. At last they had made a connection.

"He fancies you," Mary stated.

"Don't be silly," Cat scoffed as she stole another look towards him and met his eyes again.

"He so does! I may not be good at making conversation, but I am an expert at reading body language and he definitely has the hots for you." Mary turned to look at Cat as she passed her drink to her. "And if I'm not mistaken, I think you fancy him too."

"Oh behave yourself!" Cat laughed. "I can assure you that I am not in the mood for a man in my life at the moment, thanks very much. However, I have a sneaky suspicion that he may be in the web design business so I'll go and introduce you."

"Oh, I'm not sure about that!" Mary exclaimed and picked up her drink and went to return to the group of people she had just met.

Cat laughed and caught her by the arm. "Come on you, this will be painless." And they walked towards the blond web designer who was just finishing his business card transaction.

"Hi!" Cat said brightly. "I'm afraid I can't remember your name," she lied shamelessly, "but we've been looking at each other's profiles on Ecademy recently and I seem to remember that you're a web designer or something?" "Yes, hello Cat. I'm Jonny and yes, web design and copywriting is my game."

"I told you," Mary whispered to Cat. "He knows your name."

"I'm sorry?" Jonny asked, thinking he had missed something.

"This is someone I would like you to meet," Cat said swiftly, bringing Mary forward before she could put her foot in it. This is someone with a brilliant business idea, a dating agency for shy people, run by none other than a very shy person!"

Jonny laughed, thinking that it was a joke, but then saw Mary's mortified expression. "Hang on," he said with a puzzled expression. "That has a definite ring to it. After all, who else would be able to persuade shy people to come out of the closet as it were, than a shy person who has been brave enough to set up the business in the first place?"

Cat flashed him her best 'thank you!' smile. "That's just what I thought," she said, very much relieved that Mary had recovered her composure.

"So do you think you'll be able to help me?" Mary asked Jonny.

"Absolutely," Jonny agreed. "And although you'll expect me to say this, I could be the perfect choice for you as I'm a copywriter as well so we can work out an eye-catching, user-friendly site and the perfect words to intrigue your target audience."

"But will I be able to afford it," Mary asked solemnly.

Jonny laughed. "My rates are very reasonable and to be honest

I have only recently set up my own business, so if you agree to write some testimonials for me, then I'm sure we can come to a deal that suits both parties." He held out his card to Mary, but had to wait for her to fish her business card out of her handbag. He and Cat exchanged slightly awkward glances before Jonny offered Cat one of his cards and she returned the favour.

"It's good to finally meet you, Cat," he said keeping eye contact with her. "I've noticed you around on Ecademy and we seem to live in the same area."

"I'm sorry if I'm being daft here," Mary said, "but if you live close to each other and keep looking at each other's profiles, why haven't you contacted each other before? You both seem such nice people, you should do business together."

Jonny and Cat both laughed awkwardly.

"Well, I would have done," Jonny started and paused.

"But?" Mary prompted.

"I did think that, as Cat hasn't got a web site yet, she might be a potential customer. But I was wary of approaching her with a sales pitch, because I know it's not done to do that in networking circles and, to be honest, I keep doing the wrong thing; selling when I should be listening and listening when I should be selling and..." Jonny paused, obviously looking for a way to end his ramble before it reached epic proportions. His eyes lit up as he spotted Julius walking towards them. "Aha! Here's someone you both should meet! This is Julius, corporate film maker extraordinaire and my networking mentor."

"Wow, what an introduction!" Julius smirked. "Nice to meet you both. I see he's finally broken the ice then?" he asked Cat.

"Well, I..." Cat muttered, looking a bit bemused.

"I was just asking Jonny why he hasn't contacted Cat before, what with them both living so close to each other." Mary said with just a hint of fake innocence.

"It's no big deal," Julius assured them, earning a grateful glance from Jonny. "He fancies you," he said to Cat causing Mary to almost spit her mouthful of drink across the room. Jonny's face burned bright scarlet, clashing vividly with his hair while Cat flushed more subtly and failed to stop a little giggle as she looked at the floor.

"It's not like that," Jonny blurted out. "It's just that I didn't want to approach you and have you thinking that I just want to sell to you or come onto you. Especially as you live so close."

Mary looked at Cat. "I think I've found a new customer," she said, prompting another burst of giggles from Cat. "Would you be interested in joining *Shy to Shy*?" She asked Jonny.

Jonny opened his mouth like a constipated goldfish as Julius chortled beside him. Cat felt sorry for him and let him off the hook.

"So whereabouts do you live Jonny?" She asked, managing to keep a straight face.

"Well, that is just about to change as I'm moving into a new flat," Jonny explained, grateful for the change in subject. "It's above the Dog and Bacon in Overchurch. Do you know it?"

It was Cat's turn to try not to spray her mouthful of drink across the room. "Know it! My little sister runs it!"

"Who? Kelly?"

"Yes!"

"Oh, that's just too weird," Jonny said in shock. "She keeps saying to me that I should meet you."

Cat laughed. "And she says the same about you to me!"

Julius rolled his eyes and caught Mary's eye. "Something tells me that we're not needed here," he said as he guided her a short distance away and started asking her about her business venture.

Cat and Jonny looked at each other warily for a short time. They had made the connection at last, they had a combined network of over 750 and they had over 200 people in common. However, from now on the two of them getting together was not about what other people do, it would just be down to the two of them. Or would it?

It was some time before Cat broke the silence.

"This is very strange," she said.

"It's one hell of a coincidence," Jonny agreed, causing Cat to laugh heartily.

"What?" He asked.

"Have you read book *The Celestine Prophecy*?" She asked.

"No."

"Good." She laughed. "Neither have I." She thought for a second about coincidences and random connections before asking, "What can I do for you?"

"Excuse me?" Jonny replied, somewhat startled by the question.

"It's what we're supposed to ask each other as networkers."

"Oh right. Well, I would have said that I needed businesses who want both their web sites designed and their advertising copy spruced up, but you seem to have brought that straight into my lap. Was she for real about this shy dating thing?"

"Of course she is!" Cat said defensively.

"It's just that she doesn't seem that shy to me," Jonny observed.

"Ah, I think that might be due to the effect of vodka and diet coke. She's been sipping quite frequently."

"Fair enough," Jonny laughed and then brightened. "I know what you can do for me. I, or rather, my friend Julius, needs to be able to talk to a farmer in Ohio."

"Why on earth would he want to do that?"

"It's a long story," Jonny grinned, "but that's my answer to your question."

"You don't want something for yourself?"

"As I said, you've already come up trumps there and Julius has helped me out a lot. It would be good to return the favour."

Cat was pleased with the answer, but had no idea where she was going to be able to contact an American farmer let alone one specifically in Ohio. "You don't ask for easy favours do you?" she said. From the corner of her eye she saw an impressive moustache come into view. It was Dennis, (18,535) the networking guru who she had the Skype call with on the weekend. "I'll see what I can do," she said before making her way towards Dennis.

Thirty minutes later she found Jonny who had caught up with Julius and was taking him to task over landing him in it with Cat. She had a very slim lady (241) by her side with barely visible curves who seemed to glide along the floor in her flat shoes, her auburn hair gathered carelessly, yet elegantly at the back of her head with an oversized clasp. Her cheeks bore two small parallel lines around the edge of her mouth that suggested she was not averse to smiling.

"Jonny and Julius, meet Melissa," Cat crowed looking very smug.

"Nice to meet you Melissa," Jonny said in a puzzled tone, reaching forward to shake her hand.

"And you Jonny," Melissa drawled with a thick American accent.

"No!" Jonny exclaimed with a laugh that Cat instantly joined in with.

"Julius," she beamed. "Melissa here is a very talented dance teacher who can hold dance lessons of many different styles as well as corporate team bonding events that encourage people to explore their creative side through teamwork. She also happens to have recently moved to the UK from America where her parents have a farm in Ohio!"

"So what d'ya wanna know about farmin' in Ohio?" Melissa asked with a big grin on her face.

It was Julius' turn for his chin to hit the floor.

As the evening drew to a close and the numbers had fallen to a selection of people who had stopped flitting from one person to the next and were either building new friendships, or cementing existing ones, Jonny and Cat found themselves isolated in a corner of the room.

"That was some stunt you pulled earlier," Jonny laughed. "The look on Julius' face was priceless. I get the impression that he's not used to people getting one up on him."

"Ah well," Cat said with a knowing smile. "If I hadn't had a chat with someone on the weekend I wouldn't have thought of giving it a go. It was very jammy, but you know what they say? If you don't ask, you don't get."

"Very true," Jonny agreed and then paused. "I don't suppose I can be cheeky and ask you for a favour, can I?"

"Now that Jonny, entirely depends on what you ask."

"A very reasonable answer," Jonny replied with a grin. "It's just that I was supposed to be getting a lift back with someone here, but they seem to have disappeared, and you said that you had driven up with a local florist?"

Cat laughed. "Now that is cheeky! But I can't see a problem although it may be a bit of a squeeze. We came up in her van."

Jonny did make an effort to try and disguise the instant smile on his face when he had the mental image of being squeezed up next to Cat for an hour and a half. However, it was too little, too late and Cat picked up on it instantly and she couldn't help releasing a little smirk herself. She was starting to take a shine to Jonny.

The moment was broken by the appearance of an attractive woman with wavy blonde hair who rushed in without acknowledging Cat and kissed Jonny on the cheek.

"Hey Blondie!" She said laying a possessive hand on his arm. "It's been manic here. Just been talking to someone who knows a big, big, big, BIG! Company who are putting out a tender for a big fat contract. Only problem is that I need to get the proposal in tomorrow so I'll be up all night. And not in the right way if you know what I mean. So, I'm sorry babe but I'm going to have to take a rain check, again!" She kissed him on the cheek again. "I'll call you!" She said before smiling a thinly disguised evil 'hello' at Cat and walking quickly out of the venue.

"So," Cat said after a pause that was so long it had gone past the pregnant stage and had moved on to adolescence. "That was your girlfriend?"

"Not exactly." Jonny said slowly, wondering why all good things have to come to an end so quickly when he was involved. "That is someone who I have been networking with and keeps threatening to go on a date with me, but never actually goes through with it."

"Oh." Cat said which was followed by a silence and a pause that had nothing to do with pregnancy and a lot to do with abstinence. It lasted most of the way home.

The House of Fun Blog

Diary of a mad house
Date Tues 5th July 2006

The sound of silence

VIKING – It's quiet in here. Too quiet.
I'm sitting here surrounded by silence and
thinking about a silence that got in the way
between me and a certain foxy lady that I'd
like to get to know a lot better.

However, the good news is that I can now
watch what I want on my crap telly, I can
even pop downstairs to catch the sport on
the big screen. Perhaps best of all, my
kindly (and admittedly very foxy) landlady
often feeds me with the leftovers from the
pub kitchen so I'm cooking less and eating
more.

I may soon put on so much weight that I will
be unable to persuade a woman to share my
bijou flat with me!

CELT – Oh stop it Viking! We miss your
cooking! Can you come round for dinner?

SPANIARD – Don't come back hombre, the
place has been turned into a girl's place –
there's cushions and flowers and everything!

And remember, silences are golden in the
world of selling. Don't be the first to
speak – if she breaks the silence she's
interested.

GUEST – Ute: You're talking rubbish
Spaniard. Women like to be talked to.

SPANIARD – So do plants apparently.

GUEST – Ute: Be careful Don Juan or you
might find that the Celt's not talking to
you! ;)

Chapter 21

Jonny (230) was in the middle of a working lunch although it wasn't really him who was doing any grafting. He was tucking into a big plate of leftovers in the pub while Kelly (182) sat beside him clicking her tongue stud against her front teeth as she flicked through the *Shy to Shy* web site he was developing. The theme centred on a clickable Cupid that did all the work for the members by launching virtual arrows at them and pointing out anything they had in common.

"This is really wicked," Kelly laughed. "I did have an image of a group of wallflowers all smiling shyly to each other across the room, but this looks cool."

"Thank God for that," Jonny sighed. "She may be a shy person, but she certainly knows what she wants and is certainly not going to settle for anything less than the best."

"I should think not," Cat (513) said as she appeared round the side of the bar. "And I would hardly call my little sister an ideal guinea pig for road testing the site. She wouldn't know what shy was if it tweaked one of her piercings."

"Hey Top Cat!" Kelly grinned. "So do you know what this secret meeting with the boys is all about?"

"I haven't got a clue, but Julius has just driven into the car park so I expect…"

"Afternoon all!" Julius (671) chirped as he hurried in. "And you must be Kelly." He said extending his hands towards Kelly. "I love the look. Really suits you darling. Just that bit scary, but with a soupcon of femininity to keep it sexy."

"Oh," Kelly blushed.

"Wow Julius," Cat smiled. "I think that I am going to like doing business with you. There's not many people in the world who can effortlessly leave my sister lost for words."

"I just say what I see," Julius smirked. "And I would compliment you, but I bet you look as good as that every day, don't you?"

"Sit down for Christ sake," Jonny groaned. "Let me guess. You're in character?"

"Oh Jonny! You noticed!" Julius squealed. "For your information, today I am Rupert, a slightly camp, womaniser who thinks he has a way with women and the gift of the gab."

"What on earth?" Cat exclaimed.

"I'm researching a character. I find it helps if I try to be them for a day to work out what they're really like."

"You're mad!" Kelly laughed.

"And you, my dear are interesting on the eye, now should we get things started?"

"Is your girlfriend coming?" Cat asked Jonny innocently with more intensity than she planned.

"A girlfriend!" Julius spouted in shock accompanied by stereotypical camp movements of his arms. "I'm not sure we have heard about our dear friend Jonny here sharing his tender heart with a *lady*. This is certainly something we should examine in great detail."

"Oh please," Jonny moaned as the girls exchanged amused glances.

Julius sprung to his feet and paced around the floor. "Members of the jury," he motioned grandly towards Cat and Kelly, we are gathered here today to establish whether the suspect here, one Jonny Philips, is currently involved in a romantic liaison with someone of the female persuasion."

"Shut up Julius," Jonny said curtly.

"Silence in court!" Julius screeched. "And when I do allow you to speak you will kindly refer to me as Rupert, as this is my name. Now, let us consider the evidence. Cat, please can we have the name of the accused's accused girlfriend?"

"I'm sorry Jonny," Cat giggled. "It's just that at the end of the meeting the other day that woman kissed you and..."

"A kiss!" Julius squealed. "A kiss in public! Well Jonny, we do seem to be skating on somewhat precarious ice my dear, don't we? Please continue Cat."

Cat gasped for air in between her laughs. "She just mentioned something about a date."

"Ah, a date! This truly is deep trouble indeed. So tell me Jonny, in your own words. Were tongues involved in the kiss?"

"No!" Jonny cried, joining in the mirth despite his embarrassment.

"And have there been tongues in the past?"

Jonny hesitated.

"Remember that you are under oath old sport, and that perjury was important enough to send Lord Archer to jail, for which we should be forever grateful. Amen."

"Old sport?" Kelly queried.

"Don't interrupt! Answer the question defendant, old sport."

"Yes, on one occasion. Some time ago."

"And has there been a romantic liaison? A date?"

"No."

"Has there been a date arranged?"

"No."

"And has there been any phone sex?"

"No!"

"Please remember your oath, old sport."

"No. And 'old sport' really doesn't fit your character."

"I'll ignore that. So you have both been fully clothed at all times when conversing on the telephone?"

"Ah, no."

"What!" Kelly exclaimed.

Tears started to trickle down Cat's face as she tried to stop herself from laughing.

"Please elucidate, Mr Accused."

"She phoned me once when she had just stepped out of the shower."

"So she was naked?"

"For some of the call."

"Why some of the call."

"She was getting dressed."

"And were video phones involved at all?"

"No!"

"So there was no hanky-panky?"

"None at all your honour."

"Right!" Julius exclaimed grandly and banged a salt shaker loudly on a table next to him. "This court concludes that the defendant is not guilty of having a girlfriend and is thereby sentenced to being single until such time as he does find someone of a female persuasion who will perform a full range of girlfriendly duties not just cheek kissing, one snog and conversing via the telephone whilst being bereft of clothing. These will include..."

"I think we should stop there shouldn't we," Cat said wiping a tear from her eye. "I hate to ask again, but is this cheek kissing person going to be joining us today?"

"No," Jonny said, eager to move the conversation on. She is not involved with this, but Melissa is."

"Who is Melissa?" Kelly asked. "Is that Julius' girlfriend?"

Julius stopped short in his movements to retake his seat.

"I don't know," Jonny said smugly. "Should we find out *Rupert*? Is Melissa your girlfriend?"

"No," Julius said defensively.

"Come now, Rupert, old sport, don't be shy!" Kelly exclaimed. "Why the change in tone? Pray answer the question properly."

Julius grinned as he realised he had been cornered.

"As of this moment there is nothing to suggest that our hearts are intertwined," he replied grandly.

"But you do fancy her?" Cat teased.

It was Julius' turn to blush. "Yes, my heart has indicated a certain fondness for her," he admitted.

"Blimey," Jonny said. "So those yanks aren't so bad after all then?"

"This one has certain good qualities."

"And what are they?" Kelly probed.

"I think we ought to adjourn there," Jonny said quickly, not trusting Julius, or rather Rupert, to refrain from drifting off into sexual fantasies. "The *real* point is that you're going to hold a networking event here aren't you?"

"Are we?" Kelly squealed.

"Yes," Cat smiled. "I was going to go over it with you after this."

"Oh thanks Cat!" Kelly gave her sister a big fat kiss.

"Ouch!" Cat said, pushing her away. "You be careful with those piercings."

"Well, we were wondering whether you would like to hold a cinema night here." Jonny said earnestly.

"A cinema night!" Kelly's eyes opened wide in anticipation.

"You have some of the facilities with your footie screen," Jonny continued.

"And we can source the film and the kit and get all the legal stuff done," Julius chipped in, forgetting to be his alter ego in his excitement. "We won't be able to get the current releases, but I've got my eye on a Brit flick rom com that has only just left the cinemas."

"A Brit flick what?" Cat asked.

"Sorry, romantic comedy," Julius explained. "Melissa suggested that it would be the ideal thing to get couples in. You could tempt them to eat here before the film and there would be a brief interval in the middle for them to get more drinks in and, hopefully, they won't be in a hurry to leave at the end."

"How much would it cost the pub?" Cat asked.

"Nothing," Jonny said. "We thought we would offer it on a profit share basis to start with. Charge the punters three quid to come in which can be offset against food if they eat a meal beforehand. Then you can pay us back from your profits for the evening and we can divvy up the extras. We just want to test the theory to start with."

"The aim is to get a regular screening so we can show excellent British films that don't make the cinema play list," Julius explained. "Melissa suggested that rather than trying to change how the cinemas operate, we should show what could be done, and hopefully make some cash in the process."

There was a pause as Cat and Kelly digested the information.

"Can we? Can we Cat?" Kelly squealed.

Cat laughed. "I'll have a think about it, but there is one thing that worries me."

"What's that?" Julius asked with a concerned look on his face.

"What happened to Rupert? When you go all serious he disappears."

They all laughed, but Julius groaned as a text came through on his phone. "Duty calls I'm afraid," he sighed.

Forty minutes after Julius had left, Jonny had shown Cat his mock up of the Shy to Shy web site and was trying to think of ways to keep her there. He got the feeling that Cat was enjoying his company, but he was running out of ways to keep the business conversation going in order to keep her with him. As he feared she started to collect her things together.

"I'm sorry about dumping you in it about your girlfriend earlier," Cat smirked to herself as she gathered her notes.

"She's not my girlfriend!" Jonny exclaimed a little too quickly. "Sarah's a nice girl, but she always seems to be in a hurry to go somewhere and it's usually away from me. I'm sorry if it made things a little awkward the other night."

"You're a big boy now Jonny," Cat said. "You don't have to explain yourself to me. Who you see is your business."

"But I'm not seeing her," Jonny protested.

"Well perhaps you had better tell her that, because it looks to me as if she thinks that you are," Cat said firmly. "Now you go back upstairs and away from Kelly's bad influence or you will never get that web site finished."

Jonny gave her a mock salute with a grin. If Cat found it awkward the other night then she must have thought of him as more than a friend at some point. Things were on the up.

You have a video email from Sam Surname

Sam is sitting in her chair looking frazzled. She is not wearing makeup and her hair hasn't been styled and is sticking up wherever it pleases. She is clutching a dirty baby bib and is wearing a baggy tracksuit that bears an interesting collection of stains. Regardless of her haphazard appearance she looks very happy.

"G'day Sheila!" She beams. "Thanks for video email. Wow! You looked stunning, I bet you knocked them all dead! I showed your message to my hubby and he was lost for words for a while. He went all red when I teased him about fancying you. I put my foot in it then by saying that it was alright because you looked so good that I practically fancied you.

"I've had trouble with him ever since, he keeps asking me whether I fancy Angelina Jolie, or heaven help us –Kylie! Why do men always have to take things so literally?

"Sorry that I haven't been in contact sooner but I've been really busy, hence my rather glam appearance here. If I waited for when I was looking respectable then I would never get the time.

"I'm earning some useful beer money from this video email lark, although not in the way I imagined. It's been a big hit with new mums! We can send each other footage of our tots, not to mention to grandparents and friends. Of course the grandparents love it and want to respond so they're signing up as well!

"Anyway, enough about me. How did the big networking do go? And more importantly did you meet that Jonny bloke? Ah, it's good to be matchmaking again."

There is the high-pitched wail of a hungry baby in the

background.

"Aha," Sam grinned. "That will be his majesty wanting some food I expect. I'll have to love you and leave you sweetheart. Enjoy yourself!"

Sam blows a kiss to the camera and the footage stops.

Chapter 22

"Was it this badly organised last time?" Cat (515) asked Kelly (184) as she surveyed the Carrot Woman's attempt to hold court over a group of disgruntled local business owners who were not taking too kindly to the arguments that they should pay a membership subscription.

"There was much more of a buzz last time," Kelly puffed as she served up drinks at high speed. "I think it was a mixture of hope and fear, they seem to be more resigned this time. They're still drinking the same amount though, which is a result."

"Aren't you an eager capitalist?" Cat grinned, but the corners of her mouth soon slipped sideways when she saw Tim (519) making his way through the throng towards her at the bar. "Oh shit!" She said. "He's here."

Kelly looked up to see Tim pulling his most hard-done-by face.

"Piss off, you're barred," she growled as Cat deftly disappeared behind the bar.

"But there has been quite an unforgivable misunderstanding!" Tim whined. "Please can I see Cat?"

Kelly noticed that the people around Tim were starting to take notice of their exchange. "No!" She hissed "Now get out."

"But that hardly seems fair," Tim argued "I am a member of this business group and I can hear them discussing a subscription level. I can hardly pay money to be part of the community if I am not allowed to join in, now can I?"

Kelly started to fluster, as the people at the bar started to grow impatient to order their drinks. One of them was Jonny (237) who raised his eyebrows as if to check that she was all right.

"Okay," she conceded. "But you're not allowed within ten feet of my sister."

"If those are your terms then I fear I will have to abide by them,"

Tim sighed and shrugged theatrically at his fellow drinkers as if it was all a mystery to him. Jonny gave him a very suspicious look.

"A pint of lager top, please." Tim said graciously and handed Kelly a ten pound note. She snatched it, quickly poured the drink, passed it across the bar and took the next person's order.

"Excuse me Kelly," Tim said politely, "But I fear you may have forgotten my change."

"Special prices just for married losers who try to play away from home," Kelly snapped. "Ten pounds a pint. If you don't like it you can take your custom elsewhere."

"That sounds a reasonable request to me," Jonny butted in with a cold stare at Tim who looked at him without recognition until the penny dropped.

"Ah! I remember you!" He crowed. "A web designer or something? We met at a meeting a while ago."

"So we did," Jonny agreed. "I remember you talking about your wife at the time."

Kelly shot Jonny a winning smile as she caught up with the drinks orders and Tim attempted to make a graceful retreat to the far corner of the pub. "Thanks Jonny," she said. "Can you do me favour and go and check on Cat? She's round the back." She smiled as Jonny immediately sped off behind the bar.

Cat was not so pleased to see him. She was sitting on the stairs trying to control her anger and didn't really feel like explaining her personal life to him.

"Are you okay Cat?" Jonny said, a concerned look on his face. "Kelly asked me to come back and check on you."

"She did, did she?" Cat sighed. "She never did know when it was best to leave people alone. I suppose if you're born with a big mouth you always want to use it."

"Hey, I can leave you alone if you like," Jonny said hurriedly. "I'm only trying to help."

Cat smiled at him. "Can't win really can you? I'm sorry, didn't mean to snap, I just had a visit from someone who..." she paused and looked away as she tried to work out how to phrase it, "very nearly made a complete fool of me."

"That will be Tim, who Kelly has just charged ten pounds for a beer, then," Jonny said as he sat down next to Cat on the stairs.

"Did she!" Cat exclaimed. "I really think that my hippy sister has turned into a capitalist pig."

"She certainly gave Tim a going over," Jonny grinned. "I met him the other week. I didn't like him much then."

"It's a shame he didn't try and get you into bed then."

"How do you know he didn't?" Jonny quipped.

Cat's head snapped round to look at him with her mouth open. When she saw his expression, she relaxed into a smile. "I never really know where I am with you," she observed as she smiled despite herself.

"I'm quite straightforward really," Jonny said with a theatrical sigh. "I'm the bloke who lives in your sister's flat. I've got a network of over 200 people but I don't have many friends. I've been booted out of a flat that I shared with my best mate because he's loved-up with a woman who pretty much treats me as a father figure. I moved in with said best mate after splitting up with a long term girlfriend who had an affair with her boss and his bulging bank account. I soon realised that she had quietly persuaded me to lose contact with my friends and swap them with her friends. Although, strangely enough, when we split up they stopped wanting to go out for a drink with me. You can just think of me as a walking cliché."

Cat whistled. "Phew, it looks like we have more in common than we thought. Except that my ex had an affair with my young and beautiful, assistant and then Tim, well, who cares about him? Walking clichés the pair of us." Cat felt Jonny lean into her and she let herself relax against him. "I know what you mean about losing your friends," she continued. "If it's any consolation I've re-found a fair few of them via LinkedIn."

"What's that?" Jonny asked.

"It's another networking interface. It's less personal than Ecademy, but it's easier to use to get introductions to people."

Jonny groaned. "I think I'll stick to what I've got. Then again," he added thoughtfully "I do believe that there is some missing information. "Isn't it time that you appeared in court?"

"What are you talking about?" Cat asked.

"I had to appear in court to explain my lack of proper girlfriend so I feel I have every right to cross examine you." Jonny laughed and Cat found that she was unable to stop a smile spreading across her face. "So was there a kiss?" He asked.

Cat dug him sharply in the ribs. "You can't ask me that!"

"Ouch! I'll take it that there was, and that it was in public?"

"Yes, there was a kiss."

"And were tongues involved?"

Cat gasped and dug him in the ribs again. "Yes, but only once."

"When was this?"

"Oh, some time ago," Cat replied airily.

"And has there been a date?"

"Just the one."

"And was there been any phone sex?"

Cat gasped again.

"I'm sorry Cat, but I had to go through this in front of an audience."

"Oh, you win your honour," Cat sighed in exasperation. "He's married, but told me that he was single."

"I'd guessed that much," Jonny said. "I can tell that you're not the sort of person who would be someone's mistress."

"And how do you know?"

"You just seem like a really nice person."

"And how would you know?"

"I'm a good judge of character."

"So why don't you seem to know what is going on with your pseudo girlfriend?" Cat teased.

Jonny looked lost for what to say so Cat decided to help him out.

"Come on you," she said getting up and pulling him to his feet. "Cheering up duties over, it's time to get out there and face the enemy, or at least pretend that he isn't there." She found that she liked the feel of Jonny's hand in hers, especially the way he was in no hurry to let her hand go.

*

"Well that was an interesting evening," Kelly observed as she finished wiping down the bar and came to join Cat and Jonny, carrying a drink for them both.

"It's not every day that the landlady pours a pint over one their customers just for trying to talk to their sister," Jonny agreed. "Although I thought that Cat telling that Mr Wills bloke to check whether Tim had a will was a touch of genius."

"Oh right, and you telling our orange-haired leader that the meeting was boring, too long and had no chance of improving your bottom line was your idea of being subtle was it?" Cat laughed. "I thought she was going to burst a blood vessel."

"Yeah well," Jonny argued. "She had been banging on at me for ages, telling me how she was going to save the world. What is the point of making endless plans that no-one will ever follow up on?"

"No point at all Jonny," Kelly agreed, "but your film night

announcement did seem to lack a certain amount of, say planning?"

Cat cackled with laughter.

"I didn't know I was going to have to do it until the woman of the moment here introduced me," Jonny objected. "Why couldn't you just make the film announcement after your themed networking announcement?"

"It's your big plan," Cat sighed as she got her breath back and took a sip from the gin and tonic that Kelly placed in front of her.

"Well I'll leave you two to argue it out over your drink," Kelly said waspishly. "I'm knackered. Can you lock up when you leave Cat?"

"That's silly Kel. We can go now. You'll need your keys."

"I've poured out your drinks now. I'm not wasting them." Kelly looked pointedly at Jonny. "Perhaps you could drink them elsewhere?"

"Kelly!" Cat objected.

"Oh come on you two," Kelly sighed. "You're both mature, not to mention nice, adults and you are obliviously not ready to end your evening yet so why not go upstairs? I'm sure that Jonny will not assume anything and will be the perfect gentleman. Won't you Jonny?"

"Of course," Jonny said seriously.

*

Ten minutes later and Cat was standing behind Jonny holding her drink as he unlocked the door to the flat. She had certainly not expected the evening to end in this way and she knew that Kelly was being a clumsy matchmaker. However, something had stopped her simply going home, and it was not just that she didn't want to offend Jonny. She did trust him not to jump on her, but part of her was half-hoping that he would.

However, she was quite shocked when she saw the state of the flat. Half unpacked boxes lay scattered amongst small piles of possessions that had been unpacked and then piled up in corners. The only things that didn't have things piled up on them were two cheap, plastic garden chairs that were aimed towards a very dated TV set in the corner. She looked at Jonny and realised that he had spotted her surprised expression.

"Sorry about the mess," he said. "I've been busy with work and to be honest I'm a bit wary of putting everything away. I never realised how empty my life was until I moved in to my little flat for one. If I tidy it up, I think my one bed flat will echo."

"Hey, my house is just as messy," she assured him, "but yes, I do have lots more stuff. In fact when I moved my stuff out of my ex's house it was practically empty. You boys don't seem to have the knack of accumulating stuff the way we do."

Jonny ceremoniously dusted off one seat and gestured for Cat to sit down and he slumped down in the other chair looking demoralised.

"Yes we do, but at Antonio's I didn't need anything. He was always buying stuff, new games, music. There wasn't much point me buying it because he always had to have it. The latest album, DVD whatever, he's a hoarder."

"Aha," Cat smiled. "That's not like me at all. I just see something that I like and end up buying it. I believe the marketers classify me as an impulse buyer. Mind you, it might help if you had the occasional impulse to buy a sofa or something. Is this all you sit in to work at all day?"

"Not the best solution is it?" Jonny admitted. "I've ordered a sofa, I'm just hoping that my cash flow allows me to pay for it." He sighed. "Oh, who am I kidding? I'm broke. It took me too long to get work once I left Sunshine. Not to best way to impress a woman who ventures up into your flat after closing time."

"Oi you," Cat scolded and she prodded him in the ribs. "Don't you start getting all morose and putting yourself down. Anyway, due to the technicality of us not having kissed there is no way that I can be classed as girlfriend material."

"What about when the sofa arrives?" Jonny asked with a wink.

"Well that would have to depend on what type of sofa it is," Cat laughed.

"You'll have to wait and see. So I need a sofa and more stuff. Anything else?"

"You could tidy up a bit, or at least unpack," Cat reasoned. "I'm not sure you need the extra stuff unless it's stuff you really want."

"My music collection has certainly got a big hole in it, but I suppose I'll have to get some ornaments or something to make this seem more homely."

Cat didn't respond, she was gazing into space as she finished her drink.

"I think you were supposed to take the piss out of me then," Jonny prompted.

"Sorry," Cat said as she snapped out of her trance. "Miles away. I was thinking of someone at that networking do. Dennis, the chap who found Julius' farmer in Ohio. He's says that he's got about 18,000 people in his network. I don't see how he can possibly be useful to all those people."

"It's a bit like having loads of stuff, I suppose," Jonny said. "You keep it around because you never know when it will come in useful."

"That is very profound for this late at night," Cat said.

"I have hidden depths," Jonny sighed theatrically. "Do you think that when this film night takes off that we'll have loads of friends? A huge network?"

"I don't see why not," Cat laughed.

"It's just that I don't seem to be good at creating a support network. When I split up with my ex I had very few friends and when I was living with Antonio we were partners in crime and didn't really need anyone else, until Heather turned up of course."

"I know just what you mean," Cat said and gently touched his arm in support. She found herself staring into his eyes and decided that it was a now or never moment. "Right I should be making a move," she said, springing to her feet.

Jonny didn't make any objection, he just saw her to the door.

"The question is," he said. "Can I kiss you goodnight? Or do I have to wait until I get a sofa?"

Cat laughed and offered her cheek. Jonny kissed it gently, but didn't pull his face away afterwards. Cat felt his warm breath on her cheek and didn't feel too compelled to move her face either. Jonny gently put his fingers up to her cheek and stroked it and Cat lips started moving closer to his, but he didn't make any further move. She leaned in and met his lips with hers and they kissed very gently, only to kiss again and again, with gradually increasing intensity. She slipped her tongue inside his mouth and felt his arms around her back and neck, pulling her into him. It was another now or never moment. She pulled back gently and kissed him on the lips again. "Mmm," she murmured. "We had better watch out. That's your first step to being my boyfriend." She smiled at him and slipped away into the night.

The House of Fun Blog

Diary of a mad house
Date Thurs 7th July 2006

One for the ladies

VIKING – What do you say to win over the perfect woman? Especially if she thinks that you already have a girlfriend.

CELT – Who is your girlfriend???

GUEST – Ute: Sounds like a classic case of not wanting what's on offer. You've got to choose what you want and go for it!

CELT – C'mon Viking are you and 'blondie' an item now? Who's the perfect woman? I should know these things I'm your friend!

GUEST – CapnJack: You're going to have to define perfect woman here. Is the perfect woman gorgeous, clever and rich, or gorgeous and rich with low standards? ☺

VIKING – That's the problem, she seems to have high standards…

GUEST – CapnJack: Ah well, at least she's nice to look at and she might feel sorry for you and buy you a drink!

Chapter 23

Living above a pub has its own share of temptations, but Jonny's (257) mind was fixed firmly on the film night from the moment he woke up. Well, almost. His grey matter wasn't only absorbed with the business logistics of the event, as Cat also featured quite heavily in the firing of his thinking neurones. Especially their previous late night conversation.

However, Cat was not the only woman to cross his mind before his alarm clock reached the hour of eight o'clock. He was shocked out of his ponderings on the probable colour of Cat's nipples by his mobile phone demanding his attention.

"Hiya Blondie, it's Madame Scarlet Pimpernel here," Sarah (998) said chirpily. "So, so sorry for standing you up the other night. Good news is that I got that contract! How cool is that? Also my books are full now so instead of spending time looking for work I can do more enjoyable things with you."

"Oh hello, Sarah," Jonny said slowly.

"You don't sound pleased to hear from me," Sarah pointed out, her super confident demeanour cooling just a little.

"Oh no, no, it's just that I've only just woken up," Jonny mumbled unconvincingly.

"Yum," Sarah sighed. "Perfect way for a man to be; sleepy, mellow and hard. Do you have a tent pole situation going on there?"

Jonny lifted the duvet slightly to look at the erection that was so recently created on Cat's behalf. It was certainly not in danger of diminishing at the moment. "Erm, yes, I do," he admitted.

"Oh yum!" Sarah exclaimed. "Don't worry, I'll soon knock the stuffing out of him. I know I've let you down so I'll make it up to you. I may be a bossy cow during the day, but at night I can play the submissive one if you know what I mean? I'm free tonight. Isn't that the night of your slide show thingy?"

"It's not a slideshow, it's a cinema film," Jonny with a touch of petulance.

"That's the one! I'll see you there. What would you like me to wear? I've just bought a fab, strappy summer dress, or I can do a short skirt and boots combo, or maybe as it's a film premier I can wear a very sharp and sexy, little black dress?"

"Er, the boots and skirt sounds fine to me," Jonny said weakly.

"Just knew you were the kinky type!" Sarah laughed. "See you tonight tent pole boy!"

*

Jonny managed to stay in his flat until lunchtime, trying to keep his mind on the *Shy to Shy* web site and away from images of either Cat or Sarah in kinky boots. While he did manage to get a fair amount of work done, the flat also got a good sorting out and was now looking tidy, if bare. It was all ready for the arrival of his sofa. Jonny was just praying that his business would actually get some money through the door before the credit card bill landed on his doormat.

He almost ran out of his flat the moment Julius called him to say he had arrived with the kit. He charged down the stairs to find the rest of the cinema crew waiting for him. Julius (673) was looking remarkably hip with a carefully propagated stubble line, shades and three-quarter length shorts that only seem to suit very few people, him being one. Melissa (261) looked very artfully fit with a loose baggy shirt over a vest top and shorts, but Cat (519) took the biscuit in a T-shirt dress and high-heeled sandals. Jonny made an effort not to stare, but was unable to drag his eyes away from her as he greeted everyone. Fortunately Ferrero distracted his gaze before it became too obvious by leaping up at him, placing Ferrero-sized paw prints on his best summer shirt and short combo that he had spent ages ironing.

"Oh God, I'm sorry about that," Cat giggled. "I'm afraid he always does that to people he likes. It's a compliment. I think."

Jonny grinned and got down on one knee to make a fuss of Ferrero who reacted to the attention by producing his best rolling-on-back-with-paws-in-the-air routine.

"Looks like he's made a friend too," Kelly (186) remarked from behind the bar with a smirk. "Do you lot always dress up like this to shift dirty equipment about?" She grinned knowingly at the various claims that they had just thrown on whatever was to hand and left them to get on with it.

The group busied about their work like a class of excited school children preparing for their first night of an opening play. There was lots of giggling and flirting, not least because Julius had arrived in the persona of an adolescent American teenager.

"This is, just like, way so cool," he exclaimed excitedly. "What with working with you, like total babes and stuff."

Melissa groaned. "You're way off *dude*," she scolded. "You need to start watching way more American movies. You obviously don't get enough of them over here." She ducked as Julius aimed a scrunched up ball of gaffer tape at her. "Geez you Brits, just don't understand irony!" She laughed.

"So how is the film writing training going?" Jonny asked.

"J's a really talented guy," Melissa replied. "He just needs to get over his hang ups about having so much talking in his scripts. Talk, talk, talk. That's all they do. Show, don't tell is the golden rule. Then even us stupid Yanks will understand."

"J hey?" Jonny smirked.

"Julius is just *so* old fashioned," Melissa laughed. "I mean, didn't that name like go out with the Romans?" She turned round to see that Julius was making a yapping mouth sign with his hand behind her.

"Yap, yap, yadda yadda. That's all these Yank dudes seem to do and you have the balls to tell me to cut down on dialogue." He said shaking his head as he plugged the speakers into the amp for the cinema equipment and they all jumped with the resulting burst of feedback.

"But he thinks that words are the answer to everything!" Melissa complained. "You don't need words, all you need is love!"

"You two are like a feuding married couple," Cat laughed.

"Melissa has a point," Kelly butted in from behind the bar where she was filling the fridges in preparation for the evening. "I don't need to listen to you lot to know what is going on here. To start with Ferrero, he's fallen in love with Jonny, in fact any minute he's going to start humping Jonny's leg. Jonny is happy to play with Ferrero as he is in lust with Cat."

"Kelly!" Cat exclaimed.

"What?" Kelly replied nonchalantly. "Would you prefer me to say that Jonny wanted to hump you?"

Jonny and Cat exchanged a quick embarrassed glance, but Kelly continued.

"Cat is playing it a bit more cool, but we know that she likes Jonny as her current summery, yet cool and casual look takes absolutely *ages* to perfect, and she has chosen to do it for the mucky job of setting up the kit."

Julius snorted with laughter.

"And Julius here, or is it J for short?" Kelly continued with a big grin on her face. "He would like us all to believe that he is playing wingman for Jonny's seduction of Cat, but we all know that he fancies the pants off Melissa and is doing everything possible he can to impress her, and Melissa..."

Kelly's summarising was cut short by a burst of loud music from the stereo system as Julius loaded one of Melissa's CD's, sticking his tongue out at Kelly as he did so. Cat laughed and applauded him.

"Well done J!" She shouted over the music.

"Nice taste in music dude, not! My Mom wouldn't even dance to this." He exclaimed, turning it down to a more manageable level.

"The Argentinean tango! The music of love and passion!" Melissa exclaimed. "Come, come!" She ordered gesturing the others to her. "I'll show you." She pulled Julius to stand opposite her. "Come on you two, stand opposite each other," she ordered Cat and Jonny and they obeyed. "Now lean in towards each other and turn your faces towards me." Melissa leant into Julius and pulled him towards her so they formed a pyramid meeting at the chest. Julius's eyes bulged noticeably and Jonny did his best not to gulp as he and Cat took up a similar position. He held his breath as he felt Cat's soft breasts through her thin cotton dress cushion the force between them. They found themselves nose-to-nose and Jonny had a huge urge to kiss her, but she giggled and turned her head to look at Melissa as instructed.

"Put your left hand around Jonny's neck," Melissa instructed as she did the same with her hand on Julius. Jonny was unable to repress a tremor as the soft contact of Cat's fingers on his neck sent shivers across his back. She gave a little smile in response.

"C'mon Jonny, don't be such a stiff! Put your left hand around Cat's waist. You too," she said to Julius, who seemed more than happy to oblige by placing his hand on Melissa's slender waist. "Now you must hold her firmly to help her balance, but still be gentle enough to allow her room to move. It is like a pyramid meeting at the top, but not at the bottom. The tango is completely led by the man. It caused a huge scandal when it first came out because of the close contact and the way the man invades the space between the woman's legs."

Cat burst out giggling and had to step back releasing her hold on Jonny who was tempted to step forward and grab her back again. "I'm sorry," she said and raising her eyebrows in her best 'we had better behave' look and stepped back into their embrace. Jonny felt himself twitching again and he knew that Cat could feel his reaction to her hands on his neck.

"Right!" Melissa commanded. "The man takes a step with his right foot to the side and then brings his left foot to meet it before returning the left foot to the original position. The woman mirrors his movements." Melissa played the male role and demonstrated the moves with elegant steps. The couples just about manage to achieve this and Melissa went on to the next step.

"The man puts his right leg forward, then his left leg forward while the woman steps back with the corresponding leg each time. Cat you need to stretch your leg back as far you can each time. Keep your bottom in and never pause with your legs apart."

That was too much for Cat who developed such a fit of giggles that she was forced to sit down.

"Jeez, I sure hope y'aal take the event tonight more seriously," Julius grinned.

*

Unfortunately, they all took the main event very seriously, it was just a shame that very few other people did. Julius was forced to start the film before an audience of 12 people not including the organisers and this included four people who just happened to pop in.

"I can't believe it," Kelly moaned. "All that work for nothing. I'm going to make a loss tonight."

"We're all going to make a loss," Julius sighed as he looked on at the small huddle of people watching the action on the big screen.

"I s'pose it was a gamble screening a movie that's only just finished its theatre run," Melissa said quietly. "P'haps we shoulda gone for a cult film that people will wanna to see again?"

"Next time?" Kelly said in a huff and went to collect some glasses.

Jonny just watched his friends as they bemoaned their collective business failure. He was aware that he had drunk too much already, firstly through excitement before the screening and then through depression when the lack of audience, and thus profit became apparent. He knew he should stop investing in beery liquid assets, he had no idea how he was going to pay for his sofa now, but it seemed like a good night to drown his sorrows. He was also desperate to say the right thing to Cat as the buzz between them fizzled out when the night started to go downhill. But he didn't know where to start. He was the person who had actually convinced Cat of the merits of the venture and neither his ex-flat mates or his ex-work mates from Sunshine that he invited had shown up.

He was just about to order himself another drink when Sarah (998) walked in looking amazing in her skirt and boots coupled with an off the shoulder summer top. She was with a woman (441) who looked like a celeb from a gossip magazine lurking mysteriously behind dark glasses. Sarah mouthed her apologies for being late across the room to Jonny and blew him a kiss as they quietly grabbed their seats.

Jonny smiled back at her trying to look nonchalant in the face of glares from both Cat and Kelly. Sarah may have significantly boosted their audience and she did look very foxy, but he fervently wished she hadn't come. He then noticed Sarah giving Cat a particularly cold look. He suddenly didn't know where his life was heading, but he had the distinct impression it was not under his control.

Just before the end of the film Cat sighed and quickly gathered her things together. "Shall we meet up tomorrow morning to clear this lot up and debrief as to what to do next?" She asked the others.

"But the film hasn't finished yet!" Jonny protested. Awkward situation or not. He didn't want Cat to go.

"Already seen it," Cat replied curtly. "And the lovers always get together in the end."

"Not in my films they don't," Julius remarked, but no-one had the energy to make any response.

Jonny sadly watched Cat leave and ordered another beer on his tab. At this rate it was going to be a bigger debt than his sofa.

When the credits finally rolled, the customers followed their example and made their way out of the door, all except for Sarah who made a beeline towards Jonny.

"That was different," she said in a manner that stopped well short of complimentary, but was intent at avoiding offence.

"Yeah, different as in a failure," Jonny grumbled.

"Least you tried, Blondie," Sarah soothed. "I hope you haven't been hitting the booze too hard. I have big plans for you tonight."

Jonny just looked at her, his groin yelling at him to go into Casanova mode, while his brain was still humming along to the rhythm of the tango from that afternoon and the electric feel of Cat's fingers on his neck.

"C'mon," she smiled. "It's time that I took a look at your groovy new flat."

Jonny looked around the room and was acutely conscious of Kelly's eyes boring into the side of the head.

"Oh so now that you're ready to hang around you expect me to do exactly what you want?" He said petulantly. "Perhaps I don't want to be picked up and put down whenever you feel like it. Perhaps I have other things on my mind, other women who are more reliable."

Sarah looked surprised. "Touché," she said slowly. "Does that mean that you'll be seeing me around?"

Jonny didn't know how to respond. His groin was screaming at him, yelling, 'Look at her you fool! She's gorgeous! She's randy! This morning she offered you no strings sex!' In the end all he managed was "I don't know."

"Oh don't dither, Jonny," she commanded. "Either you want to have sex with me or you don't. Now which is it?"

Jonny was bamboozled by her directness and his inner conflict between reason and pleasure.

Sarah frowned and stiffened. "I'll take that as a no." She said before adding loudly "The least you can do is walk me home."

Jonny looked at her and at Kelly who was still staring at them. "Okay," he said just as loudly, "but no funny business."

Sarah snorted. "That's supposed to be my line."

As they walked out of the door together Jonny mouthed "I'll see you later," to a stone-faced Kelly.

Sarah changed gear into work mode the moment they left the pub telling Jonny all about her work exploits as if their previous conversation hadn't happened. She was full of praise for a mystical management guru who she claimed put her on the path to success. It was hard going for Jonny after his business failure that evening so he was relieved when they eventually reached her trendy flat on the posher side of town.

"Hey," she exclaimed, grabbing his hand. "You must borrow his book, it helps you stay one step ahead of the competition!"

Jonny hung back, in a dilemma as to whether to go in her flat.

"Oh behave Jonny!" She laughed. "Do you think I'm going to jump on you!"

She unlocked the door to the flat and walked in and Jonny shook his head and followed her.

His first view of the flat was that it was an office that someone was trying to live in. The lounge was dominated by a table full of computer equipment complete with scanner, printer, fax and a myriad of wires. The room was dotted with skyscraper piles of paper, while the focus of most people's lounge, the television, was hidden in a corner, a leather sofa angled carelessly towards it. Half of the sofa was also covered with paper and folders and a squat filing cabinet was fulfilling the role of a coffee table by being home to an assortment of mugs with varying levels of dark fluid in them.

"Something tells me that you like to bring your work home with you," Jonny observed as he looked round the room.

"Very funny," Sarah sighed. "I'll get that book for you," and she walked out of the room.

Jonny walked warily into the room, gingerly stepping between the piles of paper. He wasn't sure whether he should have a look around or not. He reasoned that some of the information stacked around him could be confidential.

"There you go," Sarah said and Jonny turned round to see Sarah standing between him and the front door holding out a management textbook. However, there was something distinctly different about her. She was dressed in nothing but a black, strapless bra, silky, black French knickers and her boots. "It's your choice Jonny. You can take the book and go home with a tent pole in your trousers and a sure-fire method to improve your bottom line. You can take me *and* the book with the biggest smile you've ever had, and believe me the book is not that funny, or you can just take me. I highly recommend one of the last two options."

Jonny's eyes bulged so much they threatened to pop out of his head and bounce on to one of the teetering piles of paper littered around him. "That's not fair," he muttered, his eyes taking in every curve of Sarah's lithe body.

"It's totally fair Jonny," Sarah laughed. "I've given you a range of options; perhaps you would prefer the executive summary? Option one no sex but some very useful business tactics. Option two mixing business with exquisite pleasure. Option 3, nothing but pure unadulterated sex. I might throw in breakfast as well. You said you wanted to make your own decisions. Those are the available options, but I should warn you. I am accustomed to getting my own way."

Jonny just stood and stared at her, inner turmoil raging inside him between his groin and his head. His heart was also involved, but mainly by beating about 180 bpm. Most of the blood it was expelling was heading straight towards his trousers.

Sarah shrugged. "You obviously need more information in this due diligence exercise before you make a decision." She reached behind her back with her free hand and effortlessly undid her bra, letting it fall to the floor. Her small, pointed breasts fell slightly lower than Jonny anticipated, but his drink affected gaze followed their fall from grace and determinedly stayed fixed upon them. The arguments from his brain were beginning to sound incoherent, like a drunk that knows exactly what he wants to say but lacks the coordination to arrange the words in the correct order.

Sarah smiled. "We have at least a passing business interest so perhaps we can at least continue? Perhaps I should start by telling you more about my personal portfolio, by reminding you of my terms and conditions? She held the book behind her back with both hands, pushing out her breasts, before walking from side to side in front of him as if she was presenting to an audience. Each step involved a solid heel-strike from her boots.

"It has been noted that Sarah Evans enterprises has not acted in a strictly professional manner during previous negotiations. In order to turn this into a true win-win situation she is willing to bring some extra incentives to the negotiating table. Sarah Evans Unlimited is a forward thinking and open minded organisation that will not deliver anything less than full satisfaction to her preferred supplier. To that end, as previously suggested, she is prepared to go along with anything that Jonny Philips suggests."

"Anything?" Jonny stammered.

"Anything," Sarah replied airily, facing him and clicking her heels together sharply, causing her breasts to bounce gently. "I am very open minded to new experiences and opportunities. This is your chance to live out your fantasies Jonny boy, but like every effective sales pitch this is a time-limited offer." She held the book in front of her groin and wriggled her knickers down her hips with her other hand so they slipped down her legs. They caught on the top of one of her boots and staying there at half mast, just below her knees. The glaringly corporate cover of the book being her only remaining modesty. "As one of my favourites songs go. 'It's now or never!'" She purred, with a triumphant expression on her face.

Jonny just stood there staring, his mouth going, but no sound actually escaping.

"Is that a 'yes' vote from the Trouser Department?" Sarah asked looking at his groin with an innocent expression. She threw the book to one side, stepped out of her knickers and walked confidently towards Jonny wearing nothing but her boots. "It is always good to identify areas of constraints in the system," she purred as she ran a finger down from his neck to just above his belt. "Because releasing that constraint can make the whole system function much more efficiently." She dropped to her knees and deftly undid his belt.

Jonny knew then that in terms of influencing his actions, his groin had just completed a hostile takeover.

You have a video email from Cat Forsythe

Cat is looking smart if a little tired and is pulling her hair back into a ponytail as she starts to speak.

"G'day Sport, or should I call you Cupid? Sorry to keep you in suspenders by not responding sooner, but what with my new business, Kelly's pub and this networking lark I've hardly sat still recently. It's now coming up to 2am and on a school night too!

"Well the big news for you is that I snogged Jonny the other night!" Cat smiles. "I bet you're cheering now, well to be honest, it wasn't supposed to happen and it nearly led to a whole lot more, but common sense prevailed. Would you believe it that he is the new tenant in the flat in Kel's pub? It's a bit like getting it on with your neighbour. Kel is dead keen on it but me, well…"

Cat shifted in her seat and looked away to a corner of the room. "Guess who I saw in the street today? Give up? My ex! Not the ugly not funny one, the very fit bastard one who shagged my assistant."

Cat released her hair from the ponytail again before looking back up to the camera. "Would you believe it? I still fancied the bastard. Kel told me that he's been hassling Mum to try and get my new phone number. Apparently he wants to get back with me. He was in a razor sharp suit, he always looked good in a suit, he hardly wore them when he was with me. My brain is screaming no, but my heart and rude bits are shouting yes! I probably shouldn't say this, but he was fantastic in bed."

Cat sighed and swept her hair back again. "This Jonny bloke seems nice. Well he was at first, very honest and straightforward, but now, well he seems to be on a big charm offensive, and I liked it when he was just being himself. And there seems to be another woman on the scene as well, and she doesn't look like the sort of woman you want to be in competition with."

She yawned, delicately covering her mouth as she did so. "Who knows what to do? Kelly just thinks I should shag Jonny; that I can't think straight until I relieve my sexual frustrations." Cat rolled her eyes. "Sounds like a typical bloke's response to me, so I'll sleep on it and see how I feel in the morning. Too much going on at the moment. Just had a shocker of a day on the business front. I hope everything's going well with you and your Aussie cottage industry. Laters sport.

The footage stops.

Chapter 24

Cat (520) was determined to cheer her sister up the next morning. She was often irritated by Kelly's self-obsessed nature, but she knew how much her sister was worrying about the success of her business. Of course, Cat had a few issues of her own to sort out, like the arrival of that Sarah woman last night, but it was easier to focus on other people's problems than her own.

She smiled sympathetically as Kelly (187) answered her knocking by throwing open the door with a grimace against the bright July sunshine.

"Hiya Top Cat," Kelly growled. "So, any ideas on the next big money spinning idea?"

"Easy Kelly," Cat said reassuringly. "We all took a hit last night, and if you don't try these things you don't know, do you?"

"Well, we certainly know now," Kelly pointed out. "I also know that my git of a husband still hasn't come back from Scotland like he promised."

"When is he due back?"

"Yesterday, he reckons he'll be another week or so. Apparently it will all be worth it in the end. It had better be. He's missing out. When are you expecting the others?"

"I'm not sure," Cat said. "We agreed to meet up this morning to pack up before you have to open, but apart from that I don't have any specifics. Judging by the drinks Jonny put away last night I doubt he will be up too early this morning."

"Hmm," Kelly replied vaguely as she poured them both a cup of coffee.

"What?" Cat asked sharply.

"He walked that Sarah bird home last night. If it makes it any better, she did ask to go up to his flat, but he refused and then she played the old 'I'm a woman alone late at night' ruse to get him to walk her home."

"You're acting as if it is big deal to me," Cat said casually.

"Oh c'mon Top Cat! I know you like him and I also know he really likes you. It *is* a big deal."

Cat was just trying to find a non-committal answer to this when Julius (673) and Melissa (261) walked into the pub. Julius sported a face akin to a hurricane thundercloud and Melissa rolled her eyes at the women as she followed him in.

"Ladies, we officially have a bear with a sore head in our midst," she sighed theatrically and laughed when she saw Kelly's questioning face. "Oh no, we didn't take the tango one step further last night! We're just doing our bit for the environment by car sharing."

They all turned to see Jonny (257) stagger in clutching a management textbook. He looked just as if he had been run over by a succession of beer barrels all night. They all stared at him, taking in his dishevelled appearance and the fact he was wearing the same clothes as yesterday. Jonny looked at the others and winced. Cat's attempts to keep her expression casual failed very quickly and she emitted a barely audible gasp, before she made an effort to harden her face into a 'couldn't care' look. Jonny wasn't able to look her in the eyes and was obviously very relieved when Julius broke the spell.

"Right!" Julius said briskly. "Let's get things packed away and then work out what we're going to be doing from there. Jonny, go and get showered and then come and join us."

Jonny shot him a grateful look and scuttled off to his flat wincing again as he noticed Kelly's deadpan stare following his progress across the room. Cat shook her head and tried to busy herself in the task of dismantling the cinema equipment.

The equipment was stowed at lightning speed due to the way that everyone wanted to move on from their collective business failure, not to mention Jonny's failure to make it back to his own bed at the end of the evening. The result was that everything was almost finished by the time Jonny reappeared, looking much more presentable and human. He helped Julius carry the kit out to the car while Kelly made some coffees.

"What a little shit!" Kelly exclaimed, a ferocious frown on her face.

Cat smiled despite herself. "That's what you get for putting your big nose into other people's affairs," she pointed out.

"That's so rubbish!" Kelly snorted. "Why don't you stand up for yourself? Everyone could tell that you two had something going on and he ruins it by shagging some cheap tart."

"Hey you guys," Melissa said cautiously. "I don't wanna to get into the middle of a family row here, but I do know that Jonny is pretty keen on Cat here."

"Not that keen, obviously," Cat pointed out. "Can we just drop the subject please? We've got other things to discuss here."

"Just as long as you give him a bollocking when we finish here," Kelly muttered. "If you don't I will!"

"Look Kelly," Cat snapped. "Jonny is free to shag whoever he wants to!" She winced as she turned to see that Jonny and Julius had just walked back into the bar.

Jonny's jaw dropped and he stopped in the doorway, unsure of whether to come in or disappear into the street.

"Oh just come in Jonny," Cat snapped again. "Get yourself some coffee to wake yourself up. I presume now that your balls have been emptied you will be able to think properly?"

Kelly snorted with laughter and Melissa turned away to try and hide her grin. However, Jonny still looked as if he was going to take flight at any moment.

Cat sighed with exasperation and walked towards Jonny and took his arm and led him to the chair next to her and sat him down. Jonny looked like a five year old who was being put next to the teacher for being naughty. "You sit there Romeo and give us some of this inspiration that you're supposed to have. Kelly, coffee here quick! Now let's start the meeting."

Cat took a deep breath. "Last night was crap to put it bluntly. It was a complete and costly failure. We need to work out if the idea is a dead duck or if we need to do things differently. Perhaps we can start with a show of hands. Hands up who thinks we should walk away now?"

All the women slowly raised their hands while Julius just looked miserably in front of him and Jonny looked at Julius.

"Okay, so we have a majority decision if we are going to do this democratically," Cat continued. "But perhaps we ought to push for a unanimous decision? Jonny, excuse the blunt question, but are you going along with this because you know that your mate is so keen on it?"

"No," Jonny said thoughtfully. "I think we should have another go, but..."

"But what?" Kelly snapped.

"But I really can't afford for us to make a loss again," Jonny said miserably. "And if I can't afford it then I can't pay Kelly's rent and I don't think that's fair."

"Okay, so it's not looking good," Cat replied. "Julius, any words from you that can help us to see why we should invest more of our time and money in your venture?"

"It's just so frustrating!" Julius snarled and slapped his hand on the table, making everyone jump. "I know it will work, it just needs investment, and I don't have the cash."

"Julius, honey," Melissa said soothingly. "You know I think it's a swell idea. After all, I helped you think of it, but you saw it last night. Why would people pay extra to watch a movie in a pub when they can see it earlier in the theatre, rent it dead cheap or watch it on cable? Don't you Brits go to the pub to socialise? Not to sit and stare at a screen."

"But it's providing a new service," Julius argued. "It's adding value."

"Where is it adding value, Julius?" Cat asked gently. "What is your – what do you call it – Elevator pitch?"

"Pub cinema is something that brings together two of our favourite pastimes, drinking and film watching," Julius started. "It, er, it..."

Jonny suddenly jumped to his feet with a determined look on his face, knocking his chair back and making them all jump. He winced and put his hand to his head briefly, but then the determined look returned.

"I'll tell you where it adds value," he said and stomped towards the door where he turned back with a flourish. "You walk into the cinema and what do you get? A queue. You have to wind round those stupid roped off lanes. Then you get to buy an expensive ticket off some gormless teenager." He made a gesture at a fruit machine as if he was collecting his ticket. "You then walk towards the screens and there's the food." He gestured against the side of the bar. "It's processed crap, it's a rip off and you get far more than you could ever want to eat or drink, but people still seem to defy logic and spend money there."

He looked around at the others, obviously on a major caffeine buzz. "Then you go and find your seat after handing your ticket to another vacant teenager who has an obvious phobia against soap and water. This kid grunts at you and tears your ticket in half. You enter the auditorium and they've made a token effort to clear up the crap from the previous audience, but it's hardly clean. It's the same teenager staff again who have walked around with a bin liner picking up the huge, empty coke buckets and bugger all else. Your feet stick to the carpets, there's popcorn on the floor and the place smells of exactly what it is. A closed off room that is periodically filled with people eating junk food, a room that never sees daylight or fresh air."

He grabbed a chair and swung it round to face them. "You get your seat, you've either had to squeeze past a row of people who really don't want to let you past, or even worse, you are one of those people, and you get your toes mashed by big fat pie eaters, or women with daggers for heels. And then what? You have to sit through ages of dull slide screens of adverts telling you to eat at

Raj's Curry House and to buy your Ford Mondeo from Honest Guv's on the corner.

"Just when you think you're going to go insane they start the proper adverts, but they're just the same as the ones you get on the telly, they're just on a bigger screen. Only then do you get the film trailers. By the time the film finally starts your arse has gone numb and you start to need a piss because you managed to drink half a bucket of watery coke syrup in your boredom.

"Where can we add value? We give people a service, we make them feel as if they are welcomed, not just someone for a kid with greasy hair to grunt at. We give them quality food and drink at reasonable prices. We decorate the place a bit for them, something to do with the film, make it feel as if it's been just for that visit. We show them a decent film and we serve them *booze!*"

Jonny sat back and looked at them. They were all grinning at him. Julius started clapping and then stood up and applauded. The women reluctantly joined in the clapping.

"Jeez," Melissa whistled. "If that was your elevator pitch I'd sure hate to be stuck in a confined space with you."

The women laughed, but Julius shot out of his seat to stand next to Jonny.

"Calm down ladies, calm down," he said in a dodgy Eastend London accent. "My pal Jonny here, he might still be pissed from last night, but he's hit ver china on ver 'ead."

"Hit the what?" Melissa laughed.

"You wouldn't know sweet'eart," Julius growled. "It's a gangster fing init?"

"That's supposed to a gangster accent?" Cat groaned.

"Shut yer cake 'ole for a minute darlin'," Julius grinned. "An lemme get to ver point, like. My associate 'ere has just made an 'andsome speech. One which I fink has answered your previous question. So 'ows about us all 'aving a nice little vote again eh?"

"Not so fast *darling*" Cat scoffed. "Jonny's speech was indeed passionate and more than just a little bit fired by booze and caffeine. However, while he did make a good case for why people should have come to our event, it doesn't change the fact they didn't."

"We should have just made it a networking do," Kelly sighed. "Those nutters go to anything as long as there's food and booze."

"That's it!" Jonny exclaimed, jumping to his feet again. "We make the next one a networking event."

"Have you been taking too many alka seltzer?" Cat laughed. "Isn't the idea about networking that you talk to people rather than sit next to them and ignore them for an hour and half?"

"Trust me on this one," Jonny urged her.

"And why should she do that?" Kelly said pointedly.

"It would be a good advert for our skills," Jonny continued, ignoring Kelly's comments. "Here we have Kelly, the landlady of the perfect place to network or to bring clients."

"Creep!" Kelly muttered.

"Next we have Cat, event organiser extraordinaire."

Cat rolled her eyes at him.

"Julius here is terrible at acting, but he makes a mean advert that can be broadcast using video emails. I may appear to have a drink problem, but I can show people a thing or two about creating a web site that is easy to find and use. And Melissa, well…"

There was an awkward pause as they watched Jonny's battered brain trying to dig himself out of his hole.

"I don't believe it," Cat exclaimed. "He's got it!"

"I have?" Jonny replied instinctively before wishing he had kept quiet.

"Melissa!" Cat said excitedly. "What's your favourite film?"

"Easy. Moulin Rouge. I told you yesterday."

"That's right! And would you like to see it on a big screen rather than on your own TV?"

"Sure I would."

"And would you like to have some French inspired food? With some wine perhaps? Maybe even some Champagne if your man was going to treat you?"

"Damn right I would!" Melissa laughed. "I've got where you're going now!"

"But that's just the start!" Cat exclaimed. "What better after having some wine and watching the film than having a go at what you have just seen? Karaoke would be naff, but wouldn't it be great to try a little tango dancing with a Latin disco?"

"Sold to the babe with the dark hair!" Melissa exclaimed. "You're a genius!"

"But it doesn't stop there," Cat said breathlessly. "Jonny talked about adverts, we can cut our costs and increase the profits by getting other people to advertise."

"Are you suggesting that we have people standing up and spouting their elevator pitches?" Julius laughed.

"That's the trouble with you Julius," Cat laughed. "You can never keep in character. What happened to the East End gangster? Did he end up with a pair of concrete wellies? We don't advertise, well not here anyway, we can on the web site that Jonny's going to make us by the end of today," Cat paused to give Jonny a meaningful look. "But we don't have to advertise here. We can however, sell stall space to people with products that are linked to the theme. I'm sure the travel agents would love to have a space to sell discounted trips to Paris. Then there's the lingerie seller that's in my network. Just imagine a stall selling corsets after people have watched Moulin Rouge over a few glasses of wine. She'll make a killing!"

"She is a genius," Jonny said softly.

"Alright then 'ands up all those who are in for 'avin anover go,"

Julius said, his hand already raised. "Go on, get 'em up where I can see 'em!"

Julius was rewarded with a full show of hands.

*

In the middle of that afternoon Jonny tiptoed down into the bar to see if he could escape to the shops for some more coffee. By the look of him it was obvious that his eyelids were succumbing all too easily to the effects of gravity. He stopped dead when he saw Cat and Kelly discussing some paperwork in a corner of the bar. They both looked up and saw him.

"Ouch," Cat winced. "Looks like last night has caught up with you then."

"I'm on a mission to get some more caffeine," Jonny admitted. "The film web site is coming on well though. I should have a template to show you by the end of the day."

"I was only joking about finishing it by the end of the day," Cat said. "Come and have a coffee with us, we're trying to work out the food and booze orders."

Kelly scowled at her sister. "If you want a coffee you have to pay for it. Your slate has officially terminated and I want it paid by the end of the week."

"Of course," Jonny said to Kelly. "I think I had better leave it thanks Cat."

"No you don't," Cat said. "I'll pay for your coffee. I want to know how that web site is coming along."

Kelly growled and went off to get the coffee leaving Jonny and Cat alone.

"Look Cat, I really need to talk to you about last night," Jonny said urgently.

Cat just turned away. "Who you sleep with is none of my

business."

"But I want it to be you!" Jonny blurted out, his jaw dropping with shock as he registered Cat's startled reaction. "Oh God, I'm sorry," he stammered. "My brain, it's not working properly today, needs sleep."

"Comments like that are not helping," Cat said in disbelief.

Jonny took a deep breath. "Look, last night was a nightmare. It shouldn't have happened. I can't believe it did happen. I was weak and I've never done that sort of thing before."

"All men are weak. What's the saying? A standing cock has no conscience. Anyway, it's not as if we really had anything going. I like you Jonny, but I'm not going to come running to you when you click your fingers after you have shagged someone else. If I let someone into my life I need to be able to trust them. I've been cheated on before."

"That's better," Jonny sighed.

"What?"

"You're getting angry. Before, I didn't think you cared."

"Don't get cocky Jonny, it doesn't suit you."

"I'm not being cocky Cat, it's just that, well, I really like you."

"You what! You slept with that Sarah woman and then you come up with this crap!"

"I'm not interested in Sarah."

"I'm sure she'd be delighted to hear you say that after last night."

"That's not fair. She tricked me. I think she was jealous of you. She just wanted to close the deal, win the transaction. She's not interested in me as a person. I turned her down twice."

"Third time lucky was it?"

"She told me that she had a textbook that would really help my business. I only went into her flat to get the book."

"Oh pull the other one!"

"You may not have noticed, but I need help with my business Cat. I can't even pay my bar slate, let alone my rent. I turned her down, she took it well and then she started acting like a mentor. She got me into her flat and seduced me."

"Oh please!"

"I can give you the full details that I'm sure you don't want to hear, but the gist of it is that she stripped and then blocked the way out of the flat."

"She didn't!" Cat exclaimed, intrigued despite everything.

"She was starkers except for her boots. And I must confess to having a bit of a fetish for boots at the best of times. Look Cat, I have never been so miserable after sex in my whole life. The reason I'm so knackered is that I lay there most of the might thinking about you and how I've screwed things up."

"Quite literally," Cat observed.

"I want you Cat. I want to be your boyfriend. I want us to cuddle up on the sofa that I've ordered and can't afford. I can be trusted. It's not all about sex. We can start again. I'm lonely Cat. I want a soul mate and I can see that in you."

Cat was momentarily lost of words by Jonny's speech and was pleased when Kelly returned with the coffee.

"What are you to up to?" Kelly said suspiciously, handing the coffee to Jonny. "I've put it on your slate."

"Fair enough," Jonny said looking intently at Cat, but Cat had been distracted by the arrival of a man in the bar. He had dark hair, slicked back immaculately and was wearing a smart striped shirt, worn open-necked for a recklessly casual look, partnered with perfectly ironed slacks. Even the few days of beard growth just served to accentuate his superhero jaw line. This Mr Suave appeared to know Cat and judging by the shock on her face the recognition was mutual.

"No way!" Kelly exclaimed. "You're barred!" She yelled at the man.

"Kelly!" Cat screamed. "Will you stop interfering in my life?"

The locals all turned to look as Cat walked outside with her ex-boyfriend.

Kelly put her head in her hands. "I can't believe it!" She wailed giving Jonny a look of despair. "I thought you were bad!"

Jonny didn't say a word. He picked up his coffee and took it upstairs to his flat.

The House of Fun Blog

Diary of a mad house
Date Weds 21st July 2006

The smell of the shit hitting the fan

VIKING – There is a very old joke about an old man who confesses to a priest about having sex with two gorgeous 18 year old twins. The priest tells him what he must do for forgiveness, but the old boy doesn't care. He told the priest about it because he wants everyone to know.

It's the opposite with me. I had a series of fantastic sexual experiences last night but it was with the wrong woman. And all I can think of is the other woman.

CELT – Jonny!!!

VIKING – Don't use my name!

CELT – Sorry, but well!!!!!

GUEST – Ute: You men bring so much extra stress on yourself. Hope the sex was worth it!

GUEST – CapnJack: I was joking with my previous definition of the perfect woman! Sounds good though! ☺

SPANIARD – I've got two thoughts on this.

As the song says 'If you can't be with the one you love, love the one you're with' (and let's face it she's muy bonita). However, once an Ex, always an Ex – get in there hombre!

Chapter 25

Jonny (298) was discovering that as well as his mild fetish for kinky boots, he also had a soft spot for having a hand curled around the back of his neck. While, he felt ridiculous in his 'bohemian' outfit that consisted of a trilby hat, a suit jacket worn over flared jeans with a long scarf, he had nothing but compliments for the appearance of the slutty, yet trendy can-can look of the woman opposite him, but he quickly realised his spine only developed the shivers when it was Cat's hand that was doing the neck curling. It didn't help that the owner of the hand kept telling him what to do.

"C'mon Jonny, you're supposed to be taking charge here! Show me what to do and I'll do it. You lead and I'll follow. You're the boss, anything goes. It just has to be within our set rules."

Jonny broke out of the embrace and took a few steps back. "Look it's not working," he sighed. "I think we had better end this. It's not as if it's getting us anywhere."

"Uh, uh. You don't escape that easily!"

Jonny found himself pulled back in the embrace, his brain was whirring with what to do next. Right foot out. One. Left foot next to right and back. Two. Right foot forward. Three.

"That's better!" Melissa (285) encouraged. "Remember, le tango es mucho macho. It's all about the guy. You gotta just know what you wanna to do and go for it."

Jonny broke away again. "What do you think I'm doing this for?" He exclaimed.

Melissa simply laughed at him. "Don't have a go at me Jonny. I'm not the one who slept with the wrong woman!"

Jonny rubbed his forehead. "I'm sorry Melissa. I do appreciate you helping me out."

"No sweat," Melissa said and patted his arm reassuringly. "Perhaps we'd better call it a day and go and check on the others?"

They walked downstairs into a pub that was transformed with bright lights, dark corners and freestyle French tricolore flags. They also walked into an argument between Kelly (194) and Cat (549). It was at an impressive volume due to the fact that Kelly was the only one of the sisters in the room at the time.

"I can't believe you're so stupid!" Kelly shouted up the stairs behind the bar. Her heavy make up and bustling wench's outfit making her look even more intimidating. "You shagged him after the way he treated you like shit, cheated on you?"

Jonny and Melissa paused in their entrance.

"I guess she's not talking about you?" Melissa said softly to Jonny who simply shook his head. "Well that's levelled up the playing field," she sighed.

Kelly turned round to see them, her face a vivid red with her anger. "And what the hell have you two been up to?" She exclaimed.

"You'll see soon enough," Melissa reassured her with a smile.

There was a loud knock on the door.

"We're closed!" Kelly screeched.

"Er Kelly. I think that might be the local paper," Jonny said in his best soothing voice. "I've persuaded them to do a photo feature on our big night."

"How did you manage that?" Kelly exclaimed, her anger forgotten as she hurried towards the door.

"Oh you know? I know a man who knows a woman," Jonny said airily.

"Madames et monsieurs," Julius (691) called out grandly as he entered the pub looking every inch the absinthe-soaked bohemian by wearing clothes he didn't have to search too hard to find in his wardrobe. "I 'ave just sold zee last tickets! We 'ave a full 'ouse!"

His fellow bohemians all cheered.

"Thank God for that!" Kelly exclaimed.

"Where's Cat?" Jonny asked. "She should know this."

"You'll see her soon enough Romeo," Kelly pointed out, "and try not to drool when you do."

"What's all the noise about?" Cat asked as she walked into the bar wearing a pink, satin corset, a very short, ruffled skirt and Jonny's favourite boots with the killer high heels. Not to mention an impressive array of gaudy make up.

Melissa wolf-whistled furiously while everyone else clapped and Jonny did his best to follow Kelly's previous instructions.

"Oh behave!" Cat laughed. "Look at you lot, you look fantastic!"

"Julius has just sold the last tickets," Jonny informed her.

"Ahem, mon petite chou, I think you will find that I am called Toulouse tonight," Julian scolded him. "And I 'ave not only sold zee last ticket pour tonight, mais aussi pour le repeat showing next week!"

"Oh fantastic!" Cat squealed. "Well I think that calls for a pre-event drinkie!" Cat exclaimed and she went behind the bar and came back with a chilled bottle of Champagne and a tray full of glasses.

"Cat!" Kelly exclaimed. "Don't forget that I need to make a big enough profit here to cover the last fiasco. Not to mention the fact that our poor bohemian Jonny boy here can't pay his bar bill. Not that I'm supposed to mention that of course."

"At last!" Cat kissed Kelly hard on the cheek leaving a vivid scarlet lipstick mark. "My little sister has developed some business acumen. I've paid for the bubbly. I just want to say how nice it is to work with people like you, compared to the power obsessed freaks in the corporate world."

"Welcome to the real world," Julius grinned. "You have chosen to take the blue pill. You are now out of the matrix."

"That has to be the next film!" Jonny declared as Cat popped the cork and started pouring the Champagne.

"And what food am I supposed to serve up with that?" Kelly snorted. "Cold gloopy porridge?"

They all looked at each other and laughed.

"Good point," Jonny conceded.

"Here's to the bohemian values! Love, beauty, freedom and truth!" Cat declared.

"Ze greatest thing you can have in life is to love and be loved in return!" Julius crowed and they all laughed and toasted their impending success.

"What on earth is going on here?" Asked a man (241) dressed in a more modern bohemian look of a tie dye shirt, long shorts and a colourful woollen hat.

Kelly squealed and launched herself at her husband. "Malc!" She cried. "You've made it at last!"

"I think it was probably your threats to insert hot needles into my testicles that did the trick," Malc admitted ruefully.

"Well you should have come back earlier," Kelly said sulkily, although she still held him tightly by the arm. "There's lots of news to tell you."

"You're telling me," Malc said as he took in the costumes and the decorated pub.

"Not the pub you loser!" Kelly moaned. "And you lot are no better," she scolded at the rest of the group who looked at each in bemusement. "Not one of you has noticed that I've been off the booze for the last two weeks. That I'm not drinking Champagne now…" she looked expectantly at them.

"Congratulations!" Cat cried as the penny finally dropped.

"What on earth is going on?" Malc demanded.

"I'm pregnant!" Kelly announced with a huge grin. "And there was no way I was telling them before you knew. And I couldn't tell you that on the phone so I've had to keep a secret for two whole weeks!"

"Oh my good God," Malc muttered, before slumping down on a chair.

"Pass that man some Champagne," Julius laughed. "It looks like he needs it."

Jonny sat on the barstool next to Cat watching the raucous crowd who were drinking, singing and generally joining in with the film in a manner that would be frowned upon in the average multiplex cinema. The bohemian team knew that the big tango dance number to the vamped up version of Roxanne was the crucial part of the film. If that left a big impression then the tango lessons were much more likely to be a big success.

He was delighted when the crowd fell silent with the build up as the broad-chested, narcoleptic Argentinean started to strut and sing. As the scantily dressed dancers hit their feet in unison on the floorboards he felt a prickle of excitement as he saw their punters sucked into the cinematic moment. He desperately wanted to quietly take hold of Cat's hand and squeeze it. Partly because of their joint success, but mostly just because he needed to touch her.

He looked to his right and saw Cat's annoyingly good looking ex-boyfriend Luke (169) sitting in a corner, the epitome of good GQ style casual grooming. There was no chance of him joining in the fancy dress theme, he looked like James Bond on a relaxed mission to seduce a few stunning Russian female spies. He wasn't looking at the screen at all, but was staring intently at Cat and Jonny.

Jonny snapped his eyes away and moved them to Sarah (1002) who was totally engrossed in the film. She had vamped herself up for the occasion and Jonny found his mind filled with images and sensations from the passionate night they spent together. He recalled the smell of her perfume on her naked body, the same perfume that had entranced him when she gave him a lift when he was still on crutches. This has to be serious, he thought to himself. He had a sure thing with a gorgeous woman and yet he was very willing to risk it all on the outside chance of a relationship with someone else. Someone who was currently sitting very close to him.

His eyes moved on towards Antonio (1263) and Heather (180), cuddled up together on one of the small sofas. Trust Antonio to get the best seat in the house, he thought to himself, before remembering Melissa's words from earlier. 'You've gotta to know what you wanna do and go for it.' That's much easier said than done, Jonny thought to himself.

His eyes drew back to Julius and Melissa who were sitting just in front of him. As the dance routine reached its crescendo Julius quietly reached out for Melissa's hands and softly grasped it. Melissa turned to look at him with a surprised expression that read 'Oh yeah? You'll be lucky!' Julius winked at her and turned his attention back to the film. Melissa grinned and quietly placed their entwined hands on her lap.

Le tango es mucho macho, Jonny said to himself. It was time for a Brad Pitt moment. He reached his hand out slowly and gently grasped Cat's hand that was resting on her lap. As he did so he saw Luke's eyes boring into him. He gently squeezed Cat's hand and she turned to face him her eyes wide with excitement.

"I know," she said returning his hand squeeze. "It's just amazing. I can't believe we have pulled this off." She let go of his hand and returned her attention to the screen.

Jonny pulled his hand away, trying to ignore the gloating expression Luke's face.

When the credits started to roll accompanied by applause from the crowd and a sudden rush to the bar, the team moved into the more demanding part of the evening. They needed to get the crowd interested in the other events and persuade them to hang around so they could spend more of their money. They opted to bring on the dancing sooner rather than later as the guests had tucked into the wine and might be more in the mood so soon after the film. Melissa herded some people up towards the area they put aside for the dance floor and she launched into her teaching routine.

"She's brought some ringers," Cat smiled as some of Melissa's friends showed people how it should be done and slowly more and more couples drifted out towards the dance floor. Jonny was desperate to take Cat onto the dance floor, to place his arm round her corseted waist, to feel her fingers touch his neck, but his feet seemed to be set in concrete.

He suddenly found himself being none too gently pushed to one side as Luke appeared, taking her arm. "Shall we?" He asked while already leading her to the dance floor with a secret agent's swagger. Jonny felt himself crumple as he saw Cat's elegant fingers curl around Luke's broad neck. As they took their positions they looked like a perfect couple. Bond and his latest exotic babe. He was glad to be distracted by the sight of Antonio making a total mess of trying to dance with Heather. His usual arrogant swagger replaced by a total inability to balance on one foot and lead Heather with the other. It was so bad that they left the floor within minutes and headed towards Jonny.

"You're gonnae have tae get lessons or something pal," Heather warned Antonio. "I dinnae see why I should sit it out when everyone else is having so much fun."

Jonny laughed. "That was terrible EO! Absolutely awful. And I thought you were good at everything."

"I just need a bit of practice that's all," Antonio muttered, looking a lot smaller than usual with his air of dejection.

"Is the tango too macho for you?" Jonny teased. "Too Spanish? Perhaps you're more English than you thought?"

"Watch it hombre!" Antonio snarled.

"Now, now you two," Heather laughed. "Remember that we have something to tell Jonny?"

Antonio brightened suddenly. "We're getting married!" He

exclaimed. "And you, hombre, are going to be the best man!"

"That's fantastic news!" Jonny exclaimed kissing Heather on the cheek. She gave him a big hug.

"Don't go too near EO," she warned. "He's got a cold again."

"Oh shit." Jonny laughed and stepped away from Antonio.

"I hate to point out the obvious hombre," Antonio said quietly. "But isn't the senora of your dreams dancing with someone else?"

"Ooh yes! Who's the woman who is better than sex with Sarah?" Heather exclaimed.

"Mr smarmy James Bond is her ex," Jonny said glumly, ignoring Heather's outburst.

"At least he's nearly as bad as me," Antonio observed as they watched the couple struggle to master the dance steps before coming to a standstill that led to Cat walking off laughing, her ex in hot pursuit. "You considered forgetting about Cat and enjoying yourself with Sarah?"

"No way!" Heather cried. "Go dance with her Jonny," she urged and pushed Jonny towards her. He resented the push but still started to stride towards Cat with a forceful air. However, his matador approach was blocked by Sarah.

"Hiya Blondie," she smirked. "You going to ask me to dance or what?"

Jonny took in Sarah's knowing look and then at Cat making her way towards him through the crowd closely followed by Luke. "I don't get you Sarah," he said. "What do you want from me?"

"Oh come on babe," Sarah laughed. "You telling me that you didn't have a fantastic time the other night? If that wasn't the best sex you've ever had then I'm a nun!"

"I'm not going to disagree with you," Jonny said quietly. "But how much of a kick did you get out of winning?"

"I always play to win Jonny. You should know that by now. I

may not always play fair, but I don't get too many complaints when I play dirty."

"That's just it. You know that I like Cat. Did your interest in me suddenly peak because you saw that she was on the scene, or do you genuinely have feelings for me?"

"Oh Jonny!" Sarah exclaimed. "Just quit the super sensitive stuff will you? Surely you've got an inkling of what I'm about? Yes, I play to win, but I don't bother unless I think it's going to be worthwhile. I like you Jonny, you're a nice guy, a bit naïve maybe. And yes, we are different. And yes, I am bossy and my work probably takes up more time than it should, but I'm not hiding anything from you. If you like that Cat woman, then you need to sort it out with her. But I'm warning you. I'm not the sort of person who plays second fiddle. Just remember the old saying, 'a bird in the hand is worth two in the bush'. She smiled mischievously and took hold of Jonny's hand. "If you decide to go after Miss Glam over there then you lose me. It's quite simple."

Jonny looked into Sarah's face. He could just make out the small scar on the bridge of her nose that signified their first meeting. "I'm sorry Sarah. People have been giving me endless advice over the past few months, but in this case I'm just going to follow my heart and take the consequences."

He sidestepped her and just managed to catch Cat's hand as she walked past. She stopped with a start and saw Sarah standing behind Jonny. Luke bumped into Cat and pushed them all together and Jonny found himself holding Cat's hand, being the meat of an ex sandwich.

"You got time for a dance?" He asked her, trying to ignore the glares being flashed their way by Sarah and Luke.

Cat looked flustered, not appreciating the situation they were in, but she managed a wan smile. "Why not?" she said and turned back towards the dance floor dropping Jonny's hand. Luke stood in her way, and she paused only to side-step him and walk in a large loop around him. He tried to step into her path again and took hold of her arm but she jerked herself free. Jonny followed her stepping round Luke on the opposite side, but he still had to deflect a shoulder charge from Luke as he glared at Jonny, his dark eyes furrowed with hatred.

They took their positions on the dance floor and Jonny twitched again the moment that Cat's hands touched his neck.

"Your hands send a shiver down my neck every time," he said.

"I know," Cat said. "I can feel it."

They concentrated on their steps, Jonny relishing the close contact between them even though the corset formed a rigid barrier between them.

"You've been practising!" Cat accused him as he swirled her round.

"Guilty as charged," Jonny admitted with a smile.

"That's what you were doing with Melissa earlier," Cat guessed with a laugh.

"I wanted to be able to dance properly with you," Jonny said seriously as they stood face-to-face.

"You slept with Sarah," Cat pointed out.

"You slept with your ex," Jonny replied. "We all make mistakes. He looks a nice bloke by the way. I'm hoping he's not quite as aggressive as he looks because at the moment he looks quite capable of ripping my arm off and beating me over the head with it."

Cat laughed. "That's for me to know and you to find out. Anyway, if looks could kill then Sarah would have me dead and buried long ago."

"Sorry about that. I don't think that Sarah is used to not getting her own way."

"That makes two of them," Cat sighed. "I wish he would just leave me alone."

"You don't want to go out with him again?"

"I'd rather eat my corset," Cat exclaimed and she missed her step. "Oh! Sorry." She said. "And we were doing so well."

"Don't worry about it. I've got a plan," Jonny said mischievously.

"I'm having enough trouble remembering these steps," Cat pointed out. "I don't need any more complications."

"It's not about us," Jonny winked "it's all about working with our competitors."

"Sounds intriguing," Cat observed.

"Jonny!" Melissa screeched beside them. "Get your back straight! Come on lead your partner. Show her where you want to go."

Jonny and Cat shared a naughty school children look and improved their postures.

"I want to be your boyfriend," Jonny said softly as he pushed her back briskly across the dance floor.

Cat swung round to the side of him. "How can I trust you?" She said with a sad expression and they joined in the applause as the song finished.

Jonny and Cat walked off the dance floor and when Cat saw Luke waiting for her she took a diversion and nipped behind the bar. However, Jonny continued on his course and walked up to Sarah.

"You had so better not be trying your luck with me now," she warned.

Jonny just smiled at her, and also at Luke who was standing beside her glowering at Jonny.

"You may not know it," he said to them both, "but you are both separated by two degrees of separation, as it's known in the trade."

"Are you taking the piss?" Luke growled, puffing himself up alarmingly.

"Not at all," Jonny assured him quickly. "It's just that there's a fair amount of history between the four of us. Sarah and I have had a fling, but I've only got eyes for Cat. And you are Cat's ex, so we are all joined. Except that you haven't met each other properly yet."

Sarah and Luke exchanged puzzled looks.

"Okay," Jonny sighed. "I'll put it very bluntly. Sarah, this bloke looks like James Bond. James Bond, Sarah would make a very sexy Bond girl. Now I suggest you take the next dance together to see if there is any likelihood of you going on a secret mission together."

After a shocked pause. Sarah recovered her composure and daintily offered her hand to Luke. "Do you accept your mission?"

Luke took in Sarah with a long lingering look. "Certainly Miss Moneypenny." He said, recovering his poise and giving her a salacious look.

As they walked towards the dance floor Jonny heard Sarah remark. "Excuse me 007, but there's no way in the world that I'm being your secretary." He grinned to himself and wished them well, but he was wishing harder for his own success.

You have a video email from Cat Forsythe

Cat is beaming at the camera. Her face is heavily made up, her hair is a mass of mad curls nestling around a bling tiara and she is wearing a pink satin corset.

"You are a complete star!" She grins before swishing her arms out to emphasise her outfit. "What do you think of this? Can you believe it that I now have someone in my network who sells corsets! Can you guess what it's all for?

"We're having a Moulin Rouge cinema night! I'll send you some video footage of the event. Although I haven't worked out what to wear below this corset. I'll stay sitting down as I haven't got a skirt on and I don't want your hubby perving over me! I can't believe you showed him the previous email!

"Right, back to business. I don't care about men. Mr Ugly And Not Funny was always babbling on about coincidences and there have certainly been a few between Jonny and I.

"Thanks for your wise words about my ex, but I'm just going to go with flow. He will have to do a hell of a lot more than just look fit in a suit to get me back and who knows who else I will meet? At the moment Jonny is looking a good prospect, but I'm open to suggestions!"

Cat laughs and put her hand over her mouth. "Did I really just say that? It must be the corset that makes me feel saucy, or should I say slutty! Anyway, enough about me. I see that you're quite the busy on-line networker. I always knew you'd be a shrewd businesswoman. You just needed the right product to sell to the right people!

"Well, I had better get changed before I get the urge to hang around on street corners like this to boost my own income! A bientot ma cherie and just remember the can-can, can!

Cat sends the camera a theatrical kiss and then winks.

The footage stops.

Chapter 26

Cat snuck behind the bar for a breather from the pressures of being a host while being pursued by two men she had mixed feelings about. She looked across at the busy pub in front of her. At the people she had helped to entice into the pub on the notion of doing something new and more importantly to spend their money. She loved the fact that people were having a good time but she was also thinking that now was a good time to feel loved. The trouble was that she had big issues with the notion of trust with the two men that she cared about.

She winced as she thought back to the moment she overheard Tim's callous comments about her at the Bridal Fair. If that's how men think, how could she ever learn to trust one?

She was snapped out of her thoughts by the arrival of the Jenny, the Business Link hostess (681), looking every inch the sparkling courtesan with a bejewelled outfit that was finished off by the tiara she was trying out at the Bridal Fair.

"I'm sorry to sneak round here when you're having a breather," she said with a warm smile. "I know exactly what it's like when you have to be the hostess with the mostest all the time, and I won't keep you. I just wanted you to know something." She took one of Cat's hands and looked at her kindly. "We all missed you at the last meeting and Tim got the cold shoulder from a number of people there. I think we all knew he was a bit of a flirt, but a whole string of deceptions have emerged since Gladys and you made your stand. Quite a few of our members are refusing to pass on referrals to Tim and I think he is going to have to work very hard to win back their trust."

Cat was both embarrassed and pleased at the news and started to lead Jenny back out into the public area of the pub in a subtle attempt at changing the subject. However, the host still had hold of Cat's hand.

"I just want to tell you something Cat," she said with a coy smile. "I was in a situation very similar to yours, however, I actually had a relationship with a man who was, unknown to me, married. I thought my world had ended when I found out but here I am, engaged to be married to a wonderful man. I'm so excited that I'm sad enough to wear my wedding tiara to a fancy dress do!" She laughed. "Don't waste time stressing about what Tim did to you Cat. He's just not worth it, and there'll be another man out there who is." She kissed Cat on the cheek, hurriedly wiped off the resulting lurid lipstick mark and disappeared back into the crowd.

Cat followed her out into the public bar deep in thought and was surprised to see her shy friend Mary (231) appear in front of her. It was not actually the appearance of her friend that surprised her, but well, her appearance. She was wearing perhaps the most audacious outfit of the night in the type of dress that is normally only seen at film premieres. It was bright red and while it reached down to her calves, it was open at both sides, revealing her skin in between a wide mesh of twisted rope from her thighs to her armpits. It was also backless down to the base of her spine. It was not a dress that was compatible with underwear of any sort.

Her 'shy' friend giggled when she saw Cat's expression. "I know!" She said breathlessly. "A few of us at the club got together and decided that this was the ideal event to be brave in. We chose each other's outfits and mine's only held together with tape and string!"

"You look amazing!" Cat assured her. "I just can't believe that you're brave enough to wear it."

"I've had quite a few vodkas." Her shy friend admitted. "And there are a number of us here so we can all cluster together and hide if need be."

"And is there anyone special here?" Cat asked with a grin.

"There might be," her friend replied with a fake air of diffidence. "I must say, I thought he was a bit shy, even for me, but he is the most amazing dancer!"

"Well, you know what they say," Cat said with an air of conspiracy. "You always have to watch the quiet ones! She laughed at her friend's expression and then resumed her mysterious look. "Have you got a few minutes?" She asked. "I've got a question for you."

Cat was just musing on Mary's answer to her question when she felt a tap on her shoulder. She turned round to see Mr Wills (395) standing there wearing a surprisingly smart tuxedo, his grey Elvis-like quaff smothered tightly back to his head with Brylcreem.

"May I have the honour of dancing with our most glamorous host?" He asked with a stiff little bow and the offering of a nicotine-stained hand.

"How could I refuse such a polite request?" Cat responded and they walked together towards the dance floor.

"You will, I hope, forgive me if I indulge in a more restrained dance," Mr Wills said as they took up their dancing positions. Me, myself, I am used to a more sedate style of dance." He led Cat into a brisk waltz and she had to concentrate on her steps.

"You dance very well," she observed when she gained sufficient confidence in her footwork.

"I herald from an era when we were taught to dance at an early age. In fact it was the main way of meeting young ladies. Now we have conventions such as speed dating and I believe the younger generations even court by text. We now have a great many ways of forcing people to make social interactions."

"That's a good point," Cat agreed. "Do you mind if I ask you a question?"

Cat was asked to dance once more after Mr Wills and was quite relieved to leave the floor and make it back to the bar area for a much needed G'n'T refresher. The ice cubes were just brushing her lips when someone pinched her bum, making her jump. She spun round to see Gladys winking at her suggestively. She was doing glamour old-school style with a long green velvet dress and a chunky pearl necklace.

"Well, hello there Gorgeous!" Gladys cooed. "Now don't you look absolutely stunning?"

"You made me jump out my skin!" Cat exclaimed.

"I'm sorry Cat, but if you dress up in an outfit like that you deserve to get your bottom pinched." Gladys scoffed good-naturedly. "I have noticed that an impressive number of male eyes have been rolling around your contours. Have you detected anyone that takes your fancy?"

"I'm sure that the men are looking at other women here besides me," Cat pointed out. "It's a relief not to have Tim here, my evening is complicated enough already."

"Ooh, tell me more!" Gladys gushed.

"I'll fill you in later," Cat smiled, "but first I need to ask you a question."

*

By the time the last punter finally left the team were nearly dead on their feet.

"What a difference to ze last event," Julius said in his clumsy French accent, determined to stay in character this time.

"I'd say that there is an obvious conclusion here," Cat observed and was rewarded with expectant faces. "That it's a lot easier to sell to networkers than the general public."

"Zat is very true," Julius agreed. "A beeg lesson for us all, non?"

"I'm going to leave this lot until the morning," Kelly declared, pointing at the dozens of empty glasses littering the pub. "Can I be really rude and tell you all to bugger off home? I am pregnant after all. Not to mention the fact that I've got a hubby to shag."

They laughed as Malcolm's eyes lit up.

Cat and Jonny watched Julius and Melissa slope off arm-in-arm. They found themselves enveloped in an awkward silence that threatened to hang around indefinitely.

"So, Sarah left the party with my ex," Cat observed. "Did you have something to do with that?

Jonny looked as innocent as possible. "I think it's probably called networking insider trading," he admitted.

Cat snorted with laughter. "Oh, that was attractive!" She giggled.

"I can put up with it," Jonny assured her.

"Can I have a word with you?" Cat said softly.

"Of course," Jonny replied and gazed at her expectantly.

"No, not here, Kel has to close up." Cat paused. "Can we go up to your flat?"

"Only if you promise not to seduce me," Jonny sighed theatrically.

"You behave yourself!" Cat scoffed as they headed up the stairs.

"You've got a sofa!" She exclaimed as they walked in the door and were met with a large sofa that dominated the room.

"Sure have," Jonny agreed. "Second hand mind you but I've picked up a few leads tonight so I might even be able to pay for it. Have a seat."

Cat winced as she sat down on one far corner of the sofa. "I've got to take this corset off!" She exclaimed.

Jonny disappeared into his bedroom, reappearing with a black t-shirt. "It's clean," he assured her. "And it won't clash with your skirt. Do you want to use the bathroom?"

Cat laughed. "Nice to know that you don't want me to look like a fashion victim," she said before disappearing into the bathroom.

She reappeared a few minutes later looking a bit embarrassed. "I'm sorry, but I think I'm going to need a hand. I can't get the top clasp undone. Can you do it?"

Jonny stepped forward with his heart throwing a wobbly in his chest. He carefully placed his fingers on the clasp that was sitting snugly on her spine. He noticed her tremble slightly.

"It's you who is shivering now," he grinned as he deftly undid the clasp.

"I'm just ticklish!" Cat said without turning round as she escaped to the bathroom.

She reappeared five minutes later wearing Jonny's T-shirt and holding the unfurled corset. "This thing is a killer!" She declared holding the t-shirt up slightly so Jonny could see the marks it had left around her waist and stomach.

"You looked stunning in it," Jonny assured her and told himself that she looked even more stunning out of it, even if there was his t-shirt in the way.

"Behave you," Cat grinned. "As I said, I've got some things to say to you."

"Fire away," Jonny said settling back into the sofa.

"Hang on, are you playing tango music? Are you trying to seduce me?"

"Erm yes and no."

"Glad to hear it," Cat smiled. "Oh well, we seem to be able to have frank conversations when we're dancing, so shall we?" Cat took up the starting position and a very confused Jonny took up his position. He shivered the moment her hand touched his neck.

"It is every time, isn't it?" Cat chortled.

"I'm ticklish!" Jonny objected.

However, they both had no doubt about his reaction as he flinched the moment that Cat leant in with her soft breasts against his chest.

"Right!" Cat said authoritatively as if to keep the conversation on track while they started to dance. "It seems that you are quite the efficient little networker. I asked loads of people tonight what they thought about you and no-one had a bad word to say."

"That's nice to hear," Jonny said as he walked Cat a bit close to the wall and had to check his stride.

"Julius said that you were definitely Ed Norton and not Brad Pitt which completely lost me."

"You know J," Jonny smiled. "He doesn't live in the real world."

"I see," Cat said, not sure whether to force Jonny into explaining the comment or not. She decided that she had more potent weapons in her arsenal. "You might also be interested to hear that there is someone out there who would like to marry you."

"You what!" Jonny exclaimed, stopping his dance moves.

"That's what I said," Cat replied calmly, giving him a look as if to say, 'carry on'.

Jonny started dancing again, allowing his face to continue to register shock now that Cat couldn't see his expression.

"It was Heather. Yes I know she's getting married to Antonio but she told me that you were the perfect boyfriend and that if she wasn't attracted to arrogant, chauvinistic men she would want to marry someone like just like you."

Jonny couldn't think of anything to say so he swirled Cat round instead.

"Did you really make her chicken soup when she was ill?"

"Guilty as charged."

"You have to admit that does put you somewhat in the perfect boyfriend category."

"But I'm broke."

"Your network seems to think that you have potential. I need someone to write my web site and I can see us getting lots of business through our cinema nights." Cat checked their dance steps. "There's one other thing that I want to know. What do you think of Ferrero?"

"He's dead cute."

"You're not just saying that?"

"My parents always had dogs. It's great having him around."

"Are you just saying that?" Cat asked again with a suspicious look in her eye.

"No!"

"And you haven't been talking to Kelly about this?"

"No! Why should I?"

"And you can cope with the fact that I slept with my ex last night?"

Jonny involuntarily gripped her more tightly but he managed to keep his face neutral. "I don't really have much choice. It's not as if I'm in a position to pass judgement."

"Actually, I didn't sleep with him!" Cat said impishly, maintaining eye contact as she swirled to one side. "I had great pleasure in turning him down. Flat."

"But why...?"

"Kel just jumped to the wrong conclusion earlier, and I wanted to see how you would react. I don't do stupid impulsive things, even if I am tempted sometimes."

Jonny stepped forward into her space, his leg between hers, his nose almost touching hers. He didn't move into the next step, but held the position.

"You appear to have forgotten your steps Jonny," Cat observed calmly, but Jonny could feel her heart thumping.

"Antonio was telling me the other day that when you reach a certain point in closing a deal you keep quiet and the first person to speak loses the initiative. Keep quiet and you make the sale."

"But you just spoke," Cat pointed out reasonably still maintaining eye contact.

"But you spoke first." Jonny smirked.

"You do realise that if we go out together that Kelly will expect you to baby-sit for her?" Cat asked, her face brimming with fake innocence.

Jonny strode her into the next step and she laughed, missing her steps and coming to a halt. However, she maintained her tango hold and tickled the back of his neck. He trembled on cue.

"Don't believe everything that the sales experts tell you," she advised. "Sometimes it's better just to ad-lib."

"I think you're right," Jonny agreed. "I might even become a bohemian. There's beauty for a start." He said as he set them off round the room again, their eyes locked together.

Cat smiled. "And truth?"

"Always truth." Jonny agreed solemnly.

"And what about freedom?"

"Freedom to work away from a corporate regime," Jonny reasoned.

"So what about love?" Cat asked with a coy smile.

"Sound like a natural step to me. How could I not fall in love with someone who looks so good in kinky boots?"

Cat stepped back and aimed a playful slap at his head that he ducked easily. "You do realise that I have six different pairs of boots?" She smirked. She was enjoying herself. After all her previous indecision she now felt fully in control.

Jonny just beamed, not knowing, or caring, what to say. Cat moved back in close and drew him into a deep, passionate kiss. Jonny held her tight against him and Cat responded by pulling his body into hers, enjoying the feeling of Jonny's instant and obvious arousal.

"That seemed quite impulsive to me," Jonny suggested when she finally moved away, back into the tango hold.

"Either that or a playful kiss good night," Cat pouted.

Jonny said nothing but gently started to undo her skirt. Cat took a sharp intake of breath but resolved to remain in charge of the situation and moved her hips round slightly to make the process easier.

"I only said that I never do anything impulsive," she added as her skirt fell to the ground. "If someone else wants to be impulsive, well, that's quite another matter."

Jonny smiled and deftly pulled up the oversized t-shirt, taking her arms up with it in one quick, smooth movement.

Cat was left bare-chested and more than a little surprised at the speed of his manoeuvre. "Oh!" She exclaimed. "I'm not ready to be standing naked in front of you. Can we go to bed?"

"I thought you'd never ask," Jonny said urgently as he danced over to the bed. "You can leave your boots on if you like!"

Cat laughed as they fell onto the bed and thought that perhaps now was a good time to lose her tightly fought control.

The House of Fun Blog

Diary of a mad house
Date Friday 23rd July 2006

Viking's ship has entered the harbour

SPANIARD – Just thought that our readers might like to know that Viking has not been seen out of his flat for the last two days. Neither has a particular bonita senora…

GUEST – Ute: Result! Which girl has he 'moored up' with?

SPANIARD – The one he wanted.

GUEST – Ute: The perfect woman! Nice one Jonny! Tell us all about it. ☺

GUEST – HornyBoy: Yeah yeah its all talk with you lot.

You have an instant message from Sam:

SAM: Cat! You there! It's been ages! How did the party go?

SAM: Cat!

SAM: If you don't answer this then you're no longer my friend!

SAM: You dirty stop out. I'm appalled by your behaviour. I suggest you either contact me IMMEDIATELY to assure me that you have not been acting like a strumpet or you contact me when you raise enough energy and tell me all about it! ;)

Networking Resources

Whilst this book is fiction it reflects the issues that I faced when I found myself entering the world of business networking. My first experience was a small village business meeting in Hampshire for the Overton Business Association (www.overtonbusiness.com). From there I was recommended to join **Business Link** (www.businesslink.gov.uk) where I received lots of helpful advice, both from the staff and from fellow business owners. It was at one of these breakfast meetings that someone told me about **Ecademy** (www.ecademy.com) and my on-line business career started from there. I now work in a tiny village in the Scottish Borders – my commute involves walking into my home office.

The concept of **Ecademy** was thought up by a husband and wife when they were at a pizza restaurant with their children. It has since become a worldwide phenomenon with members across the world and the aim of creating a 'friend in every city'. Members pay a fee to use the services that include free advertising, member profiles and online business clubs. They also run a monthly meeting in London and many regional meetings that are organised by the members. You can see my profile at www.ecademy.com/user/russking

One of the biggest clubs on Ecademy is the **Beermat Entrepreneur Club** that also has its own web site www.beermat.biz. This runs free monthly meetings just like the one described in the book. You can join the club for free on Ecademy or via the Beermat web site.

LinkedIn (www.linkedin.com) is a free business networking site that concentrates on finding, sharing and re-discovering contacts. You create what is effectively an on-line CV and you can search for contacts from your old work places or university. You can also search for specific people and find out who other people in your network know so you can arrange an introduction. You can find my profile at www.linkedin.com/pub/1/282/4bb

MySpace is a social networking site that is aimed at younger generations. It's free, fun, and has over 150 million members. You can listen to, and download, music from new and current bands, but it's not all about teenagers, video clips and glamour models. There are also a lot of people who are using cheap, modern technology to boost their business. Come and 'add me' at www.myspace.com/russwrites.

Shooting People is a huge community of filmmakers, including anyone associated with making films. You can sign up to receive daily email digests on specific topics that all members can post comments on. My profile card is at www.shootingpeople.org/cards/Russ

The **Chamber of Commerce** is a business organisation (www.chamberonline.co.uk) that aims to support and promote businesses in the UK and abroad. It also raises business issues from their members with government. There is a fee to join and the benefits include discounts on services and networking with other members at regular meetings.

That's all the organisations I belong to, but the choice is endless so find the right ones to suit you! I've listed a few of the main ones below:

BNI – Business Network International is a club where the members meet on a regular basis to share business knowledge and to pass on business referrals. The concept is that only one member of each trade is allow in each local 'chapter' and all the members seek business for the other members as well as their own. Find out more at www.bni.com.

BoB – Business over Breakfast www.bobclubs.com

BRE – Business Referral Exchange www.brenet.co.uk is similar to the BNI.

First Monday - www.firstmonday.com

Friendster - www.friendster.com

orkut – www.orkut.com

Ryze - www.ryze.com

Squidoo - www.squidoo.com

Xing (previously OpenBC) - www.xing.com

YouTube – www.youtube.com

Books

There are loads of useful business books so I've only included books that I have referred to for this book; or that I have actually used to improve my networking.

Networking

...and death came third! The definitive guide to networking and speaking in public. Andy Lopata and Peter Roper. www.bookshaker.com. 2006.
Full of useful advice for taking the fear out of networking and public speaking, while keeping an eye on your return on investment.

A Friend in Every City. One global family – A networking vision for the twenty first century. Penny Power, Thomas Power and Andy Coote. Ecademy Press. 2006
Views on the future of networking from the founders of Ecademy.

Six Degrees. The science of a connected age. Duncan J Watts. Vintage. 2004.
A scientific look at the six degrees of separation theory.

The Wisdom of Crowds. Why the many are smarter than the few. James Surowiecki. Abacus. 2004
An intriguing insight into why crowds have better judgement than the most qualified individuals.

The Celestine Prophecy. An adventure. James Redfield. Bantam Books. 1994.
My character Tim abused this book. It's one of those love it or hate it novels, but there's enough in it to make you think about your own life and goals.

How to Make Money on Ecademy.com. By Fraser Hay. Ecademy Press. 2006.
Tips and methods for making a profit out of on-line networking.

Why Men don't Listen and Women can't Read Maps. Allan and Barbara Pease. Orion Books Ltd. 2001.
There's no excuse for not understanding the opposite sex when business is involved!

Body Language. How to read others' thoughts by their gestures. Allan Pease. Sheldon Press. 1997.
It's amazing how many people don't pick up on body language in the business environment.

Advice for Entrepreneurs

Sales on a Beermat. Mike Southon and Chris West. Random House. 2005.
My character Jonny really needs to read this book! Every business owner should read this book.

The Beermat Entrepreneur. Turn your good idea into a great business. Mike Southon and Chris West. Pearson. 2002.
Good, solid (and fun) advice for starting a business venture.

Millionaire Upgrade. Lessons in success from those who travel at the sharp end of the plane. Richard Parkes Cordock.

Capstone Publishing Ltd. 2006.
If you want to keep up with my character Sarah then this is the book to help you tune into the millionaire mindset.

We All Fall Down. Goldratt's Theory of Constraints for healthcare systems. Julie Wright and Russ King. North River Press. 2006.
A business textbook written in the style of a thriller novel that shows you how to find the Core Problem of your business and solve it.

Printed in the United Kingdom
by Lightning Source UK Ltd.
121344UK00001B/1-33/A